10534763

TEMPT ME

THE MACINTYRE BROTHERS SERIES: BOOK ONE

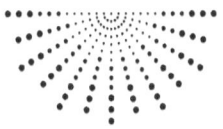

S. E. LUND

ACADIAN PUBLISHING LIMITED

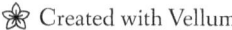 Created with Vellum

CHAPTER ONE

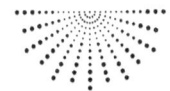

Ella

I couldn't take my eyes off her butt.

It was currently bare and resting atop the dark cherry wood desk. She was my fiancé's secretary. The cherry wood desk was my fiancé's desk in his office in Concord, New Hampshire.

It was Saturday morning, and I'd felt so bad for poor Derek, who had been working extra hard to get as much work out of the way before our wedding ceremony, which was only months away. He'd been putting in fourteen hour days six days a week. He even slept in the office a couple of times, because he was working late to get everything caught up.

That Saturday morning, I decided to drive down from Dartmouth College where I was finishing my BA and pick up some bagels and coffee, bringing them to the office so we could at least have breakfast together. He was going out of town that night on a business trip and weekends were the only time we had together while I was finishing up my spring term. A week after I was done, I would graduate with my Bachelor's Degree in English with a

1

concentration in creative writing. Then, we were getting married a month later.

He usually drove up to Hanover to stay with me Friday and Saturday night, but he was going out of town so I thought I'd surprise him with bagels and coffee, and maybe get in some hot sex before he flew to Washington.

That was when I realized the picture-perfect life I thought I had was a sham.

Wealthy family, great education, attentive best friend, and on top of it, engaged to a handsome, well-educated corporate lawyer working for my father. Square-jawed and firm abs -- the whole package. After graduating with a BA in English, I was planning on getting a job as a business editor in Concord where Derek and I would live and start a family. We were the couple everyone else wished they were. We went to charity events and gala openings. We were invited to all the most important parties.

Even my father approved, and he was a stickler for credentials and breeding. My father, *the* Emmet Carlson, Governor of New Hampshire, was hard to please but Derek Marshall pleased him. The two of them couldn't wait to be Father- and Son-in-Law.

We were engaged to be married at a resort in July in Bermuda, with our closest friends and family in attendance. Then, I'd start my new life as Mrs. Derek Marshall, wife to the future Congressman and maybe even, one day, first lady to the President of the United States of America. Why not?

Everything was truly perfect.

Or so I thought.

Then I saw her naked butt on the cherry wood desk and was as much mesmerized as I was horrified while Derek pumped into her, her butt cheeks squishing and jerking in unison with each of his grunting thrusts.

Yes, I found Derek, who henceforth and forthwith shall be

known as Jerkface, boinking his *sex*retary on the desk in his huge corner office.

Jerkface was in the last throes of passion and *Bunni* was all, "Oh, baby, *baby*, pound me, pound me harder..."

I dropped the bagels and coffee on the floor in the doorway to his office, interrupting him while he was ramming into her, her bare ass on the Johnston file. Then I turned on my heel and left the office, jamming my finger against the elevator button, my world collapsing around me.

I was too shocked to know how to respond. I only knew I had to get out of there and fast.

"Ella!" Jerkface grabbed his slacks and managed to slip them on, covering up his now limp dick, and caught up with me at the elevator just as the door opened. "Ellie, baby, I'm so sorry! Don't get the wrong idea about what you saw," he said, actual panic in his voice, practically tears in his eyes. "Oh, Ellie, sweetheart, don't look at me like that! I love you. She means nothing to me. It was just a one-time thing."

"I heard that," Bunni called out from the depths of the office.

"Ellie, it means nothing. I was anxious about the wedding and the work has been overwhelming and--."

He got to my side, the waistband of his slacks in his hands. "Ellie..."

"Fuck off, you fucking jerk." I stepped inside the car and pressed the down button, my vision blurred from my tears. He was still zipping up his slacks as the doors closed and I was finally alone.

"Ellie! Don't do this!" he called out as the elevator began its descent.

Luckily, his voice soon faded and before I knew it, I was out of the building, running down the street, wiping my cheeks and trying not to sob out loud.

I arrived at my car and opened the door, sliding into the driver's seat before locking the doors and letting my tears flow.

Jerkface arrived at the car door just as I was pushing the start button, having taken the other elevator. His white shirt was open and his feet were bare. I swear I hated him so much at that moment that if I could have driven over him and gotten away with it, I would have.

"Ella, don't do this to me!"

"You did it to yourself, Jerkface," I yelled through the window, giving him the finger. I drove off with a squeal of tires, wishing I was on gravel road so I could kick it up into his cheating face, but I wasn't.

I managed to drive back to Hanover without crashing. Once inside my dorm room, I packed a bag and made hotel reservations. For the first few days, I didn't tell anyone exactly where I was – not even Steph, my bestie and dorm mate. All I said was that Jerkface and I had split and I needed to spend some time alone with the Movie Channel and a tub of Dutch Chocolate ice cream.

Then, I cried my eyes out.

As I was lying on the hotel bed, the movie Get Bill playing on the television screen, a huge chocolate fudge sundae with whipped cream for supper, I heard my cell chime for the tenth time. I would have ignored it but I decided to check, see what new excuse Jerkface had concocted. Other than more panicked texts from him, vowing undying contrition and loyalty forever and ever, there was one from *her*.

BUNNI: He was only marrying you because of your father. He doesn't love you. He really loves me but wanted to use your father to get ahead in politics. Be thankful you found out now before it was too late.

I stared at the text, then punched out a response.

ELLA: I don't want a cheating jerk like him anymore. He's all yours.

FOR THE FIRST WEEK AFTERWARDS, I lurked around my dorm, waiting for commencement ceremony and spending time with my bestie, Steph. After commencement, I moved back to Concord with my parents and tried to figure out my life. A month passed and then two. My mother tried to talk me into giving Jerkface a second chance, but I refused, steadfast in my determination that he'd had his chance. Now that Jerkface and I weren't getting married, I was free to figure out what the hell to do with my life.

For the past year, I thought I had everything planned out but now my life was wide open.

A year earlier, I had gone to a writer's conference in Manhattan and it was there I met the woman who would change my life. Sharon Rogers, an editor with a publishing house in Manhattan, read my resume, looked at my credentials and suggested that if I wanted to be an editor, I should consider doing an internship with her in Manhattan. They hired one each year for a one-year term. The next opening would be the following fall so I could keep it in mind.

One night as I sat alone in my bedroom, I got a text from her asking if I was still interested in an internship with her company. I realized that I had to do something to move on so I was ecstatic that she considered me.

She'd been without an assistant for two weeks after her last intern informed Sharon that she took a paid job and didn't even give Sharon twenty-four-hours-notice.

ELLA: How soon do you want me to start?

It took a while, but she finally responded.

5

SHARON: Ella! Are you serious? I can't believe my luck. I was worried you would have already found a paying job and wouldn't be interested in an unpaid internship.

ELLA: I want to move to Manhattan and get into the publishing business. I have some money saved so I could do an internship for six months.

SHARON: Well, then, come! It's perfect timing. How soon can you be here?

ELLA: As soon as I can get a place to stay and a ticket there, I'm your man. Can we say next week at the earliest?

SHARON: Oh, thank God. Call me as soon as you know when you're arriving. We'll talk about your start date and terms of employment.

ELLA: Thanks, Sharon. You're a lifesaver.

SHARON: No, the thanks are all mine. I can't believe my luck that you want to work as an unpaid intern. I was looking through the resumes of other candidates a friend of mine in the head-hunting business brought me but you have the best credentials. Bachelor of Arts with an Honors in English, experience editing your school's literary magazine, your own work published. I'm so glad we met at the conference.

ELLA: I can't wait to start.

I sent the message and leaned back onto the bed, my focus now on finding a place to live in Manhattan. It wouldn't be an easy task, but if Sharon was willing to take me on as an intern, I'd do whatever I could to go to Manhattan.

I'd leave New Hampshire and all the memories of cheating Jerkface behind me and never look back.

My father wouldn't be happy about it, and my mother would weep and moan, but I had to make my own life, on my own terms. I had always wanted to move to Manhattan and get into publishing, but had postponed it all because Jerkface was so insistent we get married and settle down. He was so persuasive that I let him

6

talk me out of going to Manhattan for a few years while he finished the term working for my father.

I'd learned my lesson well. Don't compromise on your dreams for a man.

I wouldn't make that mistake again.

CHAPTER TWO

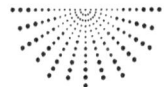

JOSHUA

THE LAW OFFICES OF COVINGTON, Covington, Covington, Peters, and Franklin occupied the entire thirty-third floor of a building bordering Central Park. The view from the boardroom overlooked the park and was one of the most exclusive locations in all of Manhattan.

One of the Covington brothers – I could never remember which one was which because they all had identical bald heads and glasses and all had names starting with "G" – George, Gregory, Gordon – sat at the head of a huge polished wood table in the boardroom, my father's last will and testament on the tabletop in front of him. In my hand was a letter from my father that we were all supposed to read before we read the will.

I scanned it, wondering why he had written us a letter, but my sense was that it wouldn't be good news.

I was right.

To my dear boys:

9

. . .

IF YOU ARE READING THIS, I am dead.

YOU HAVE all lived exceptionally privileged lives by virtue of having been born lucky – to wealthy parents. You have all gone to the best schools, lived in the most affluent of neighborhoods. You have lived the bachelor's life since graduation, sowing your wild oats, and traveling around the world in pursuit of your dreams. While I love you, and am proud of each of you, it's time to grow up and be men.

YOU KNOW that I have no respect for trust fund babies. I don't believe in inherited wealth. None of you did anything to deserve my fortune other than being born and as a result, none of you will receive a dollar of it upon my death; it will all go to charity. I'm sorry if you had plans that included some share of my fortune. Luckily for you, your dear departed mother made me promise I would include you in my will despite my distaste for inherited wealth but I worked for my fortune and I expect you to work for yours.

TO THAT END, I have created trust funds for each of you. They are called "Incentivized Trusts" and one of the Covington brothers will explain it to you in detail. The funds have certain incentives that, once satisfied, will result in the disbursement of instalments. As to the remainder of my overall fortune, it will be divided into five equal portions. Each of you will be the head of a foundation in your name so the wealth I amassed during my lifetime will do some good in this world. It's up to you what kind of charity you *create with the foundation revenue. You will receive a healthy salary for being CEO, but nothing more.*

My one piece of advice on how to have a happy life? Marry well. Have a family with many children. Love your family with all your heart, the way I did you and your mother.

I know this will be a very unsatisfactory outcome and that you were probably planning on how to spend all my money, but that's not the way life works.

Love,

Your Father

What the...

He hadn't, as we all expected, divided his huge fortune among the five of us. I glanced around the table at my four brothers to see if they were as blindsided as I was by its contents.

David was the first to speak up. The youngest of my brothers, David was never afraid to say exactly what was on his mind, no matter where he was or whom he was with.

"What the ever-loving *hell* is this?" He held up the sheet of paper and glared at Covington. "What the hell is an incentivized trust fund?"

Covington shuffled the papers in front of him and avoided David's eyes. He cleared his throat before speaking.

"It's intended to provide disbursements when certain requirements are met and not until."

"He cut us out of his will," my second-youngest brother Christian said, a note of disbelief in his voice. At twenty-nine, he was just establishing himself as an adjunct professor at Columbia Law, and had political ambitions. He could have probably used some of my father's fortune to fund a future campaign for political office.

"No, he didn't. You'll each have a considerable salary from your foundations. If you satisfy certain requirements, you'll receive annual disbursements from your trust funds."

"Such as?" Christian asked.

Covington flipped a few pages. "On the anniversary of your wedding day, and on each anniversary afterwards, you will get twenty-five million dollars."

"What?" David's expression was almost comical. "That's peanuts! He's worth what -- ten billion dollars?"

"He's been very generous, considering his views on inherited wealth. He's divided up his fortune into two equal parts. One will be used to create five foundations. The other will be used to fund you and your brothers."

"He's paying us twenty-five million dollars to get married and stay married for a year?" David asked, stuck on the marriage part. "He can't really do that, can he? I mean, I could just marry some girl from the bar and divorce her the following year."

"You don't have to get married, but if you do, you'll get a disbursement on each anniversary of that date as long as you stay married to your spouse. Twenty-five million a year for up to twenty years."

"He's paying us to get *married?*"

Covington almost rolled his eyes. "Your father wants you to find spouses you will be happy with and so you can't just enter into a marriage of convenience. If you do, it will only be worth

12

twenty-five million of the one billion fund. Your father hopes you won't divorce, but understands that it might be beyond your control, but only three marriages are permitted in total over your lifetime. Once you have divorced your third wife, that's it. No more money."

"That's like," David said, struggling for words. "It's slavery! He's enslaving us to our wives."

He stood up from his chair and went to the large picture window overlooking the city. Tall and well-built, David looked every inch the rock star with his longish black hair and tattoos covering his arms. He played lead guitar in an alt-metal band that was currently touring the US. They'd signed a big contract and had a new album coming out in the fall. He had groupies—lots of them—and girlfriends in every city waiting for his return. It would be especially hard for him to settle down, considering all the women willing to sleep with him on a moment's notice.

I could see Covington fight to keep from smiling. "You don't have to get married, David. You can stay single for as long as you want but then you forfeit access to your half a billion-dollar fund set aside for your married life, which your father believes is far too much. Plus, there are incentives for having children. On the birth of your first child, or on the date you adopt if you are unable to have your own biological children, you will receive another disbursement of twenty-five million on that date and on each subsequent year. All told, it works out to one billion dollars over twenty years. That's quite a significant sum."

We were all expecting to inherit one-fifth of his fortune. That would mean each of us would become a billionaire.

I stared at the letter in my hand, and thought of my father. He really wanted us to replicate his own life.

David turned to stare at the rest of us, his mouth open wide, expecting us to respond.

"What do you think, Michael?" David asked.

Beside me, my brother Michael shifted in his seat uncomfortably. At thirty, Michael was the owner of a construction company he'd started when he finished his degree in engineering. He didn't like family disputes and avoided them at all costs growing up.

"He made it clear to us he didn't believe in inherited wealth. Said it was against the principles of meritocracy."

David stared at Michael for a moment in disbelief.

"Did you know about this?" David asked in an accusatory voice. "Did you know he would blackmail us into getting married and having families?"

"No, but we talked about it before he died. He made it clear to anyone who might have listened."

David was clearly upset – more so than any of the rest of us. He returned to the table and picked up the letter once more, re-reading it.

"Your father was a strong family man," Covington replied, his tone patient. "He wanted you to follow the same path."

"I'm a fucking rock star," David said, slamming down the sheet of paper and sitting back down into his chair. "This is America! We have this thing called freedom. Forcing us to marry and have children is *tyranny*."

I could see Covington fight to stay neutral. "No one is forcing you to do anything. Your father didn't want to give you boys *any* money, but your mother made him create these funds, which are still considerable, given the average income for this country."

"I'm only twenty-eight, for Christ's sake," David protested. "I need a few more years before I have to settle down. I have groupies, not a wife!"

Covington cleared his throat, his patience apparently wearing thin. "Your father was married at twenty-eight and your mother gave birth to Joshua within the first year of their marriage. You boys can wait as long as you like but you won't get any of the money until your first wedding anniversary."

"We're men, not boys." Nash, my second-oldest brother and a former military pilot who now ran his own airline, frowned while he read over the will.

"Precisely," Covington said, glaring at Nash over top of his reading glasses. "Your father supported all of you while you pursued your personal goals. He funded your college educations. He gave you a home. You had ample allowances and he helped you when you wanted to start businesses or travel the world. If you don't approve of his terms, you can always continue your own way but if you want your share, you must marry and have children."

Nash grimaced like he hated the very idea of marriage and family. At thirty-one, he was closest to me in age. He'd bought a small jet after he got out of the service, using the money he'd saved while in the military, and started his company with my father's help. They had been partners in the fledgling airline. As a former fighter jock, my father was so proud of Nash. Nothing made him quite as happy as the knowledge that Nash was running his own airline.

I hadn't seen him for more than a year. He'd been off in the Middle East flying in relief supplies to war-torn zones. By his side was a motorcycle helmet and he was wearing a black leather jacket and black leather riding pants. He had a huge Harley, parked outside the offices. He looked like a rogue, despite being squeaky clean as a business man.

Nash was certainly a man by anyone's reckoning. He was always a rebel, despite being in the military, but you didn't fly high-performance aircraft at Mach 2 without having a wild streak in you. He was beloved by women everywhere, in every airport and military base he traveled to. I could see how the will's requirements would cramp his style.

"Do you think this can be challenged in court?" David said and shook his head in disbelief. "Isn't there some kind of civil rights issue involved in forcing children to marry and have families?"

"You're not being forced. You can choose to stay single for as long as you want." Covington exhaled. "Think of it this way: once you marry, it will all *begin*," he said and held his hands up, gesturing to the whole world.

"What will begin?" David grumbled. "Slavery to a woman and children?"

"Real life," Covington replied.

"Real life? Who needs it." David shot him a nasty look. "I prefer living the dream, thanks."

"Look on the bright side," Covington continued, undeterred. "You'll have a quite healthy salary as CEO of your charitable foundations and can live any way you wish, anywhere you wish. Once you get married, you'll have access to much *much* more."

"That sucks," David said disgustedly. "That's bribery."

Covington shrugged. "Some people would be happy with these terms. You're all good-looking young men with your own very successful careers. I imagine you'll have lots of potential mates who would line up at the chance to marry you. Surely one of them would be a good spouse."

Nash chimed in. "I've been dating since I was seventeen and let me tell you, if the right woman is out there, I haven't met her."

"Your father could have given all his money to charity if he had wanted. As it is, he set aside half in trust funds, but he wanted to ensure you did something with your lives to earn it. Namely have a family, the way he did. Besides, chances are very strong that you will all marry eventually anyway."

"That's not necessarily true," I replied, remembering a statistic I'd read about GenX not marrying until much later, if at all, compared to my father's generation of baby boomers. "Our generation is less likely to marry and we marry at a later age."

Covington turned to me. "Considering you were ready to marry only a few months ago, Joshua, I'd think you'd understand."

An awkward silence passed as we all probably thought about my failed engagement only six months earlier. I'd been engaged until my fiancée, Christie, whom I'd thought was the love of my life, decided that she preferred the company of her boss, Clint Watson, one of my underlings in the publishing business I managed as part of my father's empire.

What really sucked was that I couldn't blame it on Clint being richer or more powerful than me. He wasn't. In fact, he wasn't even close to my income or influence. She loved him.

She wanted me for my money.

It kind of soured me on the whole get-married-and-have-a-family thing. Frankly, I just didn't believe there was a Mrs. Joshua Macintyre out there for me. Sure, I had lots of sex partners. They were easy enough to find. But a wife?

Someone who could love me for me, and not for my wealth and power?

No.

Christie soured me on that possibility.

"Is there no way to contest this?" David asked. "I mean, don't we have a right to a share as his children?"

Covington shook his head. "No. In America, you do not have an automatic right to inherit your parent's wealth. It is entirely up to them how to distribute their property upon death."

"It's completely unfair."

"It's the law," Covington replied.

"Well," David said, "the law is an ass."

Covington raised his eyebrows. "Regardless, when each of the requirements has been satisfied, you will receive the first disbursements of your trust fund. Is there anything else?"

"What's happening to my father's penthouse? And his other properties?"

17

"Please refer to Appendix A. It details the division of property amongst the beneficiaries." Covington distributed several documents to us.

We all flipped to the appropriate appendix. In a list of my father's properties, I saw my name beside the beach house in the Hamptons. My father knew it was my favorite place to spend the summer. At least he had been nice enough to give me that without any strings attached.

Christian got the penthouse overlooking Central Park. Michael got the family mansion in upstate New York; Nash got the Florida estate; and David got the beachfront property in New Hampshire.

"There must be some kind of law against forced marriage..." David frowned as he read over the appendix.

"You aren't being forced to marry anyone. You can choose to remain single for as long as you want."

"He could have trusted us to want to marry and have a family and just given us the money," Christian said. "I could use ten million right now to fund my campaign for the state legislature." He leaned back, a disgruntled expression on his face.

"On your first wedding anniversary, you'll get it. You better start finding the love of your life sooner rather than later. Joshua," he said and turned to me. "You're the oldest of the brothers. You're now the head of the family. You take over as CEO of MBC. You'll get a salary as head of the corporation."

MBC, better known as Macintyre Broadcasting Corporation, was the business my father started from scratch. Originally a local television station, it grew into a huge media conglomerate with a publishing arm including print, television and radio.

I ran the print publishing business.

"I'm focused on the *Chronicle*," I replied, not happy to be taking over the whole empire. I'd just bought one of New York City's oldest newspapers, the *New York Chronicle,* which had all

18

but died over the past decade. I wanted to revitalize it and make it the go-to paper for anyone who wanted to know anything about the city, its politics, and culture. I did not want the added pressure of running the entire organization. "I could sure use twenty-five million dollars, but if I have to find a wife and run the corporation, I won't have time to achieve my business goals for the next few years, which are very ambitious. And given my most recent experience, I'm not all that keen on marriage."

"I knew your father well enough to know what he'd say in response," Covington said, his eyebrows raised.

"Yeah, I know what he'd say," I replied with a rueful laugh. I glanced around at my brothers. "Suck it up, buttercup," we said in unison.

"Exactly." Covington turned back to his documents, but I could see him struggle to hide a smile.

I glanced around at my brothers; they were smiling to themselves as well, glad for a little levity in the middle of a somber event.

Then, finally, we all laughed together, because we knew our old man exceptionally well. He was that kind of father. Engaged in all our lives despite his massive empire. A loving father with the demeanor of John Houseman in *The Paper Chase*, or Churchill. An old bulldog, in other words.

I missed him.

I could imagine my father sitting at the head of the table, his eagle-eyes focused like a laser on us, ice blue and unforgiving; his silver hair slicked back; his three-thousand-dollar pinstripe suit impeccable, a handkerchief in his suit pocket to match his tie. He had been strong, smart, and driven–building a business from the ground up. Buying up his competition, and then getting into every aspect of publishing and broadcasting news until his empire was the second biggest media company in the world. He had been formidable.

Sadly, lung cancer didn't care how powerful he was. Like a typical man, he wrote off the nausea and occasional pain in his chest as bad food from a local taco truck, and by the time he was diagnosed, it was too late. The cancer took him in less than a year, ending his reign as head of our family and his own empire.

I missed him terribly, but as much as I loved him, even I was blindsided by the will and I'm sure every brother felt the same.

The last thing I wanted to think about was finding a wife, given my recent experience with love and marriage...

CHAPTER THREE

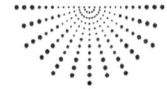

Ella

On Monday, a week after I accepted Sharon's offer of the internship, I stood outside Penn Station and debated what to do with the next three hours until I picked up my keys to my Airbnb short-term rental in Chelsea. Early that morning, I'd taken the train from Durham, New Hampshire, after a tearful goodbye to my parents and bestie Steph, and arrived in Penn Station, tired but ready for a new adventure.

My mother strongly disapproved of me up and leaving New Hampshire so soon after breaking up with Jerkface. She was afraid I wouldn't be able to make it on my own in Manhattan. My father seemed happy that I'd thrown Jerkface over. He'd even fired the bastard and sought legal counsel from another firm, and so I knew I'd made the right move not giving him a second chance. Neither of them wanted me to move away and warned me that I was unused to a city as big as Manhattan, and that I was naïve about life in general, having been sheltered and pampered.

But he did not approve of me working for Dominion Publishing.

"It's a subsidiary of MBC and you know how I feel about that bastard of a J. P. Macintyre."

I'd heard all about my father's hatred of J.P Macintyre, the chairman and CEO of Macintyre Broadcasting Corporation. Their news division had run several in-depth exposes of my father's business partner after he was caught using insider information to sell and buy stock.

Undaunted, I'd made plans to leave and work for Sharon regardless and my father had finally relented when I told him it was a minor part of the overall business empire.

"It's my chance to get my toe in the door of publishing, Daddy," I said, explaining why I had to take the internship despite it being unpaid.

He finally relented and gave me his blessing and I was filled with a renewed hope that the future I once dreamed of living could be possible. I'd do everything in my power not to return to Concord, tail between my legs.

Now that I was finally in Manhattan, I decided to store my luggage in a locker and take the subway to see the building where my internship would start on Wednesday. I grabbed a subway map from the kiosk in the underground station, bought a pass, and tried to figure out how to get to the office.

At one thirty in the afternoon, the place was packed with commuters. It was a bit of a circus, with people dressed for business, both casual and formal, as well as people who looked like they were on the way to work at the local carnival freak show.

I left the subway station and stood for a moment in the middle of the sidewalk, the pedestrian mass parting around me as I soaked up the atmosphere.

Ahh, Manhattan. Tall buildings. Great nightlife. Gorgeous men...

I walked the rest of the way and arrived at the Macintyre Building. An old Art Deco in the middle of the block bordering Central Park, the building was about thirty stories high. It was gorgeous and I couldn't wait to go up and meet Sharon, find my own office and get started.

I saw a coffee shop across the street and decided to grab a coffee before returning to Penn Station to get my luggage and go get my Airbnb. Because the traffic was backed up for the entire block, I decided to jaywalk to the coffee shop instead of going to the crosswalk. I'd barely got half-way across the second lane when I was almost run over by a bike courier in full riding gear threading his way between the cars.

I honestly didn't see him. Traffic was at a full stop and the light was red, so I thought I'd be safe. That was my first mistake. Usually, I was a law-abiding citizen, but it seemed safe enough to cross, given the traffic snarl. I felt him knock against my arm and managed to step back, his shoulder the only thing that touched me as he zipped by. I gasped and held my hands up as I backed away, but it was too late. His bike wobbled as he swerved to avoid me, and he hit the corner of the taxi ahead of him, crashing to the ground, his bike clattering to the pavement.

I covered my mouth in horror and ran to where he lay on the street, his bike in a heap beside him.

"Jesus fucking *Christ!*" he said, rubbing his elbows and knees. "Use the damn crosswalk, lady."

"I'm so sorry," I said, and knelt beside him. "I didn't see you. You came by so fast."

He stood and shook off the dust, grabbing his bike and walking it to the curb. The light had changed, but traffic was still backed up the next block and none of the vehicles moved.

I walked beside him, feeling like a total ass for not checking for cyclists. I honestly had no idea they rode in the middle of the

23

street like that. I had figured they'd use the bike lane at the side of the road.

When we got to the sidewalk, he removed his helmet and goggles and examined his knees, which were both bloody as were his elbows. That was when I got a good look at him and *ohhh...*

He was a total babe.

I felt bad ogling him at a time like that, but I couldn't help it. He had brown hair, slightly longish on top, several days' worth of beard, and the bluest of blue eyes. Add to that full kissable lips and a jaw so square you could cut your tongue on it.

It had been a few months since Jerkface and I broke up, and I was needy.

"I'm so sorry. Can I do anything?" I asked, wringing my hands.

"I don't know," he said, his deep voice frustrated. "*Can* you? Do anything, I mean?"

Can I do *anything...*

Yeah, I didn't miss it. He looked in my eyes, and I could see anger in them, but at the same time, he didn't seem mean. In fact, his lips quirked up in one corner just enough for me to see he was amused at his jab.

"Can you get worker's comp or anything for those injuries?" I asked, having no idea what bicycle couriers were eligible to receive.

"Worker's comp?" he asked, his voice slightly taunting.

I shook my head. "I'm sorry. I don't know whether bicycle couriers even qualify. Can I get you some bandages, at least? I saw a drugstore down the street. Doesn't look like you need stitches. I can call your boss, explain what happened if you need someone to vouch for you."

He glanced down at himself, then smiled. "I'm good. I can afford to buy my own bandages, thanks. Bicycle courier pay isn't much but it pays for the occasional bandages. Just make sure to check the street before you try to jaywalk, okay? Better yet, you might consider crossing at the crosswalk."

"I will. I'm so sorry. This is only my first day in Manhattan. My first hour, actually. Honestly, I had no idea bicycle couriers didn't use bike lanes." I looked at his scuffed knees and elbows. "I hope this doesn't stop you from being able to do your deliveries."

"No, it won't stop me from making deliveries." Then he did smile – a full-on smile. It was brilliant. He actually laughed.

I didn't smile. I felt my eyes tear up from embarrassment.

"Hey, it's okay," he said and reached out, touching my shoulder. "I'm fine. We bicycle couriers are used to getting knocked around by the public."

Then he got back up on his bike, which apparently was totally functional despite the spill, and drove to the front of the building out of which I had just come.

I watched while Mr. Handsome Bike Courier bent over to adjust something on his bike, his glutes straining. God, what an ass, and that cycling suit showed every very round curve of it.

It made me ache deep inside, wanting a man in my life to fulfill my needs. While I now hated Jerkface – the sonofabitch – I did miss the sex. Even writing erotica didn't entirely make up for his absence in my life. Nothing could do that like a nice hard man.

Like Garbo said, 'A hard man is good to find.' I needed to find one.

Mr. Handsome Bike Courier was a candidate, though I wasn't sure my father would approve. He had expectations that I'd marry someone rich and of political benefit to him. Not that I was going to marry someone to please my father, but still. A bike courier didn't have the same level of ambition as I did, so while Mr. Hunk had everything going for him in the looks department, I wasn't sure he and I could be more than sex buddies. Which at that moment seemed like a pretty good deal, except that there was probably no way he'd even look twice at me, considering I'd caused him to fall off his bike and probably ruin his day of deliveries.

Maybe I'd meet some cute, ambitious finance type at the local watering holes. Some MBA who didn't mind people who were nerds at heart, and who loved books as much as I did. That was the dream, anyway. As I stood alone on Fifth Avenue, my nerves finally starting to settle down after the near collision, I thought it was a real possibility, given the number of business suits walking by me.

At that moment in my life, finding a man should have been the last thing on my mind. I had to perform and impress Sharon enough that she'd be willing to give me a paid position once the unpaid internship was finished.

I had known I'd get to see a lot of man candy when I came to the Big Apple, and there, in all his glory, went my first real piece. I watched him through the plate glass windows of the building while he walked his bicycle to the elevator. I couldn't wait to text Steph, who loved to ogle handsome men on Pinterest with me.

She stayed in Concord, where we both had been born and raised. She was planning on moving to Manhattan at some point, once she saved enough money. I felt like inviting her to stay with me, but there was absolutely nowhere for her to stay in the tiny studio apartment I'd rented. When she was able, though, we might share a place.

I exhaled, deciding to walk to the crosswalk, get my coffee from the coffee shop and explore a bit more before my appointment to pick up my keys at the Airbnb in Chelsea. Despite my near-collision with a bicycle courier, I felt excited about being in Manhattan.

For the first time since Jerkface and I split, I felt a real sense of possibility – like my new life was starting and I could put the old sad one behind me.

CHAPTER FOUR

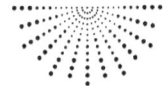

JOSHUA

I MET my brothers outside the building on Fifth Avenue later that afternoon. David was scheduled to fly back to LA and so we wanted to get together once more before he left. I slipped on a pair of aviators and watched as all four of my brothers did the same. We were our father's sons. My dad had been a pilot in the Vietnam War, and each of us had also joined the service. I'd spent time in the US Army as an intelligence officer. My other brothers had joined either the Air Force, like our father, or the National Guard, like David had.

"Come on, men," Christian said, adjusting his aviators and turning to us. "Let's go out and get drunk."

David clapped Christian on the back. "Yeah, let's get some pussy, too, seeing as we're going to be suffering a drought of it if we have to get married just to get access to our money. What do you say about Gibson's? I have a back booth reserved for me any night of the week when I'm in town. There's some really high-quality ass that frequents the place."

Everyone turned to me, as the big brother and now head of the family.

"You need a drink, after your collision," David said. "How are your elbows and knees?"

I bent my elbow, which was currently bandaged, as were both my knees. "I can hack it but honestly, a drink sounds like the perfect idea," I said, badly needing a scotch. "Gibson's it is."

We piled into my Lexus SUV and I drove to Gibson's, a very popular club with an attached high-end restaurant in the financial district. Once there, I handed my keys to the valet and we went inside. It was early, but there was an afternoon crowd there already celebrating happy hour.

David walked up to the hostess station like he owned the place. The young woman behind the counter gasped, her eyes widening when she recognized him. She was pretty in an overly-made up way, with hair piled on top of her head and a tight black dress that displayed her obviously-surgically-enhanced breasts.

"Cindy, baby," he said, and gave her a huge smile.

"David *Macintyre*," she exclaimed when she saw David, her face lighting up. "It's so good to see you again. Please come in. We haven't seen you for weeks!"

She smiled and I could tell she was a little star-struck that David was there. Hell, a lot star-struck. She glanced at the rest of us, but we weren't as notorious as David, the rock star.

"I thought you were on tour," Cindy said.

"Flew in for some family business," David said, and handed her a twenty-dollar bill. "Reading of the will. Can you take us to my usual booth?"

"Oh, I'm so sorry. Of course," she said and held her hand over her heart and made a sad face. "I read about your father's passing

28

in the paper." Then she led us through the bar to a large leather booth in the rear of the space.

"I thought he was too ornery to die," David said, "but I guess not. Hey, wanna marry me? I need a wife, and fast, so I can inherit my money." He gave her the biggest grin I'd ever seen. When her face froze, like she was trying to decide if he was being serious, he laughed out loud. "Just kidding, babe. No one's going to own this ass any time soon. Fuck the will." Then he slid into the booth next to me. Poor Cindy looked despondent that he would joke with her like that.

"Your waitress will be with you right away. Enjoy your evening." She gave us all a quick smile and then left us alone. I imagine she'd tell that story to her friends and they'd all ohh and ahh about being proposed to – even in a joking way – by *the* David Macintyre.

"You're a heartless bastard," Christian said, shoving David. "Getting that poor young woman's hopes up and then crushing them."

"I know, I know. I'm so mean." David grinned widely. "In her heart, she knew I was joking."

I turned to him and shook my head in disgust. Affectionate disgust, but still disgust.

"I hope to hell you fall madly in love with a woman and then she says, 'Just kidding.' Then you'll know how it feels."

All my brothers turned to me, and the expressions on their faces told me I'd just fucked up royally. Michael laid a hand on my shoulder. "Hey, bro. You still hurting over Christie? You need some sweet thing to take away all that pain."

"Fuck off," I said and shoved him, only somewhat affectionately. Then I softened and gave him a smile. "Just kidding."

"No, you weren't," he said, his tone serious. "You need to give it time."

"How can he afford to give it time?" David asked, oblivious as

29

usual to other people's problems. "If he wants to use some of that money, he has to get married and stay married for at least a year. It sucks ass," he said and smacked his hand onto the tabletop. "I'm not buying into Dad's man-in-a-grey-flannel-suit fantasy of marital and family bliss. I'm staying single–I'll enjoy as much pussy as I can for as long as I'm able. If Josh's smart, he will too." He turned to me. "You don't need his money. You'll make enough in stock options as CEO that you won't need it."

"You really are a scoundrel." Michael smiled and hung his arm around David's neck. "We all need our share of a quarter billion dollars. Come on, get real. Marriage won't be so bad. You're gonna do it someday. Might as well be sooner than later."

For the rest of the evening, we drank, toasted our father, and cursed his terms in equal measure.

"Have another one," David said, shoving a plate with a shot glass filled with tequila, a salt shaker and some limes toward me.

I waved him off. "No more for me. I have an early meeting with my contractor to inspect the renovations at the building on Fifth Avenue."

Despite the fact Michael was my contractor and would be meeting me bright and early at the building, he didn't seem quite as reluctant to get drunk as me and raised his glass.

"You can stay sober tonight. I'll be fine tomorrow morning. To success."

"To success," David asked, glancing between the two of us. "How's the renovation going, by the way?"

"Great," I said. "We're getting close. I've already moved the Chronicle staff out of the old building and into the new space but renovations aren't quite done."

"It'll be strange seeing the business operate out of a different building," David said.

"I know, but it'll be mine, not Dad's. No disrespect, but you know what I mean. It'll be completely mine."

"I get it," David said. "Get out from under the old man's shadow. That's why I never bought into the whole family business thing. I want to be my own person. I know Dad never approved of me, but he's gone now and I have to keep living."

"He was proud of you," Michael said, leaning over to clink glasses with David. "Dad's proud of anyone who's a success, and you most definitely are a huge success."

"Amen to that," I said and clinked my empty glass against his. "You are the man."

I watched the four of them drink down their shots and sighed, wishing I felt more like partying with them, but I didn't. I felt like driving to the Hampton beach house and spending a couple of weeks there, decompressing from everything, but I had a business to run. Maybe once the office renovations were finished and we'd finished getting the place set up, I would take some time in the Hamptons, but that wasn't going to happen for at least three months.

I really hated it but I needed access to that first twenty-five million dollars and then twenty-five million every year after. If I was going to find a wife soon, I had some serious work to do and it was work to me.

Marriage and family was the very last thing on my mind.

CHAPTER FIVE

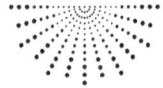

ELLA

I STOOD in the doorway of the Airbnb short term rental, my suitcase and backpack in hand, and glanced around. The room had a single Murphy bed that, when opened, dominated the space.

"This is it?" I turned to Liza, the woman who managed the Airbnb apartment. "This is a one bedroom?"

Liza handed me the key with a huge grin on her face. "Welcome to Manhattan."

"But it's a closet, not an apartment!"

"It's a room with one bed. It's a one bed room." She shrugged like she was helpless. "Did you really think you could rent a one-bedroom apartment in Manhattan – in Chelsea – for what you're paying?"

"It's twice what I'd pay in New Hampshire."

"This is the Big Apple, sweetheart. Get used to it."

I rolled my eyes, but at that moment, I had nowhere else to

stay – and besides, I had already paid in advance. I couldn't afford the insane hotel costs, so until I picked up the key to my long-term rental in Chelsea next week, it was this room or nothing.

"There's clean linen in the cupboard and there are dishes and a hotplate. No visitors after eleven. Call me if you need anything."

"Is there even a table? I'm a writer. I need something to put my laptop on and my notes."

"You can sit on the bed and work. This is the table," she said and folded down a piece of white-painted plywood on a hinge. "You can use this for a table or desk."

She smiled brightly and I looked on the rickety tabletop. "Will it even hold my laptop?"

"It's a laptop. You could use your lap."

I exhaled and tried to let the anxiety seep out of me. I could make it work for a week. Right?

I went to the tiny window overlooking the back alley and a row of trash cans, which were currently overflowing.

Word to the wise: Fisheye cameras distort spatial dimensions. I knew I should have paid attention in my physics class instead of ogling Paul Desmond, the cute football player with the cleft in his chin...

That being said, I was optimistic about life. The actual long-term apartment I'd rented had real exposed brick. It had its own bathroom. And even if it was a studio space, it was bigger than the room in the Airbnb. I hoped that the unpaid internship I would be starting would turn into a paid one by the end of six months. If it didn't, I had faith that I'd be able to find another job somewhere that did pay. The internship, paid or otherwise, had to count for something.

Right?

I'd just finished my BFA and was hoping to become an editor

for one of the big publishers one day. But my secret desire was to write the Great American Novel at some point in my career. Or at least a romantic comedy that would rival Candace Bushnell.

My dream was to be a successful author one day, but until then, I hoped my stint with a smaller publisher would develop my editing skills and networking in the business. At least I'd learn about the publishing industry. I might make connections that would help me later, when I was ready to try my hand at publishing.

So, I plopped my suitcase onto the floor, and went with Liza to check out the bathroom I would be sharing. The second-floor walkup space had a shower and toilet with an old sink that had seen better days. There were three other rooms on the floor and two on the third. We all shared the same bathroom, Liza informed me. She showed me the schedule on the back of the bathroom door. Room 2C, which was mine, had the bathroom from seven thirty to eight a.m. every morning for showering. The rest of the time after nine a.m. was first come first serve. If the seven-thirty time didn't work out for me, I was to request a different time and work something out with the other tenants, get up before six to shower, or shower after eight.

That was it.

My internship started at nine a.m. on Wednesday. I didn't know the transit system yet, so I hoped I had enough time to get there from my little closet in Chelsea. I figured I should be able to get ready in the morning and make it to midtown Manhattan with enough time to pick up a coffee and arrive at eight forty-five.

Before Liza left, I grabbed her arm.

"If I was to catch a train from the nearest station, how long would it take to get to Central Park West?"

"Depends. What time of day?"

"Say, at eight in the morning. I should be able to get there from here in forty-five minutes, right?"

35

She laughed. "You should definitely try first so you know your trains and timing. When do you start work?"

"Wednesday. Nine a.m. sharp."

She shrugged. "It's Monday mid-afternoon. You can try now, but it won't be precise. Better try tomorrow morning for a dry run. You should go a bit earlier tomorrow morning so you get a better sense of how long it takes. Good luck!"

I sighed. My real apartment was a few blocks away from the Airbnb room, so the timing wouldn't be precise, but at least I'd have an idea of how long it would take to get to work.

I thanked her and went back to my room. Or should I say, my closet.

There was a tiny shelf at the end of the room under the window. On it was a single hotplate next to a microwave and toaster. Beneath was a tiny refrigerator.

That was the extent of my kitchen. Whatever – it would do for the rest of the week.

There was one floor-to-ceiling cabinet on the wall for everything – dishes, food, linens, and other personal effects.

I sat on the Murphy bed, glad that my real apartment was much nicer. Besides, I was in Manhattan to get experience and break into the publishing industry. I had to scrimp and suffer a bit for future glory. I needed a desk, but I could use the folding table until I got my real apartment.

The smallest of air conditioners filled the top window and a thick ugly cord trailed down the wall to one of the two electrical outlets in the entire space, but at least it was air conditioned. The summers were hot in Manhattan.

I'd have to unplug and re-plug the toaster and microwave if I wanted the tiny refrigerator to run constantly. The other plug I could use for the tiny television, such as it was, and my laptop. I'd have to alternate using the plugs for my printer, which was a necessity for a writer and budding editor.

36

How anyone got away with advertising this as a studio apartment was beyond me. Wasn't there some sort of law against false advertising? This was *not* a studio apartment. It was a bedroom. Or half a bedroom. And barely even that.

My stomach rumbled and I checked my watch. It was now two forty-five in the afternoon. I'd arrived with my luggage from Penn Station and taken a taxi to the building in Chelsea to meet Liza and get my keys to the Airbnb room. Now I decided to go out into Manhattan and find my way around the place. Tomorrow morning, I would try out the subway system and take it to the building where I would be working, just to check out the neighborhood.

There was a thrift store down the street and I intended to go there and see what they had on offer. I figured I'd have to be thrifty for the next six months if I wanted my small nest egg to stretch that far. I might end up getting a part-time job as a bartender, if I could find a bar close by that needed help. Luckily, bartenders could get jobs everywhere and I had some training, so I figured I was set.

So it was that I set off to explore Manhattan after taking possession of the Airbnb room. Outside my building the street was busy with cars, and the sidewalks were crowded with pedestrians. It was a lot for someone who'd lived most of her life in Manchester, New Hampshire, where the streets were wide and the traffic much less dense. Still, there was an energy in the air that infused me and made me feel optimistic, instead of depressed because of the apartment-closet situation. I took out my cell and googled grocery stores in Chelsea, and found one a few blocks away. Score!

After a trip to the grocery store, where I purchased fruit, some yogurt, and a couple of frozen dinners, I returned to my apartment and put my purchases away.

Things were definitely looking up.

I took out one of the frozen dinners and had one for supper. The building had cable, and so I went to bed that first night in my tiny room, using every one of the four plugs: one to run the air conditioner, one to watch the television, one to power my laptop, and one to keep my food cold.

Life was good.

CHAPTER SIX

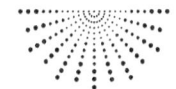

Joshua

The next morning, I met Michael and together, we walked through the renovations that were ongoing at the new site.

They were amazing.

Earlier that year, I'd leased several floors in an old building on Fifth Avenue, wanting something of my own instead of working in my father's building. I had initially thought about Hoboken, but there was something about midtown Manhattan that I loved, so when the opportunity came to get a large chunk of an old building in a great area of the city, I jumped.

Michael and I went in together as partners. The offices of Macintyre Publishing would be located on the top floors, but the rest would be high end office space. The building was mostly office space but there was some retail space on the main floor. There was even an art gallery on the main floor. I'd snagged the penthouse space as my temporary living quarters, enjoying the roof-top patio and view of Central Park.

I spent the first couple of hours with Michael, checking out the renovations, going over the numbers, and watching him troubleshoot. He was good at this. Covington was right – Michael had a successful construction business and was a good-looking guy. Theoretically, he'd have no problem finding a wife.

But he didn't sound like he wanted one, either.

"So, you sounded about as enthusiastic as David about getting married to get access to the trust fund money," I said as we took the elevator to the main level.

He laughed. "I'm too busy building my empire to get married," he confessed. We stood in silence for a moment and I was sure we were both thinking of our father on his deathbed, telling each of us how much he loved us and admonishing us to stop being playboys and settle down.

"We didn't always see eye to eye on things, but I miss him," I said, a tightness in my throat.

"Me too."

Around us, workers busied themselves, hauling drywall and gallons of paint from the trucks into the building.

"Well, I guess I better get back up to the office," I said. "Got some important work to do."

"New reporters to hire for the relaunch of the paper?"

I shook my head. "I'm meeting a headhunter today to find some new blood for the paper."

"Oh, yeah?" Michael said, his face breaking into a huge grin. "That's exciting. What are you looking for? Reporters?"

"Every position," I said, and pointed to the construction site. "I've got big plans for the *Chronicle*. I want to find new blood and really ambitious people who won't worry too much about the hours they'll be putting in to make the paper work."

"Staffing is always an issue in the construction business, as you can imagine."

"I'll bet it is but that's why I use headhunters. I've had real success with the firm I've contracted with. I only wish it was as easy to find a wife."

40

"Hey, you could always sign up for a season of The Bachelor," Michael quipped, slapping me on the back.

"Right," I said and laughed. "Maybe one of those online dating sites?"

"Bro, those are for losers," he replied, shaking his head.

"I figure there are people who do this for a living. They have fancy algorithms and psychological tests. I hire contractors when I want a building renovated. I hire electricians when I need it wired. Why not use an algorithm to find a wife?"

"Oh, man, you're taking all the romance out of it."

I exhaled. "I'm not big on romance at the moment."

"I know," Michael said and squeezed my shoulder. "I understand completely. We just have to suck it up, right?"

"You got it."

With that, I went back up to the offices. I had to do some last-minute work before I could get in a bike ride around the park before my afternoon meetings started.

I had a quick shower and dressed, getting ready for my meeting with my headhunter, who was going to start the process of finding me a whole new staff for the *Chronicle*.

I took the elevator down to my office on the forty-seventh floor. I was usually the first one into work at seven o'clock, but that morning I'd had a meeting all morning with Michael at the new build, of course, and then I had my bike ride around Central Park, so I was late getting into the office. The desks were full and my second-in-command came at me with a file in his hand and a clipboard with documents to sign. My admin assistant held out a cup of coffee from my favorite barista down the street.

I was ready for the afternoon.

"When is Marcella going to arrive?" I asked Eli, who placed the clipboard in front of me and handed me my pen.

"She's waiting in the coffee room," Eli replied. "She arrived early and asked if she could sit and use our Wi-Fi to do some work while she waited."

"Bring her in," I said and signed the checks in front of me. Then I opened the file with the label *Marcella Binetti, Staffing Specialist.* She was the owner and CEO of Binetti Human Resources, which did work now and then for MBC when we had a need for workers.

Within a couple of minutes, in she walked, dressed in her usual black jacket and skirt duo, her black hair with the silver streak done up in an elaborate style. She looked like a fashionable and much friendlier Cruella Deville.

"Marcella," I said and went to meet her, shaking her hand, air kissing her cheeks. I led her to the seating area and we sat down across from each other. She placed her bag on the coffee table, and crossed her legs, studying me carefully.

"So, you're looking to find some staff for the *Chronicle*," she said, getting right to the point. "How exciting for you to take the paper over and try to resurrect it. But lots of work, I presume."

"Marcella, you would not believe it."

For the next hour, we discussed the positions I needed to fill and what efforts she'd undertake to find the right people.

"Thanks," I said and leaned back in my chair. "You can't imagine how happy I am that you're taking on this job. There's so much to do getting the paper up and running again. Too bad you couldn't find me a wife while you're at it."

"A wife?" she said, frowning. "As if you need my help for that. Honestly, Joshua, you're the last man I know who needs help finding a wife. All you have to do is go to a society function and the women will drip off you if you let them."

"I do need help." I ran my hand through my hair, feeling overwhelmed at the prospect of spending hours on dating sites filling out forms. "I don't have time to spend on this, but at the same time, it has to be done."

Then I told her about the clause in my father's will that gave each of us boys an incentivized trust and that we wouldn't get any money until we married.

"That's too bad," she said, her voice sympathetic. "I still don't think you need any help, Joshua. It should be easy. Go out to as many social functions as you can. Meet as many young single women in your circles as possible. You'll find someone appropriate."

I made a face. "That sounds like work. I always thought that falling in love was a natural process. You meet someone when you least expect it and you fall."

"If you want, I could create a list of suitable women and then arrange meetings with each of them so you can feel each of them out. That might take care of some of your time."

"Seriously?"

"Seriously. In the old country, my family had matchmakers and they took care of everything. It would be like *The Bachelor* but without the cameras," she said and her tone was hard to read. Was she being sarcastic or genuine?

"That's what my brother said to me."

"I have access to so many young professional well-educated women in their twenties and thirties. Surely one of them would be suitable. But if I am going to try to find a wife for you, you have to tell me what you're looking for."

I raised my eyebrows, because it sounded like we were actually talking about her finding me a wife.

"You're serious?"

"I'm a headhunter. It's only one step removed from being a matchmaker."

I shrugged. "I don't know if you can find love by listing a bunch of requirements on a piece of paper and interviewing candidates. I want to fall in love."

"Who said you won't fall in love? What you have to do is

expose yourself to as many of the right women as possible. One of them will be the one, if you meet enough of them. Then the more you meet, the more of a chance you have to find the right one."

I made a face, not enamored by the idea of hiring someone to find me a wife. Of course, I thought I had fallen in love with Christie, so what the hell did I know about love?

"Tell me about your ideal woman," Marcella said, taking out her pen and opening her notebook. "What would she be like? What about her level of education?"

I shrugged. "I guess I'd be looking for someone who has either a professional degree or a degree in the arts and sciences."

"Okay, so a degree. What else? Do you want a student or someone who had work experience?"

"I don't know," I said, folding my hands. "It really comes down to the person, not the degree or job they do."

"Yes, but Joshua, you have to meet the right women. Women of your background and values. The only way to do that is to think about your perfect woman and figure out where to meet her. I can help you with that. I have resumes of thousands of women in Manhattan. I'm sure I could sort through them and find some perfect candidates."

I thought for a moment, trying to approach it like a professional.

"I'm not so sure..."

"Give me a chance," she said. "Let me bring you a few resumes to look over. I even have headshots."

"What the hell," I said and shrugged. "Give it your best shot. It's not like I have all the time in the world to spend on dating sites or in bars."

"Good, good," Marcella said. "What about your perfect woman's politics?"

"I'd prefer someone who is independent politically, not affiliated with either political party. No need to get into political fights with me."

"That makes good sense," Marcella said. "What else do you require? Things you will not budge on. What about a family?"

"She has to want to have a family," I said and nodded. "I always thought that two kids would be perfect. Three preferably. She should want to stay home with them until they are school-aged."

"Okay, that helps. What else? Any preferences in terms of appearance?"

I shrugged. "She should be fit, a non-smoker, and attractive. I don't have any physical preferences beyond that."

"You don't care about height and weight?"

"She should be fit and attractive. That's the most important. I don't care about hair or eye color."

Marcella nodded. "Anything else you can think of at the moment? Religious affiliations? Hobbies?"

"As long as she isn't a fanatic, I'm tolerant." I leaned forward. "Look, Marcella. I really don't think you can engineer a romance. Maybe on television, but in real life, it comes down to chemistry."

"Look where chemistry got you..."

She raised her eyebrows.

I leaned back, prepared to fire her for that but then I kicked myself mentally. She was right. I had let my heart lead my head with Christie, thinking that our amazing chemistry would be enough to ensure I'd made a perfect match.

Obviously, I didn't know what the hell I was talking about.

I sighed. "She should enjoy travel. Not that I've had much opportunity to do any, but when I have a family and the children are old enough, I'll want to take them around the world. She should enjoy music and have her own preferences. Other than that, I'd like her to have some serious personal interest or hobby. I don't care what it is, as long as she's passionate about something."

"I think I could come up with a great list of candidates tomorrow, in fact."

"You really think you can find me a wife?" I said, shaking my head at the prospect. "I don't think it's possible, but it would sure take a burden off my shoulders."

"I'm almost certain I could. I'll have one of my staff come and interview you for personality and temperament matters. Is there anything else you require in a wife?"

I shook my head. "Not really. I thought I had myself a wife but apparently, I have very bad taste in women."

"Then leave it up to me," Marcella said and waved her hand. "It's going to be a matter of meeting them and feeling each of them out. Seeing who's compatible and who isn't. If you want to get married in a year, you need to start right away, if possible. Ideally, I'd like my staff to come by next week and conduct a few personality tests, that kind of thing."

I raised my eyebrows at that. "You sound like you have this all figured out."

"I've often thought how similar my profession is with matchmakers. In fact, it might be a profitable side business."

"Got to love entrepreneurs," I said and stood up, escorting her out of the office. "I don't envy you the job, frankly. I can't really believe you'll be successful."

"I'll find you a wife, Joshua. Leave it up to me. I'll bet that within a year, you'll be engaged and will be on your way to your wedding. In fact, you could leave the whole business up to me. I could even arrange the reception. I could check out venues and book them in advance. That way you'd get the most desirable choices."

"Isn't the groom supposed to consult with the bride's family first?" I said, feeling a bit too mercenary about everything. "It's traditional for the bride's family to pay for and organize the wedding and reception."

"Details. Don't worry about them. I'll take care of everything once you find your bride. Is there any place in particular you would like for the wedding? A church or other venue?"

"I'm Catholic, not practicing."

"St. Patrick's would be optimal," Marcella said and I could almost see the wheels turning in her mind. "It depends on the bride, of course, so maybe I could book it now and we could change the booking if there's some serious conflict."

"St. Patrick's is very popular," I said, remembering when Christie and I booked it the previous year. "They usually book a year in advance."

"I'll get right on to it."

I held the door for Marcella, smiling at how excited she seemed about the whole business.

"Do you have a date in mind?" I said, only somewhat sarcastically.

"Summer, preferably. Say, June in one year from now. I'll go ahead and book St. Patrick's if I can. We can always reschedule if necessary."

I looked at her more closely to see if she was serious but her expression was neutral.

"As to the reception," she went on. "Where would you prefer? Your own residence or would you consider renting a space?"

I sighed. Christie and I had planned on spending a few days at the house in the Hamptons.

"At my home in the Hamptons. It would be a perfect venue and I could house a dozen out-of-town guests there."

"Perfect. We can talk about decorations and food choices when we get closer to the date."

"You seem to have this all figured out," I said, walking down the hallway with her to the elevator. "The date, venue, reception. What about love?"

"What about love?" she asked, while I pushed the elevator

47

down button. "Love will happen. It's as simple as one plus one equals two. All you have to do is meet the right woman."

"I went through all this a year ago." I shrugged. "I thought she loved me. She didn't. She loved my money and position."

"You let your heart lead the way and you'll find her, Joshua. I know." She made a sympathetic face. "I recall reading about your engagement and what happened but I thought it was mutual."

"I didn't want to hurt her reputation."

"That was very gallant of you. Don't worry. This time, you'll be successful."

"I hope so. It was a hell I'd prefer not live through again."

The elevator arrived.

"Thanks again, Marcella. My assistant will provide you with any assistance you need in this matter and regarding staffing the paper. He'll coordinate with your office on meetings and that sort of thing."

"That works for me. Thanks and good luck."

I smiled. "I'm sure that in your expert hands, Marcella, I won't need luck."

I returned to my office and sat down behind my desk, glad I'd gotten that out of the way and could forget about finding a wife and the mother of my children for a while. I had bigger and harder fish to catch and fry.

Yet something nagged at me in the back of my mind. Was I being too venal about the whole business? I felt somewhat jaded about love and marriage, especially after my recent failed engagement. I had thought I'd be living the happy-ever-after lifestyle by now, but that had all come to a crushing halt earlier that year, when I'd discovered my soon-to-be-wife in bed with her boss.

That night I was supposed to be away on a trip to California to meet with David, but I'd come home to retrieve some files I'd left on the desk in my home office. I walked in only to find that, within half an hour of my departure, after I had kissed her goodbye and we had said how much we loved each other and couldn't wait for the wedding, *he* had come over and was fucking my future wife in my bed.

In fact, the bastard was in the short strokes when I opened the door, and he actually finished. Neither of them realized I was standing there in the doorway, watching myself become a cuckold.

Our wedding was weeks off, so I'd found out in the nick of time. If I had married her and found out afterward, she would have been entitled to a small share of my income and wealth, based on our pre-nup. This way, the only thing she had of mine was the engagement ring and a lot of time I had wasted imagining that I was in love with her and she with me.

We split, and I kept the reason to myself. I told only David, who had waited for me at the airport even though I'd missed the plane. I had to take the next one after kicking her out of the apartment, her hastily-packed overnight bag in hand.

I told her she could come and get the rest the next day when I was out of town. Then I left for LA and never looked back.

I spent the next week in a drunken haze, partying with my brother in LA's finest watering holes, eating in the best restaurants to be seen in and to see other Hollywood stars and celebrities. David had a stable full of willing groupies who were only too happy to console me in my post-break-up doldrums. It was a week I soon hoped to forget because there was too much of everything – too much pussy, too much booze and pot, too much crazy dancing until late in the night. In addition, I'd had too little sleep and sober reflection on what went wrong and how I missed all the signals.

When I returned home to Manhattan, I cleaned out the apartment we had shared and put it on the market, moving into a different one owned by the company in the new building. I hadn't taken the time to find a proper apartment elsewhere and so had stayed in the apartment with my few personal possessions. I got a storage space for a year, to store the rest of the stuff I had accumulated until I felt recovered enough to search for a home of my own.

Now, I'd wait for my future wife so we could find a place together.

Part of me knew I would have to seriously focus on meeting women and being real with them, but at that moment, the sting of my breakup with the woman I thought I'd spend the rest of my life with was still real enough that I didn't want to deal with it.

So I didn't.

Instead, I'd let Marcella do the work, not really believing she could find me a wife. With the money I'd get access to, I could invest in hiring a full complement of staff and finish furnishing and appointing the offices I'd had custom built in the Fifth Avenue building that Michael and I had teamed up to work on.

In truth, I suspected that I was approaching it this way to protect myself from caring too much about the outcome, even though this was probably the most momentous life decision I could make. That small part of me that knew I was acting foolishly was shoved aside for the part of me that thought hiring someone to do the legwork was just a smart business move.

If Marcella was right, I figured that in a year or two at most, I'd be on my honeymoon with my new wife, and we'd spend the first month on a vacation, trying to get her pregnant. Then, in nine months, our baby would be born. A year later, I'd inherit the second instalment of my trust account.

I didn't believe it for a moment, but at least I could put it out of my mind.

CHAPTER SEVEN

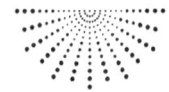

ELLA

I DID my best to organize the small number of possessions I brought with me from New Hampshire. Three sleeveless dresses, three cashmere cardigan sweaters, two pairs of slacks, five t-shirts, a jacket, boyfriend jeans, undies and bras, socks, yoga pants and sleeveless t-shirt, and scarves galore. Add a pair of pumps, a sexy pair of strappy pumps, running shoes, and boots, and that was the extent of my wardrobe. I'd have to be creative with my scarves and sweater/dress combinations so that I didn't seem to be wearing the same thing every day.

I spent that night alone in my tiny apartment, eating some curry from a take-out restaurant down the street – my one indulgence. The next morning, I'd start my new position, and I wanted everything to be perfect.

Before bed, I laid out my black sleeveless dress, a pink cashmere cardigan, my sober black pumps, and hose, hanging everything on a hanger on the back of the door. If I timed everything right, I could hop out of bed at seven fifteen, eat my breakfast, have a shower, dress, and leave the apartment by eight fifteen, arriving at the publishing house at eight fifty, with ten minutes to pick up a coffee and make it inside to my destiny.

At least, that was the plan.

Things turned out to be very not according to plan.

I stood in the middle of Grand Central Station where I had to change trains and realized I'd been robbed.

I had arrived only moments earlier, and decided to check out the subway map to make sure I was taking the right train to get to work when I got an email. I heard the *ping* and opened my backpack, then removed my cell.

Sure enough, there was an email from Sharon.

Ella!

I'm sorry but I have to cancel our meeting this morning. Can you come at 1:30 instead? My filling fell out when I was eating a pumpernickel bagel and one of the pieces of caraway must have knocked it out, so I'll be at the dentist. Please, take the morning off. I do need you this afternoon though. Bring a notebook and pen and be ready to take notes. I would usually have supplies for you, but we're in a temp office until renovations on our new one is finished, and the stock room is all packed up. I'll reimburse you for anything you spend until they finish the new office space. Thank God, you're here. I've been without someone to help since my last intern left two weeks ago so believe me, I'm so happy that I have you. Meet me at my office at 1:30. I have a 2:00 and want you to take notes, but I'll have time to show you around the office and get you set up in your temporary space before the meeting.

52

Can't wait to have you as my assistant and help organize my day.
Sharon

I sent her a response right away.
Sharon!
So sorry your filling fell out. I'll be there at 1:30 sharp.
I'm really glad to be working with you.
Ella

So there I was, having arrived downtown for my first day of work, and I had the morning to kill. I stood in Grand Central and glanced around, admiring the beautiful art deco building. Just then, a nice little old lady wearing a polka-dot kerchief over her grey hair stood beside me.

"Excuse," she said in a thick Eastern European accent. "Could you please to help me find?"

"Sure," I said and leaned closer, checking out the address scrawled on a piece of paper. Then I examined the large transit map she opened, trying to help her find a specific stop on the subway that would take her to an address in Brighton Beach.

That was my first mistake.

I mean, who was I to think I should be helping someone else find their way around the city when I had only just arrived? But I was sure I could read a map... Besides, she was such a sweet old lady.

Suddenly the old lady folded the map up. "Thank you," she said. "Now I go."

Then she sped off, suddenly and amazingly agile. The thing was, she left the station instead of going down to the platform and taking the train I'd suggested.

"Hey!" I called out. "You're going the wrong way!" I gestured to the escalator leading down to the platform she was supposed to be taking, but she disappeared out the door and into the morass of pedestrians. I shrugged to myself, figuring she must have her reasons, and leaned over to grab my backpack.

In a completely comedic fashion, I reached into thin air where my backpack had once been, only to find it was gone. Unbeknownst to me, while I was so kindly and naively studying the map to figure out how the little old lady could get to her destination, her accomplice was busy snagging my backpack. The super-fantastic backpack specially designed to contain all my most valuable possessions.

My laptop. My cell. My wallet. My passport. My freaking money order for the apartment in Chelsea – the real apartment, with the real exposed brick and private bathroom.

I turned and saw a person rushing out another door, my backpack in hand.

"Hey, you! Stop!"

I chased after the middle-aged woman, my black heels clattering on the stairs, but before I could get to the street, she disappeared into a wall of people.

Feeling helpless, I went back into the station and stood there speechless, at a loss for what to do next. I had to take a train to Fifth Avenue, for my first day as an intern. I should never have put my backpack down and let my attention be distracted elsewhere, but I was trying to be nice. The poor little old Slavic lady had looked confused and helpless. My instincts were to help her.

I was freaking out internally that I'd just lost all my ID, not to mention the cashier's check for my first and last month's rent, which represented months of savings. I was supposed to give the landlord the check when I went to pick up the keys to my new apartment on Monday after work.

I'd have to go to my bank and get another check, but of

course, since I didn't have my ID, how would they know it was me?

Oh. My. *God*...

Now, what the hell was I going to do? I'd be homeless unless I could somehow get a new cashier's check. Without it, I'd have no apartment.

As it was I had no cellphone. No laptop. Worst of all, no wallet. Even my damn keys to the Airbnb were gone. I'd have to call the landlord to get her to let me in.

But... my cell was in my damn backpack!

I went to a payphone and called Steph, my best friend in all the world, who was going to join me in Manhattan as soon as her exams were finished at Christmas.

I called collect.

As soon as she answered, the words just spilled out of me.

"Steph, oh my God, I can't believe what happened – I just arrived in Grand Central Station on my way to my new job and was just helping this little old lady with a babushka and someone who was her accomplice took my backpack and--"

Finally, she stopped me.

"Ella!" she said in a firm voice. "Slow down. Slow down. Don't panic."

Don't panic? How could she tell me not to panic? She knew me better than anyone. Panic was my middle name.

"What do you mean, don't panic?" I said, glancing around the station. "Everything's gone! I've been robbed. I have nothing. No money, no ID, no laptop."

"Nothing?"

"I have my suitcase with clothes in the Airbnb I rented but everything else is gone and I can't even get into my apartment because the key is in my backpack. That's why I'm calling collect."

"Oh, God," she said, and even she was starting to sound

panicked. "You have to call your bank immediately and cancel your credit cards and debit cards. You have to go to the police and report the theft. If you want, I'll buy you a ticket so you can come home. I'll pay for it and you can pick it up."

"I don't want to come back," I replied, glancing around the station. Even if it was big and scary, I had a job here and I was damned well not going to go running back home, tail between my legs. "I've been wanting an opportunity like this for years."

"Sometimes you have to admit defeat. Besides, the internship is unpaid. I'll buy you a ticket. All you have to do is pick it up."

"With what?" I asked, running my hand through my hair. "I can't even prove who I am."

I heard a huge sigh on the other end of the line. "I don't know what else to do. Go to the American Consulate?"

"Seriously?" I chewed my nail. "Maybe I can go to the Social Security Office and tell them my card number?"

"I don't know. My brother lost his wallet once and it was hell trying to get everything replaced, but he had his Social Security card at home. You're not supposed to carry it in your wallet, you know. Just in case someone steals it or you lose it. Identity theft? John used his Social Security number as proof of ID. Plus he had all his banking info. Letters to him from the bank. The only other option you have is to call your dad. He probably has friends in Manhattan. They could provide for you, get you some money until you can replace everything – but it'll be expensive. New cell, new laptop. All that ID."

A surge of adrenaline went through my veins. "He'll more likely to send a private plane and make me come back to New Hampshire."

"He might, but only because he loves you."

I rubbed my forehead, feeling the first tinges of a headache coming on. "I can't call him and ask for help. It'll just confirm in his mind that I can't take care of myself."

"Which, obviously, you can't..."

"Steph! I'm the victim here. You're supposed to be my bestie. You're supposed to be sympathetic."

"I'm supposed to tell you the unvarnished truth. You're clearly too inexperienced in the ways of the world to be in Manhattan all on your own. You were robbed your first week."

"My third day."

"Even worse," she said. "Call your dad."

No freaking way. Yes, I got taken in, robbed in the middle of the morning in a public space. That wasn't lost on me. But I wasn't going to give in so easily.

The very last thing I'd do was call him – Mr. Future President, as I liked to call him teasingly. He'd shake his finger at me and tell me that he was right, I shouldn't have moved to Manhattan. I should have stayed in Concord and lived with him and my mother until I found another husband.

"Look, I have to go to my job, talk to my boss. Maybe she'll accept an email transfer and give me some cash so I can at least get a new cell. I could probably get by with a tablet instead of a laptop. That would be cheaper. I could use my computer at work to access my bank account and send her my money."

"*Ella...*"

"Well, it's worth a try, right?"

"Okay, but she'll think you're a total loser if you tell her you were robbed on your first day on the job and need to hit her up for money."

"What's worse is that my cashier's check for first and last on the Chelsea apartment was in my bag. I don't even have that or my keys to the Airbnb."

"Oh, God, Ella. You are so screwed. Where are you going to stay?"

"I don't know. I'll have to contact the landlord to get into my place in Chelsea. If I can get money to my boss, maybe she can get a cashier's check for me? The least I can do is go to the meeting and explain what happened and ask for her help. If she won't help, *then* I'll call my dad."

"Call me as soon as you know what's happening. When you get back, we can get drunk."

"I'm not coming back," I said, a little too firmly. I took in a deep cleansing breath, trying to calm myself. "If I have to come back, I'm just going to do it all again, and you know it, so I might as well soldier on."

"I do know it. Why you can't be happy here I'll never know. What's Concord? Chopped liver?"

"It's not Manhattan. Manhattan is where the literary world lives."

"I know, I know. Call me collect as soon as you know what's going on. Love you."

Steph ended the call so I hung up the payphone receiver and stood there for a moment, debating whether to call my father now or later. I had about $4.95 in my pocket and wanted to save that in case I needed to eat or make another call.

First on my agenda – find a library so I could use a computer to let Sharon, my boss, know I was going to be late. Then, I had to go to the closest police precinct and report the theft.

I found a nearby public library and sat at a terminal, thankful that there was some public access to the internet in the city. I had less than five dollars in my pocket and didn't want to have to buy a coffee just to use the internet café down the street.

I opened my Gmail and sent Sharon a note, wanting to ensure that I hadn't been scammed about the internship on top of everything else. I didn't believe Sharon was a fake boss, but after the start to my morning, I was beginning to think I was the most naïve person alive.

. . .

I WALKED the ten blocks to the 17th Precinct and stopped at the front desk.

"I need to report a crime."

The duty officer, tall and older with thick dark hair shot through with grey, looked up from his roster and stared at me through his reading glasses.

"What crime?"

"I was robbed. In Grand Central Station."

He looked me over and I could tell from the expression on his face that he could barely keep from laughing out loud.

"You're in luck. We're unusually quiet right now. Fill out a form and you'll meet with an officer to give a statement." He turned to the large room where several police officers sat at their desks.

"Hey, Barnesy," he called out to a police officer sitting a few desks over. "I've got a live one for you."

Barnesy – aka Sgt. Barnes – was equally unsympathetic to my plight. Middle-aged, balding, with a tiny red swizzle stick clamped tightly between his teeth, Barnes sat at his desk and hesitated when I related to him what happened. I could see him trying to hold back a grin.

He took the swizzle stick out of his mouth and jabbed the air with it. "So, you say you sat down at a bench, and an older woman approached you and asked for help with a transit map."

"Yes. Exactly. She seemed nice and sweet. Like a grand-mother, a recent immigrant. All dressed in black like an old widow. She sat beside me and opened this big map of the subway system. I leaned over and tried to figure it out."

"And on your second day in Manhattan, you felt capable of explaining the transit system to someone else?" he asked, an expectant expression on his not-sympathetic face.

I shrugged one shoulder, feeling like a total idiot.

"I wanted to help an old lady. You know, be kind to your

59

elders? Besides, I spent hours studying the transit map before I came here, so I know it pretty well. We tried to figure it out together. Or so I thought..."

He finally cracked a smile, but it wasn't a mean smile. I thought I saw some sympathy in his eyes. He turned back to his computer keyboard. "What did she look like?"

I gave him details about the woman and watched while he typed with two fingers on his keyboard. Elderly with grey hair pulled back into a ponytail, and a black scarf over top. Blue eyes. Slavic accent. Thick black overcoat. I didn't really look at her too much, wanting to be polite.

"And when did you realize your backpack was gone?"

"After the woman left. She seemed in a hurry to leave but she didn't take the train I said she should take. I reached down to get my backpack to catch my own train and it was gone."

He glanced at his computer screen over his reading glasses. "It's a common scam in public transit spaces. Distract the target, then snag the purse or bag. Happens pretty much every day." He typed on his keyboard for a moment.

"I saw a woman leaving with my backpack in hand. I chased her but I was wearing these," I said. and showed him my heels. "I couldn't run fast enough to catch up."

I described the younger woman – dressed in ordinary clothes, jeans, a long black sweater, her dark hair pulled back in a ponytail.

"What's the chance that I'll ever see my backpack and ID again?"

He turned to me and looked me squarely in the eye. "I don't like to be the bearer of bad news, but you will probably never see any of your possessions again. It's highly unlikely that we will recover your property. In the future, keep your backpack on or keep it between your knees. The place is teeming with pickpockets and thieves."

60

I nodded. I'd already figured this crime was so common that the cops would rarely even try to do anything about it besides take a report.

"You could check local pawn shops for anything of value in your backpack, but they'll likely remove the SIM card from your cell, and wipe your laptop so you'll never see them again. The wallet?" He crossed his arms and chewed on his swizzle stick. "You have to call the bank and report any credit and debit cards. Call Social Security to report a stolen SSN. It'll take a while to get replacements. You'll need to go to the passport office and get a new passport, but that'll take a couple of weeks."

"I don't have any ID."

He shrugged. "Call your family."

"I can't."

He raised his eyebrows. "Family problems?"

I nodded and glanced away. "I'm just trying to stay independent. This is my first time away from home. I don't want to go running back to my father if I don't have to."

"No aunt, uncle, cousin, or best friend who can help?"

"Yes, but how do they get money to me here when I have no ID? I can't even go to Western Union."

He squinted like he didn't believe me. "You know absolutely no one in Manhattan?"

Of course, I did know *some* people. Or at least, some people knew me. They knew my father, who had associates here, and I had no doubt that they would be very willing to curry favor with him by helping his errant daughter. They were the last people I wanted to rely on. I was trying to *escape* my father's world. But it was looking increasingly like I had no other choice.

"I know my new boss. That's it." I sat there, disheartened.

"Do you have a place to stay?"

"I'm in an Airbnb until Monday, when I get an apartment in Chelsea, but the cashier's check was in my backpack."

"Cashier's check?"

"It was a private deal. A sublet."

He sat back, his eyes on me, his expression grimly amused. "Chelsea? Pretty swank area for a newcomer. How much you paying?"

"You don't want to know," I repeated, and took a deep breath. "I used up almost all my savings so I could afford a place in Manhattan."

"You and a hundred thousand other hopefuls. You say you have a job?"

I told him about my internship. "I start this afternoon. It's unpaid. I'm hoping to get a paid position once the internship is over."

"You moved to Manhattan for an unpaid internship?" Sgt. Barnes shook his head as he finished up typing and clicked to print the report. "That's either incredibly brave or incredibly foolish."

"Maybe both," I said with a rueful laugh.

The printer beside Sgt. Barnes hummed into action and spat out a sheet of paper. He took it and handed me a pen, pointing to where I should sign for the police report.

"You've had a very bad day. Look," he said and leaned forward, sympathy finally touching his eyes. "I don't know what's up with your family that you don't want to contact them, but this is kind of an emergency. You're broke. You have no ID. You need to call someone and get help. It's that or you start dumpster-diving and sleeping under the Brooklyn Bridge with the vagrants, but you wouldn't like the food. I can tell by looking at you that you're not cut out for the free-food lifestyle or the open-air sleeping concept."

I covered my eyes, finally overcome with emotion. "I know," I said, biting back tears. "My only hope is to ask my new boss to accept a money transfer on my behalf." I glanced at him to see his response.

62

"Are you sure the job isn't a scam, too?"

"*No*," I said, shaking my head. "That much I do know. I have a position waiting for me. I'm supposed to go this afternoon and meet my boss."

"You could ask for your boss's help, but it's not the kind of thing that will encourage confidence in you as a potential employee..." He raised his eyebrows meaningfully.

"I have to try," I said.

"Got a Plan B?" he asked expectantly.

"There is no Plan B. This is Plan A, B and C. Anyway, there's really nothing you can do, but thanks for listening."

"No problem. We do have social workers who could help you find a shelter or somewhere to stay if you need it." He handed me a card, and I tucked it into my pocket. "If you think of anything else, give me a call."

I forced a smile and then left the station house, checking the clock on the wall, not wanting to miss my meeting with Sharon. I hoped that I wouldn't have to call a social worker for help, but I was beginning to think that might be my last resort. No matter what, I wasn't going back to Manchester, but I might need to find a soup kitchen so I wouldn't have to dive into a stinking dumpster under the Brooklyn Bridge...

Until then, I had to find a cheap notebook and pen. I wandered around the streets, then went into a small bookstore to pick up a notebook and pen. The only options open to me were various superhero and toy-themed children's notebooks and pencils with toys on top that were on sale.

I chose Ironman for my notebook and a pencil with a purple-haired troll on top. I'd tell my boss it was the only notebook I could get on the fly. It would be a good story – one that we could laugh about one day.

Today was going to be one of those momentous days that you could look back on and laugh about, right?

. . .

I ARRIVED outside the Macintyre Building on Fifth Avenue, my stomach totally in knots. The building was an old Art Deco with brass fixtures and actual sculptures, some of them looking like gargoyles. There was a security desk at the front, which I went to.

A nice older man dressed in a blue uniform greeted me.

"Hello. Ella Carlson to see Sharon Rogers."

The man nodded and picked up a phone. He spoke softly into the phone and then nodded. He hung up and smiled at me. "Can I see some ID?"

I smiled guiltily. "My wallet was stolen in Grand Central Station."

He glanced at me, his eyes moving up and down over my clothing and at the notebook and troll pencil I held in my hand. "I'll need to see some ID."

"Could you maybe ask Ms. Rogers to come down? Honestly, I don't have any ID but we've Skyped before so she knows me."

He picked up the phone once more and spoke quietly into it. He glanced at me, responded to whoever was on the other end, then hung up once more.

"She said you have auburn hair and big green eyes and that I should let you up even without ID."

"Thank you," I said and mock-wiped my brow. "I haven't had a chance to go to the bank or Social Security office to get replacement cards. I spent the last few hours in the police station giving a report."

He smiled back at me. "Rough morning?"

"You don't know the half of it."

He gave me a temporary ID and pointed to the elevators. "Twenty-seventh floor. Once you get the documentation, we'll get you a permanent card but that'll work for today."

"Thanks."

64

I took the card and headed to the elevator. The doors were just closing so I called out for them to hold.

When the door re-opened, I stepped on and saw a brown-haired businessman wearing a gray suit, with his back to the door. Beside him stood a bicycle courier in full riding uniform. He was leaning against the elevator wall, his helmet in his hand, his hair wet and his bangs falling in his eyes in a very sexy way. Bandages on his elbows and knees...

It was the bike courier from the previous day. The one who almost ran me down. The one I made crash into a taxi.

Crap...

CHAPTER EIGHT

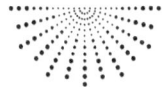

JOSHUA

I HAD A MEETING IN AN HOUR, and would have to shower and change into my business suit after my bike ride. I usually rode first thing, but today I was going to ride after a meeting at the old building in the financial district which took all morning.

I went to the apartment I kept in the building and changed into my riding suit. I donned my helmet and gloves, checked the bandages over my scuffed knees, and left the building, bringing my bike down in the elevator with me.

For the next half hour, I rode around Central Park, my usual route, and had worked up a good sweat by the time I arrived back. I squirted my face with the water bottle and walked my bike into the building.

On my way, I met up with Keith Sheppard, one of my executives. Keith and I were friends and played a game of basketball whenever we could at the gym we both frequented.

"What the hell happened?" he asked, spotting my bandages.

67

I laughed and checked my elbow. "I ran into the prettiest woman I've seen in a long time, while she was jaywalking across the street yesterday."

"Ooh," he said and grimaced. "Which one of you got the worst of it?"

"I did," I said and pushed the bike through the security gate. "I managed to miss her but didn't miss the back of a taxi. My knees and elbows got the worst of the deal. Bike's good."

"Risks of being a die-hard cyclist, I guess."

"You got it."

"But at least you ran into a pretty young woman. I guess that's one way of meeting women in this town."

I nodded. "She thought I was a bicycle courier."

He grinned. "Did you disabuse her of that misinformation?"

"No, I did not. She kept offering to pay for my doctor visit or bandages. Wondered if I could get worker's comp. I guess she was thinking that since I was a courier, I might not have health insurance. Said she would call my boss in case I needed an excuse to take the day off. She was being so sweet worrying about my health care, I didn't have the heart to tell her my family owned the building."

"Oh, that's too funny," he said. "So, she has no idea that you're one of the wealthiest business moguls in Manhattan?"

"She does not and that's the way it's going to stay." I pushed the elevator button. "It's nice not to be recognized sometimes."

The elevator arrived and we stepped inside. Before the doors closed, I heard the clack-clack-clack of high heels on marble floors.

"Wait! Hold the elevator, please!"

A woman was running to the elevator.

I pressed the door-open button, and the doors bounced back to reveal *her*– the woman I'd almost run over the previous day, standing there in all her glory. She appeared completely frazzled, a strand of her shiny hair falling out of her hair clip. When she entered the elevator, everything about her made me stand up straighter. I had noticed she was attractive the previous day, but had been distracted by my wounds – and my anger.

But now... she was lovely.

When she saw me, she stopped in her tracks. The expression on her face was so comic I almost laughed out loud.

"Oh, it's *you*. Sorry," she said and stepped back off the elevator. "I'll wait for the other elevator." Her cheeks flushed beet red.

"No, no," I said quickly, waving her on. "Come in. I won't bite. They're doing construction and the other elevator isn't in service. This one's fine."

"Okay," she said doubtfully. She stepped into the elevator and stood facing the doors, and I could tell she was utterly embarrassed to be running into me again.

She turned and looked at me. "Are you okay?" she asked, then pointed to my knees and elbows. "Did I do that?"

I glanced down at myself and smiled. "You did, actually. My name's Josh, by the way. Just in case you wanted to know the name of the man you injured."

"Ella," she said and grimaced. "I'm *so* sorry. It must be hard to keep working when you're injured like that."

"Oh, I'm fine," I said and stood up straighter, flexing my bicep like a bodybuilder. "I'm tough. Tough enough to work even with scraped knees and elbows."

I winked at Keith and we both smiled.

"Did your boss let you at least take the day off?" she asked.

I shook my head. "Boss is a slave driver."

Keith coughed into his fist and the two of us exchanged smiles again. I looked back at her, my expression solemn.

"Besides, if I want to put food on the table, I have to work, scraped knees or not."

Her expression was priceless. I felt like a cad leading her on that way, but it was only in good fun.

"If I can do anything to make it up to you – pay for your costs at the doctor, whatever, just tell me."

"Nah," I said, impressed with her willingness to make things right. "I'm good. You're too sweet."

Our eyes met and I had a good look at them... Her eyes were green with light brown flecks, her lashes long. I felt a definite surge inside, imagining us together.

"Are you just starting work today?" she asked, apparently trying to be pleasant. "You don't have a delivery bag yet."

"Yeah, I'm just going up to start the day," I said, keeping up with the lie. "Our office is in this building." I grinned.

She smiled back, revealing the cutest dimples. "For a moment, I thought you might sue me the other day."

"Nah," I said and shook my head. "Hazard of riding a bike in Manhattan. I was flying along the lane in between the rows of cars. As a professional, I should have been more careful."

The elevator stopped at the twentieth floor and Keith moved to the front of the elevator. He gave the woman a smile on his way by.

"Take care," he said and we fist-bumped before he got off. "Gotta watch out for those pedestrians. Especially the pretty ones."

"You do," I said. "I'll be on the lookout for sure."

Then the doors closed, leaving me alone with her. When the elevator started once more, I watched her out of the corner of my eye. She was hot with curves visible under her little black dress and pink sweater.

"Nice pencil," I said spying it in her hand – a troll pencil complete with purple hair. "I haven't seen one of those since public school. Where'd you get that?"

She held up the pencil and smiled. "Oh, this? It was all I

70

could find in the bookstore near Grand Central Station. Do you think my boss will like it?"

I laughed, amused at her sense of humor.

"It's choice," I said, taking it from her and turning it around. "I like the purple hair."

"I usually prefer blue hair myself, but this was all I could afford."

"So, they still sell troll pencils?" I said. "I'll have to pay a visit."

"Yeah. It goes perfectly with this," she said and showed me an Iron Man spiral notebook.

I took it from her and examined it. "Oh, man, I would have *killed* to have one of these when I was growing up. Iron Man?" I whistled and handed it back. "How come you have such good taste in office supplies? We only have the boring type in the stockroom. You know – yellow pencils, plain paper notepads."

She sighed. "I was robbed today in the subway station. Almost all my worldly possessions gone. But it's my first day at my new job. I have my first meeting with my boss, and I need to take notes."

"Oh, damn," I said, frowning. "You were robbed? What happened?"

She told me about being robbed – an old Slavic lady working with an accomplice to steal her backpack.

"That's too bad," I said, sympathy for her filling me. "It's been a fantastic morning, then."

"Absolutely stellar," she replied with a rueful laugh. "Memorable. One that will live on in infamy. A day I'll tell my children about and they'll tell their children and so on. That is, if I make it out alive."

"You have to keep an eye on your bags in Grand Central Station. In any station, for that matter. There are a lot of pickpockets and thieves in this town."

"I know. I feel like I'm like the country mouse in the big city

71

for the first time. The pickpockets and confidence men can probably spot me a mile away."

"I'm sure they can," I said. "You do have that general innocent look about you."

"You mean rube, right?"

I laughed. "I mean unthreatening and maybe inexperienced."

We smiled together – then the elevator jolted to a stop, the lights blinking out.

She screamed.

CHAPTER NINE

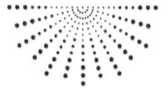

ELLA

"IT'S OKAY," Josh said, his voice calm. "The auxiliary lights will come on within twenty seconds. You don't have to worry."

"It's not the lights I'm worried about," I said, breathless, both my hands reaching out to find the wall. "It's the elevator falling." I found him instead, my hands gripping onto one of his biceps, which even to my terrified mind felt impressive. "Oh, sorry," I said and pulled my hands away, searching for the wall. "I wanted to hold onto the railing."

"No problem," he said, his voice amused in the darkness. "Always happy to help a damsel in distress. And the elevator wouldn't likely fall. If anything, it'd probably go up and hit the roof."

Of course, that sent my heart rate racing. "Thanks for those words of encouragement."

"Any time," he said softly and I could almost see his smile in the darkness.

I found the railing and held on, my eyes shut tightly. If it was pitch black, I didn't want to know it. Somehow, with my eyes closed, I could pretend it was just dark because they were shut and not because I was in a stalled elevator somewhere above the tenth floor.

It seemed like an eternity but was probably more like ten seconds before the lights did click on. Secondary lights, not as bright as the usual overhead lights. I kept hold of the railing but turned my head to meet his eyes, needing to see that he, at least, was calm.

"Power must have gone out. It happens sometimes. This building's old and being renovated," he said quickly, like he was trying to calm me. "Just internal offices being refinished. Drywall. Electrical. That sort of thing."

"This has happened before?"

He nodded, and bit his bottom lip. "Hate to tell you, but several times, in fact."

"Great," I said. "I have to take it at least four times a day, five days a week."

"So, this is your first day?"

I nodded, glad to be distracted for a moment, but I didn't want to tell him too much.

"Cool," he replied. "We're neighbors."

"Yes," I said, my throat dry. I swallowed, trying to moisten my tongue, which felt like cotton. "It's only my third day in New York, in fact. I'm from New Hampshire."

"You're having a really great intro to Manhattan. Almost killed by a cyclist. Robbed in Grand Central. Caught in an elevator with the power out." He shook his head. "I officially apologize for my city."

"Thank you, but I've wanted to live here all my life," I replied, my voice wavering. "But I really am having a great day. I have no money and no ID. And I may be homeless, if I can't get someone to accept a wire transfer for me."

He frowned. "You really have no money? No ID?"

"Yeah, someone stole my fantastic custom-made and designed backpack with slots for everything. There was a GoFundMe campaign by the creators, and I was one of the early adopters. It had a slot for a laptop, a tablet, an iPhone, your passport, a built-in wallet, places for pens and notebooks... There was even a built-in battery charger so like a fool, I put everything inside."

"Jesus. I saw those advertised on the internet. I was almost going to buy one for myself."

"They're great, but it had everything I owned of value in it. Wallet. ID. Computer. Even my cashier's check for my first and last month's rent for my new apartment."

"Crap. Do you have any friends in town who can help? Any family? Business associates?"

I sighed and ticked off imaginary numbers on my fingers. "Nope. Nope. Nope."

"Damn," he said in a low voice. "Sorry," he added. "That's really rough. Manhattan is great, but it can be a hard place to live."

"I'm going to my first meeting with my new boss and I'm going to have to ask her if she'll accept a bank transfer for me. I won't be able to eat or pay for my new apartment otherwise. The police officer who interviewed me said he didn't think I was the type to do well dumpster-diving and sleeping under the Brooklyn Bridge."

He laughed. "I would have to agree. You most definitely wouldn't do well living on the streets."

I laughed in return and then, when the moment passed, I exhaled heavily. "Maybe the local soup kitchen has room in the lineup."

He watched me for a moment and then he crossed his arms. "I can front you some cash until you can get your ID."

"You?" I glanced at him to see if he was serious. "That's so nice of you to offer, but I don't want to impose on a stranger. Especially a stranger I almost sent to the ER yesterday."

"I hate to see you ask your new boss to accept the money transfer on your first day. You should be doing everything you can to be seen as competent and capable."

"And being robbed in Grand Central Station would signal that I'm not?"

He shrugged, grinning. Then he grew serious. "It would just mean you were her problem instead of the solution to her problem."

I glanced at my Fitbit, which told me I had exactly three minutes to make my meeting.

"Oh, damn," I said. "Speaking of my boss, I'm supposed to be meeting her in three minutes."

He removed a cell from a pocket over the bicep of his riding suit sleeve. "Be my guest."

"Thanks," I replied, then I opened up a browser window and signed into my Gmail account. Then, I sent her an email.

SHARON – it's me, Ella. Just a quick note to let you know that I'm currently stuck on the elevator somewhere between the tenth and twelfth floor. I know you have a meeting so just in case they don't get us out before then, you'll have to go by yourself. So sorry!

LUCKILY, she got it right away and sent me a response.

· · ·

No problem. That damn elevator. I'll be glad when they get the other one working. Good luck. It took two hours the last time someone got stuck. See you as soon as you get here. If I'm in the meeting, just have Tate show you in.

I handed the cell back to him and sighed. "She said it might take two hours to get us out."

"That sounds about right."

I closed my eyes. "Two hours in this elevator... I *hate* elevators."

"You're really very safe. Safer than driving in a car. Or a bike." He grinned.

I sighed. "Well, there's nothing I can do. I'm going to miss my first meeting with my boss on my first day of work. What else can go wrong?"

"Shh," he said. "Don't tempt the gods." He shook his head, his gaze moving over me. "You look like you need a drink."

I laughed, but the idea of a glass of beer sounded really good to me. "I need something, that's for sure."

"When you're finished today, I'll take you for a drink and meal at Frank's Pub down the street. They have great food. Call me when you're done for the day."

"I don't have a cell."

He nodded. "I have a burner if you want to use it. "

"I couldn't impose on you."

"No seriously. You can use it until you get your money transfer and a new cell."

I stared at him, shocked that he was being so generous.

"That's really nice of you, but you don't have to," I said, a surge of gratitude going through me. He was gorgeous, and he was nice. And he was asking me to go out with him. That was a date, right? Or, at least, a sympathy invite.

"I know I don't have to, but I want to. I have a weakness for damsels in distress. They bring out the hero in me." He grinned, giving me a brilliant smile.

"I wouldn't want to deny a man the chance to be a hero," I said. "How could I resist?"

"Resistance is futile."

Just then, the elevator jerked back into action and we ascended past the twelfth floor.

"Oh, thank *God*," I said and closed my eyes. "I might just make that meeting after all."

"Thank the elevator gods," he said with a chuckle. "Usually, this takes a lot longer. You're blessed."

"I am." I smiled at him, feeling like I just might make it through the day after all.

"I'm serious about the cell and that drink and meal. Considering you lost all your earthly goods, it's the least I can do."

"It might take a couple of days to pay you back."

He shrugged. "When you get some money, I want that pencil. I must have that pencil!"

I smiled and held it up. "It's yours – once I get some money."

"Look. Come up to the apartment and I'll give you the cell."

"Okay," I said finally and only because I really needed a cell phone.

We went up to the top floor of the building. We left the elevator and there was only one apartment on the floor. Josh opened the door and pointed inside.

"Come on in," he said. "I'll get you that cell."

"Holy cow, is this *your* apartment?"

"No," he said and waved a hand. "The company owns it. I just have access because I know the owner of the company."

We went inside and I stood in awe. The apartment was amazing. Floor-to-ceiling windows on all sides, looking out over the Manhattan skyline. High-end furniture and decorations. It was worth millions, even to my unsophisticated eye for real estate.

I watched as he went to a drawer in the most amazing kitchen I had ever seen in my life – huge, with chef-level appliances. Now, my father had a great income from his position as a governor and the business he owned before he went into politics, but this – this was wealth above and beyond anything I had ever seen up close.

"Aren't you intimidated being in this place?" I said, walking around, running my hand over the marble fireplace hearth. I stood at the window and looked out over the city. "It's fantastic."

"The view *is* good," he said. He came over to where I stood and handed me an iPhone.

"This is a burner phone?"

"Not really, but it's an old model. It's been factory reset and I put a new SIM card inside so it should work. You can use it until you replace the one that was stolen. The phone number's in the contacts under This Phone. I put my contact info in as well so you can text me when you're ready to go for that drink and dinner."

"Thanks," I said and held it up appreciatively. "This is a godsend. I can phone my landlord and get back into my apartment. At least I won't be homeless until Monday night."

"Seriously," he said and looked at me from under a frown. "I know it's crazy, and I just met you, but if you need money, I could probably help you out." He went to the kitchen once more and opened a leather wallet. "I have a couple hundred that should keep you afloat until Monday."

He came over to me and held out a couple of hundred-dollar bills.

I glanced at the money, not sure if I should take it but he pushed the money into my hands.

"You actually carry that much money around?"

He shrugged. "I went to the bank today to get money out for the week. If you can't get a cashier's check by Monday, I can front

79

the rest to you. Worse comes to worst? You can stay here. I'll okay it with the owner first, of course," he said. "I'm sure he'd be pleased to think he was helping you out."

"My rent is five thousand dollars."

"I could probably get that together."

"You have five thousand dollars just lying around?"

He shrugged. "I have some savings, shall we say. Interest is pretty lousy these days, so I won't miss out if I don't have it in the bank for a couple of weeks until you can get things back to normal and get that bank draft."

I shook my head and looked at him, the money still in my hand. "Why are you being so nice?"

He shrugged. "Maybe I'm just a nice person?"

"I think you are," I said, and finally put the money away in my sweater pocket. "Seriously. Thank you so much."

"You can start paying me back by coming for a drink and meal after your first day at work. How does that sound?"

"It sounds perfect." I turned around one last time. "Well, I better go to my office or I'll be late for my meeting." I went to the elevator, feeling slightly better now that I had a cell and some cash.

"Hey," he said when I got inside the elevator. "Nice to meet you, Ella. Hope you have a better rest of the day."

"Thanks, Josh," I said as the doors were closing. Through the door, I heard him shout, "Message me later. We can go to the pub down the street for supper."

"Okay," I replied, but I had no idea if he heard me.

So, Josh's boss owned the penthouse floor and let him use it to store his bike and get changed in the morning. Josh himself was willing to front me money instead of me having to ask my boss. Part of me thought the offer was too good to be true, but maybe he was just a super nice guy.

I rode down the elevator, a skip in my heart rate at the

thought of how nice he was to offer financial help. It skipped a little more at the prospect of going out for a drink and food with him after work.

Hell, even just talking to him was more than I had done with a handsome man in – well, since Jerkface.

It felt nice.

CHAPTER TEN

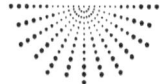

JOSHUA

GETTING TRAPPED in the elevator had never been so enjoyable. A pretty woman named Ella. Five four, one hundred and twenty pounds, long auburn hair and a light spray of freckles over her nose, big green eyes that I could imagine closing in the throes of passion while I made her orgasm for the third time...

Yeah.

Even with the troll pencil and Iron Man notebook – hell, *because* of them – she was someone I would definitely do.

I should have told her the truth about who I was, but for some reason, it tickled my fancy for her to think I was a bike courier. I was used to the women I met knowing I was one of the richest men in Manhattan, and it did something to them. They saw dollar signs.

I didn't blame them – I would, too. But it meant I could never just meet a woman as myself – plain old Josh. Not *the* Joshua Macintyre Jr. – son of MBC's Joshua Macintyre. If she had known who I really was, she would have probably acted differently. She was, after all, just a bright-eyed young woman in Manhattan for the first time, working at her first real job. Sure, it was an unpaid internship, but it showed she was more interested in getting skills and making connections than money. At least, long enough to make an impression.

A lot of people started off by volunteering or doing unpaid internships, impressing their superiors, then getting in with the companies as paid employees. I respected that kind of initiative.

I also felt bad for her – robbed of all her money, ID, and electronics on her third day in Manhattan. She said she was from New Hampshire, which wasn't anything like Manhattan, either in population or the pace at which life took place. She was inexperienced in the ways of the city and its dangers. She didn't know that you had to watch for bike couriers – and cyclists and skateboarders – threading through the narrow channels between cars in the heavy traffic. She didn't know not to leave her backpack unattended, even if only for a few moments while she examined a map to help an innocent-looking old woman in the subway station. Now she was facing the prospect of starting over, getting all her ID re-issued, and getting access to her bank accounts so she could pay for her apartment.

It was daunting.

I felt sympathy for her plight and was happy I could help. In fact, helping her made me feel useful. Handing her a couple of hundred bucks was nothing – pocket change for me. Fronting her the money for her rent was also nothing. It was a rounding error in my account books. I wouldn't miss it if she didn't pay it back – but I was sure she would. She had that air of conscientiousness about her. She'd probably get the money right away and the five grand would be back in my bank account in no time flat.

Unless I was totally wrong and she was just a really smart grifter.

But she didn't strike me that way.

While I should have been honest and told her who I was, I enjoyed the anonymity the cover story of being a bike courier gave me.

I was trying to be helpful when I suggested that I could front her money, but at the same time, I was thinking how much I'd like her in my bed. Even when I offered to let her stay in my apartment, I could tell that, homeless or not, she wasn't the type to have wild sex with some guy she had just met in an elevator.

I usually didn't give up easily when I saw something I wanted, whether it was a new vehicle, a new bike, or a new woman – at least, not without a fight. As down as I was on love, I was totally up for sex. I was already busy thinking of how I'd seduce her.

If she took me up on the offer of using the spare bedroom in my apartment, which I honestly hoped she would, I'd be a perfect gentleman. I would do nothing more than offer myself as someone who could help her get back onto her feet again – after I graciously offered to take her off her feet in my bed.

I wasn't going to be controlled by a woman ever again, no matter how sweet and sexy she seemed. I'd learned my lesson well and would make sure to find a wife who truly loved me and wanted my children. But until then, I sure would enjoy the pretty women I met along the way.

I HAD a shower in my penthouse apartment and then went back to Macintyre Publishing's temporary office, thinking about Ella and her very bad first day of work. When I arrived in my office, Keith came in right behind me.

"Look at you," he said, slapping me on the back. "Grinning like you're right in the mind for a change. Who is she?"

I frowned and gave him a dirty look. "What the fuck are you talking about?"

"You're smiling in a way that suggests you just met your next girlfriend. Don't tell me it was the pretty woman in the elevator..."

"You're nuts."

Irritated that he could read me so well, I went over to my desk and pulled out a file from the drawer, a little more roughly than was needed. Keith's words got under my skin, even though I knew he was right. I *was* smiling while I thought about pretty little Ella. Specifically, smiling at the thought of her shudders of pleasure while I fucked her senseless.

"Come on, man, spill," he insisted, standing in front of the picture window. "Tell me about her. Kaitlyn said you were caught in the elevator with her for about twenty minutes."

"You don't know what you're talking about – as usual. I was thinking about our upcoming editorial meeting," I lied, not wanting to give in too soon. "Money makes me happy. Having a sense of purpose in life makes me smile. The idea of renovating this old building makes me happy. That's all."

"Yeah, right. Tell me another one. That smile is reserved for one thing and one thing alone: pussy. And I happen to know that you haven't had enough lately. So, spill. Tell me about her."

I laughed finally, because he was right. As usual. Keith knew people. It was his superpower, as we liked to joke. He had done his undergrad in commerce before joining the Navy. We served together and when we got out, he joined the publishing company as my chief financial officer.

"She..." I said, remembering her. "She is just about the prettiest little thing I've seen in a long time."

"I knew it," he said and practically jumped on me, punching me in the shoulder. "Who is she?"

"Chill out, man," I said. "What are you? A high school freshman?"

"Nah. I've been saying you need to find someone new for a while. Get someone to lick your psychic wounds, and other things."

He grinned at me and I couldn't help but smile back.

"She's not going to be licking any psychic wounds."

"Oh, yeah? What's her name?"

"None of your damn business," I replied, smiling at his eagerness. "And don't you go nosing around her either," I said and pointed at him.

"Hey, you're going to LA next month. While the cat's away..."

He was right, of course. I was planning on going over to our offices in LA and set up the new office there. Stay there for a week to oversee it. Maybe spend some time with David in the hills around the city, getting right with myself. I didn't have to; I could easily catch a flight there and back anytime I wanted. Still, I didn't like the idea that Keith – or any of the guys in the building – would be hitting on her in my absence.

"Seriously, she's off limits. If anyone's going to do her, I got dibs."

"And how are you going to keep me away from her, when you're in LA?"

I knew he was just ribbing me, but it was still rubbing me the wrong way.

"Look, I just met her, and offered her the use of my spare bedroom, because she's currently homeless and I hate to see her being taken advantage of any more than she already has been. She's – well, she's kind of naive."

"Shit, man, you move fast. I was thinking you'd be asking her out for coffee or drinks, not to live with you. Speaking of taking advantage..." He grinned. "Is she going to take you up on the offer?"

"I hope so," I replied, opening a file, hoping he'd get the hint that I had work to do and stop with the ribbing. "You know my weakness for damsels in distress."

"That I do, that I do. She's pretty."

"Very. Long hair. Big green eyes. Nice smile. Perky little body that a man could imagine riding him all night..." I mimed holding her nice curvy torso over my hips and moving her up and down.

"Ha!" Keith said and shook his head. "You're a goner."

I laughed. "You're an idiot."

I opened the file drawer to my desk and took out a file I needed with recent financial data.

"Haven't you got anything better to do than give me a hard time?" I asked, when he seemed unable to take a hint. "Like prepare quarterly financial reports or something?"

"Speaking of which," he said, and leaned on my desk. "We just signed a big contract for that book by former Special Agent James Arthur."

"The tell-all about his time in the FBI? Great," I said, glad to see we were signing more non-fiction book contracts. I motioned to the door. "That should keep you busy and out of my hair."

I gave him a huge shit-eating grin and he laughed.

"Make sure to introduce me to this pretty little filly you're sniffing around."

"Not likely," I replied, and opened my file. I hoped he'd take off and leave me to my work, but he was enjoying ribbing me too much to go quickly or willingly.

"I'm serious, Josh. It's good to see you smiling again. I know this year's been hard."

"Yeah, yeah. Thanks, and all that. I'm a big boy. I can look after myself."

Keith winked at me and finally left my office, leaving me alone to try to fill the rest of the afternoon with enough work to keep my mind off Ella. I wasn't sure whether she'd show up at the penthouse and would be coming to live in my apartment temporarily. I also wondered whether anything more would develop between us.

I couldn't deny that I hoped it would – and when I wanted something, I did everything in my power to make it reality.

I mentally kicked myself in the head. I would be busy as hell over the next few weeks before my trip to California, tying up all the loose ends of my work. Once I was caught up, I'd take a flight to LA and set to work getting our new office set up and start working on making contacts in LA.

I loved building things – whether it was a new business or renovating an old building. Escaping Manhattan for a few weeks in LA promised to give me exactly what I wanted – escape and something meaningful.

Keith enjoyed ribbing me about a pretty little thing like Ella tempting me to get tangled up in some new woman's life, but there was no way I was going to make that mistake again.

I might make a mistake once, but not twice.

CHAPTER ELEVEN

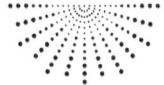

ELLA

I WENT RIGHT to reception and flashed my temporary badge at the young woman sitting there, a phone to her ear. She smiled and pointed down the hall, covering the receiver with one hand.

"Sharon's waiting for you in her office. Far corner," she said quietly. Then she returned to her phone call.

"Thank you," I mouthed and followed the hallway to the door at the end. I knocked on it, noting the name tag which read *Sharon Rogers, Manager, Acquisitions.*

I was finally here. Sharon was real and my job was definitely real, too.

"Come in," a voice called. I recognized it as Sharon's and opened the door. Inside was an unsurpassed view of the city. Floor-to-ceiling windows on two sides of the room, a huge mahogany desk facing the door, and behind it sat my new boss, Sharon Rogers. Middle-aged, salt-and-pepper hair in a tidy bob, and thick dark-rimmed glasses perched on the end of her nose.

91

She had a phone to her ear and nodded to me when I entered. She kept speaking but motioned to the chair in front of her desk.

I took it and sat down, glancing around at the office, which was huge. On the interior walls were two paintings of a rugged landscape that resembled Iceland, the hills rolling and inter-spaced with snow.

"Yes, we'll get right on it. I have my new assistant here and things will get right back on track. Yes, I realize that. We'll be up to speed ASAP. Thanks for your patience. Goodbye."

Sharon hung up and exhaled loudly. "Thank God you made it. I'm going a bit crazy without an assistant. It's been so long since I did any of the organizing, I haven't had anything new to offer our team for two weeks. I need you to get right on to it." She pointed to a chair by the door. On the seat was a file box and on top of the box were what looked like dozens of envelopes of different sizes and colors. Beside the chair were two other file boxes.

Queries from agents looking to sell us their client's books.

While reading mail wasn't what I wanted to do for the rest of my life, that file box made me more than happy. It meant I would be able to stay in Manhattan and get some experience.

"I can't wait to dig in," I said with a smile.

"You won't be saying that after the first dozen. Most of them will be ho hum manuscripts, pale imitators of books already published or books too similar to ones we have already bought. When you read over the offerings, you'll start to see how the gems really stand out from the crowd. Be prepared. Only about five percent are of any real value. The rest go in the circular file."

"I live for this opportunity."

She smiled. "I felt like you do about a dozen years ago. Reading manuscripts is tiring but exhilarating when you find a real great one. I want you to spend some time reading our newest contracts so you get a sense of what we're looking for. Then we'll do some practice evaluations, and then you'll hit the box and start separating the wheat from the chaff."

"I can't wait."

"That's cute," she said and pointed to the troll.

At that point, I decided not to bother her about the money transfer, but I would tell her about being robbed. How else would I explain the troll pencil and Iron Man notebook?

"It was all I could afford to buy on my way over. I was robbed in the subway station."

"What?" Her eyes widened. "You poor thing!"

I told her about the nice old lady and her accomplice and we laughed together for a moment.

"How are you? Do you have some money?"

"No problem," I said and waved my hand. "I have a place to stay and money. No worries."

I smiled and thought about Josh, my knight in bicycle courier armor. I hoped I could trust him. He was right. My boss had enough problems without her new hire giving a sob story about having been robbed.

We talked some more about the job and what it would entail, which involved screening manuscripts and covering the ones I felt had promise and fit with the imprints. I was also Sharon's personal assistant. I'd arrange all her meetings and make sure she had everything she needed before each one. Plus, I'd bring her the manuscripts that I thought showed promise.

She seemed nice enough, if a little frazzled, but I figured it was because the company was new and the office was temporary, as the old building was under renovation. They were trying to build the business so there would be a lot of pressure in the early days to make it a success.

I was determined to impress her.

"Come with me and I'll show you your office space," she said and rose from behind her desk. She led me through the door and down the hall to a room with no door that had a desk, chair, and filing cabinet but nothing else. There was, however, a tall picture window behind the desk. The room was about one-quarter the size of her office, but to me it was heaven.

"We don't have a computer for you yet, so I hope you can use your own and your cell until we get the new phone system up and running and our new computers come. They're on order but aren't due until next week."

"Sure," I said. "I'll bring my own computer tomorrow. Until then, this will have to do."

She smiled when I held up my pencil and notebook.

"After the meeting, you can spend the rest of the afternoon reading manuscripts, so it'll be fine."

"This is all mine?" I asked, impressed at the size of the office.

"Yes. It'll be much better once the renovations are done," she said. "Now, if you wouldn't mind bringing the file boxes in here, I'll finally be able to relax without staring at them all day, wondering if there's anything of value inside but being unable to actually contact any of the agents."

"I honestly can't wait."

For the next fifteen minutes before the two o'clock meeting, I carted the boxes into my office and spent some time reading the manuscripts Sharon gave me.

Then I joined her and went into a board room where several other people were already seated, waiting for us. She introduced me to everyone, and the meeting began. I had pulled the troll off the end of my pencil and opened the notebook so that no one could see the Iron Man cover, and aside from the fact that I had no idea what I was doing, I took notes and tried to look like a professional.

The various staff members spoke about their current list of authors, and what the executive team was looking for in the coming year as far as acquisitions. I had to pinch myself to be sure

I was really there, sitting in a meeting, discussing goals and targets. Sure, I was the lowest of the low on the corporate totem pole, but that was where I wanted to be.

Now, if only I could get a cashier's check for the apartment I rented to replace the one that had been stolen, and if only I could get new ID, everything would be perfect.

Except, nothing is ever perfect...

AT THE END of the day, I texted Josh, wondering if he still wanted to go out for dinner. I hoped so – I had called my landlady several times to no avail and I needed some place to sleep if I couldn't get in touch with her.

ELLA: *Hey, Josh. Are we still on?*

He texted me right back.

JOSH: *Of course, we are. I wouldn't leave you in your current predicament without making sure you at least get a decent meal. Have you been able to call your landlord and get keys to your place?*

ELLA: *Not yet.*

JOSH: *My offer still stands if you want to stay at the apartment tonight. I okayed it with the owner.*

ELLA: *You are way too nice.*

JOSH: *Not at all. Just trying to be a human being. Come on up when you're finished for the day. I'll be waiting.*

ELLA: *I'll be up in fifteen.*

JOSH: *See you then.*

I smiled to myself and finished up my current coverage of the manuscript I'd selected for Sharon to review. Once I was done, I packed up and took the elevator up to the penthouse.

Unlike when I had first seen him dressed in his bicycle courier's uniform, Josh was now dressed in an impeccable slate gray business suit, with a crisp white shirt and black tie. He looked like a million dollars, his longish hair freshly washed and still damp on the ends. Same blue-gray eyes and square-jawed, trimmed-beard manliness.

God. My body did all kinds of traitorous things imagining him as a lover.

"Ella, come in," he said and opened the door wide.

I entered the penthouse, passing close to him as I did, smelling his cologne in the process. Silly girl that I am, even that sent a shock wave through me.

He smelled like... like a real man. His arms were as big as two of mine, yet his hips were narrow and his shoulders wide.

Holy hell; my body warmed just from being so close to him. If I stayed at his place for the night, how hard would it be to resist him?

Did I want to?

"I was afraid you'd change your mind," he said with a smile.

I laughed lightly. "I'm glad I didn't. You sure don't look like a bike courier."

"Oh?" he said, his eyebrows raised. "Is that a good thing or bad?"

"It's just an observation. I've only seen you in your uniform. You polish up real well."

"Thanks. I hate uniforms," he said. "But sometimes you have to wear one."

He smiled and pointed to the small sofa in a seating area to the left of the desk. "Have a seat. I have to make a call, but I'll be done in a minute. Excuse me."

He left the living room and went into the back of the apartment. I heard him talking, his voice low and too soft to hear from where I sat.

When he returned about five minutes later, he pulled on his jacket. "Shall we go? I'm starved."

"Me, too." I followed him out of the apartment. His bike and

96

helmet were by the front door, next to two other bikes. I thought it was strange that the owner of the courier business had such a beautiful apartment and let the staff use it.

"Your boss is pretty nice to let you couriers use this place. It's better than most homes I've been in."

He smiled and closed the door to the apartment behind him. "He's a pretty decent guy once you get to know him, despite the very business-like exterior."

The elevator doors opened and he ushered me inside.

"Ladies first," he said.

I entered the elevator and waited for him, holding onto the rail just in case the elevator decided to stop suddenly.

He pressed the lobby button and then turned to me, leaning back against the wall, his arms crossed.

"I was serious about my offer of help. I hope you didn't hit your boss up for that cashier's check."

I shook my head. "I didn't. Honestly, you were right. I didn't want to bother her because she's in the middle of chaos right now, and helping me is the last thing she needed. Like you said, she hired me to solve her problems, not the other way around."

"Exactly. I'm glad. I'll get you a cashier's check for the rent you need tomorrow so you can pay for your new place. I've called my bank to ask about how you can get your cards replaced. They said you can come in and talk to the manager as long as you have your Social Security card, your birth certificate or passport."

"I have nothing except my Social Security card. The bank said it'll take ten days to two weeks for me to get a new credit card. I promise as soon as I get my money and ID, I'll be on my own and out of your hair."

"Don't feel you have to rush. You have enough on your plate without worrying about me."

"That's so generous," I said, taken aback by how nice he was being.

"It's the least I can do, considering how badly you've been treated by my city. Being robbed, the tiny Airbnb, and then the elevator. Plus, some crazy bicycle courier almost crashed into you..."

My chest felt tight with emotion as I realized he was my savior.

"Thank you. I was worried that I'd be stuck sleeping under a bridge after all."

"Never. It's my pleasure to help."

Of course, my mind went there, wondering if it could be – would end up being – *my* pleasure as well.

Then I kicked myself mentally. *Don't get invested...*

Thing was, he was just about the best-looking hunk of man flesh I had ever seen. He was all man, every sleek, well-muscled inch of him. It would be hard to resist if he offered or if he showed any interest, but was that getting out of the cheating-fiancé frying pan into the casual-sex-fire?

"So, let's head over to Frank's Pub and have a pint."

I couldn't help but stop, reaching out to briefly touch his arm.

"Why are you doing this?"

A second passed, the time ticking by in my head while he appeared to struggle with an answer.

"I don't know," he said finally, a quirk of a smile on his lips. "It's not like me to be nice to a stranger, but your story made me feel generous. Don't want to see you going back home the first week you arrived. Besides, it's good karma, if you believe in that sort of thing."

"You don't?"

He shrugged and when the elevator door opened, he held his arm out for me to exit. "Too many good people suffer and too many bad people get away with too much bad shit for me to believe it, but I think you have to act as if it does exist."

I left the elevator and waited for him to exit, seeing pain in his face somewhere. His smile seemed forced. Whatever the case, he was my savior; I would do my best to be an asset that he'd be glad to have around. And as soon as I could access my bank account again, I'd pay him back.

While we walked down the street to Frank's, he peppered me with questions about my family.

"I don't really like to talk about them," I said, cringing while we walked along the streets crowded with pedestrians.

"I figured you just didn't want to admit you got robbed to them – worry them – and that was why you seemed so desperate. Usually people run home to daddy and mommy when things don't work out."

I snorted at that. "Not my father and mother. My mother's a control freak and my dad is the local Gestapo."

"He a police officer?"

"No. Let's just say that he's powerful and leave it at that."

A moment of silence passed and I glanced at him, only to see a frown creasing his brow.

"Look, he's a very important person in government. He has no idea I'm in trouble and I intend to keep it that way," I said.

"What did you say your last name was?"

"Carlson." Then I kicked myself mentally. I hoped he didn't feel like he had to call my father and let him know I was having problems.

"Carlson," he said. "From New Hampshire?"

"Yes, but I honestly want to figure this out without him getting involved."

"Okay, I promise."

"Look," I said when he stopped outside the pub. "My father is a big cheese and a very important person. I don't contact him for help because I want to be free of him. That's all you need to know about me."

"Say no more." He opened the door and we walked inside.

I watched him out of the corner of my eye, still impressed with how big and brawny and handsome he was. The way my body responded to his presence suggested I had a lot to fear from myself if he ever made any kind of advance.

Of course, the thought of him making an advance sent a thrill through my body right to my core.

God, I had to get a grip on myself...

CHAPTER TWELVE

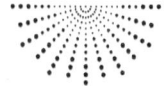

JOSHUA

FRANK'S WAS one of those hole in the wall pubs you can find down side streets in Manhattan that only the locals know about. It was busy on most nights and had a great happy hour, with snacks and cheap but good draft on tap. My staff frequented the place almost daily, after work, before a long night of meeting deadlines, or for a quick meal before going home. It felt like a second home to me, and I knew the other staff felt the same way.

When I walked in with Ella beside me, all eyes turned to us and ranged over her hungrily. She walked a little bit behind me like she was shy, but stood up straighter when we got to the table.

"Hey, guys, this is Ella Carlson. She works in our building. " Then I turned to Ella. "Ella, this is the gang. She's the one who gave me the bloody knees yesterday."

The guys all sat up straighter, saying hello to her, shaking her hand and introducing themselves. They were a bunch of management types who ran the accounting side of the *Chronicle* for me.

101

"He's a crazy man on that bike," Monroe said. "Are you joining us?"

"Nope, sorry," I replied, wanting to keep her from them. "We're going to sit closer to the front away from the music."

"Enjoy," Monroe said and held up his beer.

I led Ella to the front of the bar, into a nice booth away from the staff and DJ. She slipped into the booth and I sat beside her.

"They're pretty well-dressed for bike couriers," she said.

I smiled to myself. I was debating whether to keep up the ruse about being a bike courier, and wasn't entirely sure I was going to tell her the truth.

I liked that she didn't know who I was. It freed me in a way. In a few days, depending on how fast Marcella worked, I'd be evaluated by a bunch of high-income, well-bred women with dynasty-building on their minds. It was nice to be just a bike courier who was being kind to a damsel in distress. But I didn't want to lie to her.

"They work in the company's accounting office," I replied and folded my arms on the tabletop. "They're suits. Look, Ella, " I said and leaned closer. "I have a confession to make."

She leaned forward. "Yes? I'm all ears."

I cleared my throat, feeling bad that I'd led her on so long. "I'm actually not a bicycle courier."

"You aren't?" she said and frowned, her pretty brows knitting. "What do you do for a living? Why were you riding your bike?"

"I'm a pretty serious cyclist. I do races and marathons. I trained a few years ago for an Iron Man. I run MBC. My name's Joshua Macintyre."

Her mouth dropped open. "What?"

I nodded, feeling like a total cad for letting her believe I was a bicycle courier for so long. "My father started MBC and I took over as CEO when he died."

She sat in silence for a moment. "That means..."

"It means what?"

"I work for Sharon Rogers at Dominion Publishing."

"Oh," I said, finally putting two and two together. "You're Sharon's new intern..."

"The very one."

We both sat there, saying nothing for a moment. Her cheeks were flushed bright red.

"This is awkward," she said finally. "You're my boss."

"Technically, yes," I said.

The cocktail waitress took our food order and we turned and looked at each other. I smiled, hoping we could get past the whole boss-employee thing quickly. She was a pretty thing, with a sweet face.

"So, tell me about Ella."

"Is it legal for us to be having a drink together? I mean, fraternizing?"

"Well, I'm the CEO of MBC, but I have no real role in Dominion. I just pop by now and then to get a quarterly update and say hi. I'm not hands-on at all. I had to make a choice about what I could manage once it was clear that my father would pass. I had to let Dominion go so I could focus on the *Chronicle*."

"You bought the *Chronicle*," she said and smiled, glancing away for a moment like she was embarrassed. "I read about that a while back. I thought it was your father who bought it."

"No, we share the same name. But enough about me," I said. " My life has been pretty much an open book. Tell me about yourself. What are your aspirations? What makes you tick?"

"What makes me tick? Hmm. I thought I had my life all planned out. I was going to get married, start a family and I was going to be the wife of a Senator, and maybe the future President of the United States of America."

"Really? Your ex was a senator?"

"No, but he had aspirations," she replied. "I was going to be the good wife."

"The good wife, huh?" I said, surprised. "But he didn't turn out to be the good husband-to-be."

"Nope," she said and paused when the waitress brought our drinks. Ella took a sip of her bottle of black cherry vodka cooler, then turned back to me. "He turned out to be exactly the bad husband-to-be. I should have known, but I was naïve and starry-eyed at the whole get married and have a perfect life dream."

"And so when the dream died, you decided to come here," I said and sipped my beer. "Live life in the Big Apple."

"Exactly," she said with a laugh. "I'm going to start over. I'm just a slush and submissions reader, but some day, I hope to move up. I may go to Columbia next year, but right now, I'm keeping all my options open." She smiled. "I grew up watching Sex and the City and maybe I'll have my own 'single girl in Manhattan' adventures."

"Maybe meet your own Mr. Big," I replied, smiling inside because Christie had loved that series and used to talk about it to me.

"You know who Mr. Big is?" she asked, her eyes wide.

"I do. My ex was a big fan."

Ella nodded. She was probably embarrassed that I knew about the fantasy man who was the rich handsome guy who swept the heroine off her feet.

"What about you?" she asked. "Besides owning a huge media conglomerate?"

I took in a breath and considered what to tell her. "I aspire to make the *Chronicle* successful again one day."

"That's impressive," she said. "Did you study journalism?"

I shook my head. "Business."

She appeared impressed by that.

The waitress brought us our burgers and we both dug in. After several bites and exclamations about how great the fries were, it was my turn to ask another probing question.

"So, what do you want from life outside of living the life of a single girl in Manhattan?"

She shrugged. "I'm keeping all my options open."

"No husband and children?"

She shook her head. "I'm pretty sour on the whole marriage thing."

I dipped a fry into ketchup and frowned. "How come? You're too young to be jaded."

She sighed. "I was supposed to have been married by now, in fact. Luckily, I found out several weeks before the wedding that my soon-to-be husband was boinking his 'sexretary.'"

She raised her eyebrows and made air-quotes when she said 'sex'.

I couldn't help but laugh out loud. "Boinking?"

She laughed as well, her eyes crinkling at the corners.

"Yep," she said, her smile fading. "In the office. On his desk, to be exact. I can laugh now, but believe me, three weeks before my wedding, I wasn't laughing."

"Crap. That's terrible. How did you find out?"

She shrugged. "He'd started working on Saturday mornings, telling me it was because he wanted to get ahead on his projects so we could go on a great honeymoon. One Saturday, I thought it would be nice to bring him some bagels and coffee to help cheer him up, seeing as he was working sixty-hour weeks. There they were, boinking away, her naked butt on the Johnston file."

She shoved a fry into her mouth and chewed hard. I could still see fire in her eyes, despite the year that passed between the 'boinking' event and now.

"So, as you can imagine, I'm not all that positive about the whole till-death-do-us-part-happily-ever-after thing."

I watched her take a long drink of her spritzer and realized that she was a lot like me.

"Me either," I said. "In fact, I'm pretty sour about it. My fiancée was boinking her boss, but it wasn't in the office. It was on the bed we shared in our apartment."

"Oh, crap," she said, her expression sympathetic. "That sucks."

"It does. We called off the wedding, needless to say."

She held out a fry. "To us: losers at love."

I picked up one of my fries and touched hers with it. "To us."

We both popped the fries into our mouths and chewed, each of us probably remembering our own shock and hurt and discovering the deceit of the partners we had thought we were going to spend the rest of our lives with.

"Maybe we'll both be lucky in life," I said. "Even if we fail at love."

"Let's hope," she said. "Whatever I end up doing, I'm going to give it the old college try."

"Me, too. Turning around a failing newspaper is probably even less likely than success in love. Obviously, we're both fools." I held up my beer and she held up her spritzer and we clinked bottles.

We drank.

I had a feeling I was going to really like this woman.

One drink led to another and another. Soon the two of us were more than slightly tipsy, dancing on the tiny dance floor and going wild, like we were teenagers. We sat back down and I slid in close beside her – enjoying the moment, feeling like I'd be happy to carry on with much more than dancing. She seemed to feel the same.

"So, if you're not into marriage and happily-ever-after, what about dating? Do you favor promiscuity or are you going full celibate cat lady?" I asked, giving her a grin.

She took a drink, her eyes amused. "I'm definitely not a cat lady. If I'm going to live the single woman's dream life in Manhattan, I'm going to have to get some experience. I was with Mr. Boinking-My-Sexretary ever since my father had selected him as the perfect husband for me. The two of them were conspiring to unite their empires."

"You're shitting me," I said, frowning at the thought that her father had actually picked her husband. "You went along with it?"

"I had no idea. He was several years older than me and really handsome, ambitious, and wealthy. I was young, dumb, and under my father's thumb. I thought he actually liked me for me."

"How did you find out about the whole arranged-marriage thing?"

"I walked out of the office and he chased after me, tried to convince me that it was all just a moment of weakness, that he had panicked because of the lifetime commitment but that he loved me and only me. You know – the usual sob story of a cheater caught cheating."

"But you didn't take him back."

"Bunni with an 'i', the sexretary, texted me that he was only marrying me because of my father. I broke it off at that point."

"Her name was actually Bunni with an 'i'?"

"Swear to God. Apparently, he got her a Playboy bunny logo tattooed on her fake left boob as a birthday gift."

"That sucks," I said, thinking it was wrong to marry a person for political connections.

"Yeah. So I decided to get a revenge tattoo. A lock and key tattoo over my heart. Even if he'll never see it, it means something to me."

"You got a tattoo over your heart?" I asked, needing to see it now that I knew it existed. My dick throbbed just a bit at the thought.

She pulled her dress over to the side, just enough to display a bit of cleavage and the tiny lock and key tattoo in navy blue.

"Cool," I said – and of course, I couldn't help but gawk at her cleavage, given the chance.

She adjusted her dress and then checked her cell. I took a sip of beer and tried to rein myself in while she read. When she was done, she glanced up at me.

"I hate to ask," she said and bit her bottom lip in a very sexy way, "but is there any way I can stay at the apartment tonight? My landlord hasn't replied yet so there's no way I can get into the Airbnb."

"Of course," I said, wondering if she might like me to stay with her. "I know the boss won't mind.," I said with a laugh, now that she knew that the boss was me. "You can stay there until your landlord is able to get you the keys."

"Thanks," she said. "It'll probably be tomorrow. I'm sure she'll get the message and be willing to give me another key."

"No rush. Use it as long as you need." I leaned even closer. "There's more vodka in the apartment if you'd like another drink in a more private venue. My specialty is vodka and tonic with lime."

"That sounds wonderful," she said, a gleam in her eyes that sent a jolt of lust right to my dick, which jumped at the thought of her body. I couldn't help but imagine her naked and ready for me, that tattoo waiting to be inspected and licked, the cleavage nuzzled. "Shall we?"

I slid out of the booth and held out my hand, pleasantly surprised by this turn of events.

"If I'm going to live the life of a Manhattan single lady, I might as well start now," she said and took my hand. Together, we walked to the bar. I asked Lenny, the bartender, if I could have a couple of lime wedges. He laughed, tucked a few into a bar napkin, and gave them to me.

We left the bar and walked arm-in-arm down the street back to the building. My entry key worked 24/7, of course. We waved at the security guard and took the elevator up to the penthouse.

As soon as the doors closed and we were alone, I pushed her against the elevator wall. Her eyes widened, and I remembered her fear when the elevator jerked to a start earlier in the day. But she didn't push me away. Instead, she blinked rapidly when I took her hands in mine and confined them above her head. I leaned closer, my lips brushing over hers.

"Damn elevators," I murmured.

We kissed deeply, our bodies pressed together. All too soon, the elevator came to a stop and the doors behind us opened.

"Come in," I said and grabbed her hand, pulling her into the apartment.

"I can't believe this view," she said once we were inside. She went right to the window overlooking the cityscape. "It's amazing."

"It is," I said, and went to the refrigerator to remove a couple of iced glasses from the freezer. I poured us each some vodka and tonic, then squeezed some lime into them. I carried them to the balcony where Ella was standing, the breeze blowing her long hair.

"Here," I said and handed her one. We toasted and took a drink, standing side by side, watching the city. Down below, cars drove along the streets surrounding the building, their taillights glowing red in the distance.

"This is what I came for," she said. "The city. The sounds and sights. The energy."

She turned and smiled up at me. It seemed like the perfect time to finish my drink and move things forward into the bedroom.

So I did.

"To us," I said and held out my glass.

"To us," she said and clinked hers against it.

We both finished our drinks and I took her glass from her, then took her hand in mine.

I pulled her against me and slid my arms around her, bending down to kiss her. In response, she slipped her arms around my neck and kissed me back.

That was all the encouragement I needed.

CHAPTER THIRTEEN

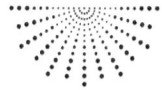

ELLA

WHEN I DECIDED to move to Manhattan, I had dreams of meeting a gorgeous man – ambitious, funny, and good in bed. Someone who would sweep me off my feet and make me forget the heartache I left behind in New Hampshire.

Josh fulfilled the order perfectly. He was ambitious, gorgeous and in fact, at that moment, he was definitely sweeping me off my feet. He picked me up, his arms under my butt, and in response, I wrapped my legs around his hips and felt his erection pressed against me. It wasn't like me to just hop into bed with a man I just met. In fact, it wasn't like me to do any of the things I had done since breaking up with Jerkface. Moving to Manhattan by myself. Getting a new job. Going home with a gorgeous man.

Jerkface had been my one and only serious relationship.

It wasn't like me at all, but that was my goal – to become someone I hadn't been before, no longer a doormat who let the powerful men around me try to control my fate.

111

Josh kissed me as he carried me through the apartment to the bedroom, where he laid me down on the side of the bed. I kept my legs wrapped around his waist as he leaned over me, kissing me intensely. His kiss was passionate from the start, his tongue exploring my mouth while his hands explored my body.

Finally, he pulled away and removed my sweater.

"I need you naked," he said in a husky voice. "Now."

I stood up and reached behind my back, trying to unzip my dress. He helped, then I let it slide off my body to puddle at my feet.

"That's better," he said as he pushed me back onto the bed, his mouth moving down my throat, lingering over the tattoo. "I've been waiting to do this since you showed me," he said and licked the tattoo, the sensation of his tongue, warm and wet on my skin, sending a shock of desire right to my clit.

He eagerly attacked my bra, and it opened much more easily, my breasts spilling out of the cups, my nipples budding in the cold air.

While he was busy licking a trail from my chin to my left breast, I heard a faint noise and glanced at the bedroom door where a blonde woman stood, her mouth open and an expression of pure hatred in her eyes.

"Oh, my *God*," I said and pushed on Josh's shoulder.

"What?" He looked in my eyes and I gestured with my chin to the door. He turned to check and his body tensed.

He helped me cover up and then stood up, facing the door.

"What the fuck are you doing here?"

"I didn't know you had anyone here..." the woman said.

Was it another employee who had decided to use the apartment?

"Christie, get the *hell* out of here."

He strode to the door, taking the woman by the arm and trying to push her out of the bedroom. Before she left, she stared at me where I lay on the bed, pulling the sheet more tightly against me.

Was it his ex?

I quickly dressed, pulling on my bra and hastily throwing on my dress, struggling to zip it back up before he returned. While I pulled on my sweater, I listened to the heated words being exchanged between them – words I couldn't make out clearly but which included weeping on the woman's part.

It had to be the ex-fiancée.

Whatever mood had existed after our encounter was now decidedly dead.

Josh came back into the bedroom and shook his head.

"I'm so sorry, Ella, but I have to take her home. She's drunk."

"Who is she, if you don't mind me asking?"

"My ex."

I sighed. "I thought so. She had a key to this place?"

"She used to work with me."

I nodded. "I'm sorry. This is awkward."

He came over and stood at the side of the bed, taking my chin in his hand.

"You didn't have to get dressed. The place is yours for the night. You can stay as long as you need. I have to take her home."

"Okay."

He pulled me into his arms and kissed me, then brushed a lock of hair off my cheek.

"Thank you," I said. "For everything."

"No, thank you for coming out with me tonight. I apologize for her. She's overly invested and can't let go."

He kissed me again and then left.

Once I was alone, I sat on the side of the bed and debated what the hell to do. It wasn't like me to go home with a man I just met and have sex, but in addition to the fact he was utterly the hottest man I had ever met, there was something about Josh that made me feel I could trust him.

He was funny, ambitious and smart. And very rich. Maybe he was my own Mr. Big.

I hoped I'd see him again. It made all the crap I'd been through in the past few days worthwhile. But at the same time, I felt weird about staying in the apartment.

I texted Steph.

ELLA: Can you book me a hotel room at the cheapest hotel you can find? I need a place to stay for the night. I mean the cheapest hotel that doesn't rent by the hour. I'll transfer you the money as soon as I get access to my account.

STEPH: Of course and don't sweat the timing. I have enough room on my Visa. Are you ready to call your father?

ELLA: Not yet. I'm going to hold out for as long as I can. Stick with me, okay? I'll transfer you money as soon as I get my card working again.

STEPH: No problem. I know you have the money. I wish I was there with you. Maybe in the new year.

ELLA: I hope! XOXOX

IN ABOUT FIFTEEN MINUTES, I got a text back from Steph:

STEPH: Got you a deal on a hostel near Columbia University. You have a bunk bed for two nights, just in case. Let me know how it goes and if you need anything else. I even told them you had no ID because you were robbed so all you have to do is show them your cell with these messages.

ELLA: I will. Thanks, Bestie. You're a princess.

STEPH: *You know it!*

THEN I TOOK a taxi to the hostel, getting a key from the front desk clerk after she examined my cell and the email in question. Then, I plopped myself down on the bottom bunk in a room not much bigger than the Airbnb and went to sleep, feeling like things were finally improving.

I could make it without calling my father.

THE NEXT MORNING, I showered in the shared room and dressed, unhappy about wearing the same outfit to work that I had worn the previous day, but at least I had a good excuse. I took the subway to the office, wondering if I'd run into Josh during the day or if he'd text me. I hoped so, because he was so gorgeous and sweet, but I was not going to wait for an email. That was the new me – not the obedient daughter to a tyrant and loyal fiancée to a cheating cad. I was a young woman in Manhattan with an internship in a publishing house and hopes of making my mark one day as an author. No man was going to occupy the prime real estate in my mind or heart for a while. A long while.

I spent the morning going over several dozen manuscripts, searching for ones that matched Sharon's criteria for the imprints the company published. The manuscript had to have a great opening and near perfect writing. Previous publications would be an asset. I sorted through the manuscripts, putting those who failed on both counts in one pile and the ones who satisfied both in another. The third pile was for those I wasn't sure about and would read over again. Why not take the best if you could have them? Then I sorted each pile by how much I wanted to read on and ended up with a stack of manuscripts ranked from the best to the worst.

My father sent me an email mid-morning, wondering why I wasn't answering my cell and I realized I'd have to tell him the truth.

I called, using Josh's burner cell, and he answered on the second ring.

"Ellie, dear, I was worried about you. Why haven't you answered my calls?"

"My cell was stolen, that's why, Daddy," I said, chewing a nail, waiting for him to berate me. "I'm using a spare cellphone a friend lent me."

"You've already been mugged and you've only been in Manhattan what – three days?"

"It's nothing," I said. "I'm going to get a new one in a couple of days. I'm fine."

"Your mother and I miss you, dear. She sends her love. Please keep in touch. It's hard for us to see our little girl move so far away."

"I know, but your little girl has to grow up and leave the nest."

"I'm proud of you, even if I wish you'd got a job in Concord."

"I had to leave," I said, sighing. We'd had this discussion before.

"I know, sweetheart, but we miss you. Keep in touch and if you need anything, just give me a call."

"I will. I love you," I said, feeling a squeeze in my heart to hear that he and my mother missed me.

"We both love you back."

I hung up, pleased that my father hadn't scolded me too much for losing my cell. What would he think if he knew that I had everything stolen? He'd freak.

I couldn't let him find out and was even more determined than ever to stand on my own two feet.

. . .

AFTER OUR REGULAR morning staff meeting was over, I went back to Sharon's office and we discussed the manuscripts. I gave her my notes, then went back to my office, ready to look over the backlog of submissions.

I really hoped Josh was serious about his offer of help, because I would need it if I hoped to keep my job.

First thing was getting a temporary loan until the wire transfer came through and I could pay him back. I'd need to buy a laptop. I usually bought Apple products because I loved them, but given my situation, I'd be going with the cheapest laptop I could find.

I phoned Liza at the Airbnb and finally got through.

"Oh, thank God," I said when she finally answered her phone. "I was robbed and don't have my key. I called and called last night but you didn't answer."

"Sorry," she said, "but I dropped my cell in a puddle and couldn't use it."

"Can I meet you at the apartment after work and get a spare key?"

"Sure," she said. "Meet me at six. Sorry to hear about you being robbed. That's terrible."

We said goodbye and I hung up, glad at least that I'd have the Airbnb back until Monday when I picked up my keys for my long-term apartment.

Then I got a text from Josh:

JOSH: Hey, why didn't you stay at the apartment? I came back, thinking you'd still be there but you were gone.

I bit my bottom lip and considered my response.

ELLA: I went to a hostel for the night. My best friend rented it for me so no worries. I felt really bad staying in your apartment. I'll be getting my replacement key from my landlord at the Airbnb so it's all good. But I could use that cashier's check for first and last month's rent if you're still willing. I'll transfer you the money as soon as the bank lets me back into my account. I need the check for Monday.

JOSH: No problem. Are you free tonight? I thought we might have dinner and maybe try again, considering we were so rudely interrupted... And my apologies for that. My ex is a little unstable. Well, a lot unstable.

ELLA: Thanks for the offer, but I think maybe we were rushing things a bit. It's not like me to just fall into bed with a strange man. Especially one who is technically my boss.

JOSH: Are you calling me strange?

ELLA: Sorry! Didn't mean it that way. But thanks for the offer.

JOSH: A guy can try. If you change your mind, just text me. What about just a meal?

ELLA: You've done more than enough already but I don't want this to seem like a transaction, you know?

JOSH: I know exactly what you mean and don't do transactions. With me, everything is voluntary. It never crossed my mind that being with me was some kind of repayment. I'm helping you only because I can. Seriously. No strings of any kind or expectations.

ELLA: Thanks. I appreciate you saying that. If I change my mind, I'll text you but seriously, thanks again for all your help. You're my hero.

JOSH: Your hero? I like that! If you change your mind about a meal, I know a nice little Italian restaurant down the street from the building with a great Italian meatball.

ELLA: A great Italian meatball? You're trying to tempt me, aren't you?

JOSH: Yes, that's my evil plan. I want to tempt you. Meatballs... MEATBALLS!

ELLA: LOL *is tempted* Okay. What girl can say no to a great meatball?

JOSH: Good. Come up to the apartment at six thirty and I'll

take you for world-famous Italian meatballs. How does that sound?

ELLA: Sounds delicious. See you at six-thirty.

I STARED AT THE SCREEN, smiling, anticipating our meal together but I didn't want it to feel like I was having sex with him as repayment or anything. If he was going to help me, I wanted it to be only that. No matter how attracted I was to him, and him to me, if money changed hands, I'd feel too much like a prostitute. Doing sex – or feigning love – for money was the very last thing I wanted to do or have done to me, considering my engagement to Jerkface.

I remembered back to the previous night and our almost hot sex. I was a little breathless as I finished up for the morning and made plans to go buy some lunch.

"Before you go for lunch, I want to take you to meet the new boss," Sharon said. "I think he's back in his office. He's been on vacation since the death of his father and is just taking over the business. He came back to work this Monday and will be here for the next week or so getting caught up with the business, so I haven't had a chance to introduce you. He's pretty hands-off with Dominion because he's too busy with taking over MBC but he does come for a couple of weeks every quarter."

"You mean Joshua Macintyre?" I said, wondering if I should admit that I already met him.

"Yes," Sharon said. "He's been named the new CEO."

"I already met him. He was in the elevator with me when it stalled."

"Oh, you're kidding," Sharon said. "I didn't know you'd already met him. He's in the office today for an update, but I want to introduce you formally."

"Okay."

"How are the manuscripts, by the way?" she asked as we walked down the hall.

"Some of them are actually pretty good. I have a pile of decent manuscripts that we can talk about tomorrow. But my eyes need a rest."

"Well, this is the perfect time, then."

I followed her down the hallway to the elevator, wondering how I should act around Josh.

When we arrived, she spoke with a receptionist, who waved us through to a hallway and a corner office. Sharon knocked on the door, then opened it and poked her head in. I stood off to the side waiting to be admitted, a little nervous, not really feeling comfortable with having to interact with him, considering he was licking my breast the night before.

"I'm here," she said. "Are you ready for me?"

"Come," came a deep and familiar voice.

Sharon opened the door wide and went inside. She encouraged me to follow her with a wave of her hand.

"Ella said you already met but I wanted to introduce you to our newest recruit. She'll be working with me as my new acquisitions assistant."

I went inside and there, sitting behind the desk, was Josh, looking like a few billion dollars. He was wearing a very expensive black suit, crisp white shirt, and dark gray tie.

"Joshua Macintyre, meet Ella Carlson. Ella," Sharon said, and turned to me, "this is Joshua Macintyre, CEO and owner of Dominion Publishing and now, CEO of the entire Macintyre Broadcasting Corporation."

Sharon smiled brightly. When my eyes finally met Josh's, his expression was pleased, even playful.

"Ella," he said and stood up, coming around the desk to greet us. "So nice to be formally introduced."

We shook hands and I felt like a real idiot feigning we barely knew each other, considering only hours earlier, his body and his very hard erection was pressed against my body.

"Nice to meet you formally, too. Do I call you Mr. Macintyre?" I asked, raising my eyebrows.

"Josh will work fine," he said and shook my hand, holding onto it for longer than he technically should have. His touch sent a thrill through my body.

It was then I knew I was going to be in trouble...

CHAPTER FOURTEEN

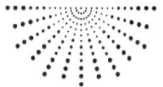

Joshua

I spent the morning trying to get caught up.

From eight until ten o'clock, I was in a meeting with my assistant manager, trying to get everything in place for my first real meeting with the paper's lead editors to discuss the paper's future. It was exciting, even if it was too much admin for my tastes. I wanted to focus on vision and new hires to get fresh blood and ideas on the paper's pages. I also wanted to improve the web presence of the paper and bring it fully into the Twenty-First Century. The previous owner had been a total luddite and had resisted going digital, but you couldn't fight progress. It meant a different business model than print alone, but it was doable.

I'd spend the rest of the day trying to catch up with the remainder of my family's business – and now my business. The business of broadcasting and publishing.

I met with the manager of the new web-based broadcaster,

which represented our response to Netflix. It was exciting but at the same time, not what I really wanted to focus on. I was more into news than entertainment, and in print than broadcast news. The written word felt real to me in a way that television news never did. I loved investigative reporting, although I had never been a reporter. I loved being part of a newsroom, even if only from management's point of view. Chasing down an important story, with national or international significance, was what really excited me. I would keep the broadcast news arm of the business of course, but my focus would be on keeping the investigative and print side alive. Whether people read on paper or on their smartphones or tablets didn't matter. What mattered was that they were reading.

Hopefully, reading my newspaper.

After a quick lunch with my head editor at the paper, I went back to the building and prepared for a couple of meetings to catch up with the latest developments on the book publishing side of the business. I enjoyed that side. Developing an author, publishing the memoir or tell-all of some public figure or important political actor was exciting and had a real impact on the world. But news was and had always been my love.

So, it was that I waited to meet with Sharon, the lead acquisitions editor of the publishing house. She'd sent me an email earlier with a summary of what had been happening in the business since my father's death. There had been some turnover in staff and she was behind but we were in a state of flux at the moment and I had to cut her some slack. I tried to focus on the memo she had written about the upcoming spring release schedule, which was months away, but it was hard. There were a dozen big books slated to be released and one of them caught my eye. It was a romantic comedy / chick lit novel by one of our bestselling authors. Right away, I thought about Ella and her dream of living the single girl's life described by Candace Bushnell, replete with Mr. Big and a cadre of BFFs.

I hoped that we'd be able to carry on from where we'd left off the previous night, but I wouldn't push. Not too much, at least. The taste I'd had of her last night had served only to whet my appetite for more.

A knock came at my door as I was finishing up writing an email to my editor in chief and so I quickly sent it and then turned to the door, preparing for my next meeting with Sharon.

"Come in," I said and folded my hands in wait.

In Sharon walked, looking her usual self. Late forties, salt-and-pepper hair, fashionably dressed, and seeming a little frazzled. I knew she was feeling guilty for being behind in her work for the publishing imprint she was managing acquisitions editor.

She motioned to someone behind her and when the woman came forward, I realized it was Ella.

Adrenaline surged through me when I saw her again. Ella had that effect on me.

"Ella said you already met but I wanted to introduce you to our newest recruit. She'll be working with me as my new acquisitions assistant."

I stood abruptly, and buttoned my jacket, putting on as calm and cool expression as I could muster.

After we were all introduced formally, I turned to Sharon.

"So, I suppose you're relieved to have a new assistant. It must have been hard to keep up with everything after you lost your last one."

Sharon spoke for a moment about what she'd done for the past month without an assistant, getting some help from another staff member but not really being able to tackle her work.

I listened with half a mind, focused in part on Ella, who stood there, her eyes wide, a smile on her pretty face.

There was no need for Sharon to know anything about what

happened between Ella and me the night before. I'd pretend that we only met that one time in the elevator.

"Well, it's nice to meet you," I said and caught Ella's eye. "I hope you enjoy your new position with Macintyre Publishing."

"Thank you, Josh. I hope so, too."

Sharon led Ella out and I closed the door, exhaling heavily. I went back behind my desk, my mind working furiously, trying to figure out how to explain to Ella why I had led her on all this time.

I grabbed my cell and pulled up her last text.

JOSH: *I know what just happened was awkward but when you get a few minutes, please come back to my office so we can talk. I know you were concerned about the ethics of us going out, but honestly, I'm not really involved in Dominion except quarterly.*

I WAITED but there was no response. Fifteen minutes later, I sent another text.

JOSH: *If you want to pretend we didn't have a great evening together and that you weren't really into what was happening last night, it's up to you. But I really enjoyed our time together and hope we can do it again. Please come by and see me.*

STILL NOTHING.

I SIGHED and turned back to the file on my desk, kicking myself mentally for not reassuring her that I would not expect anything from her that she didn't want to give or penalize her if she decided she didn't want anything else to happen between us. Given both our experiences with our exes, it was understandable she was reluctant to get involved with me. I felt that we really hit it off right from the start and it would be too bad if we didn't at least give it a try.

I could have walked to the elevator and gone to her office and demanded that she speak to me. I was the owner of the publishing house, after all, but I didn't want to embarrass her or take advantage of my position. That was what she was afraid of after all. I understood how it would look.

So I tried to distract myself, wondering if she would respond. She had to -- if she wanted the cashier's check. Luckily, my assistant came in and handed me a copy of something to sign and for the next hour, I was distracted and unable to ruminate much about Ella and how I hoped that she'd give me a chance despite technically being her boss.

THE REST of my day passed much as the previous part had -- with me busy in meetings or reading over material in preparation for more meetings.

By five thirty, when I still hadn't received a reply from Ella, I sent her a final text.

JOSH: *Look, Ella. I get that you're concerned about me being the owner of Dominion Publishing, but I really do want to help you even if you don't want to see what develops between us. No matter what happens or doesn't happen between us, I still want to give you the cashier's check so you can get your apartment on Monday. If you want, I can have it sent to your office. If what happened between us upset you, you don't have to even see me or speak to me again. Let me know.*

. . .

I SAT HOLDING the cashier's check in my hand. Made out to Roberto Bertelli, first and last month's rent, the check was for $5400.00. I googled the address and saw it was in a decent part of Chelsea, and using street view, I could see that her apartment was in an old brownstone building and was probably on the third floor. The street was tree-lined. It was close to a subway stop. The apartment would be a great choice for someone's first months in Manhattan. I envied her in a way. She was truly starting her life, and living her dream.

Work at a publishing house reading submissions. Living in a studio apartment in Chelsea. She was beautiful and young and smart. She'd have her pick of men, who I knew would be quite happy to give her the attention she deserved after being betrayed by her fiancé.

Problem was, I wanted to be the one who did that for her. I hated the thought that I'd been the one who found her and every other hungry dog standing around in the bars and clubs would be the ones who had a real chance.

Finally, at approximately 6:15, fifteen minutes before we had planned on going for some great Italian meatballs, I got a text from her.

ELLA: Sharon was able to get me a cashier's check. She totally understood my problem and was happy to help. I really think we should keep things professional between us. Thanks for everything you've done for me. I won't forget it even if we don't see each other outside of work again.

CRAP.

128

I should have just chalked it up to experience and moved on. There were hundreds of young women who would be happy enough to spend time in my bed. Besides, I had a headhunter busy trying to find me a wife.

I should have put Ella Carlson out of my head, but I couldn't.

I didn't want to.

I didn't give up that easily when I saw something I wanted.

I wanted Ella. Still, I couldn't force the issue. I'd have to try to build up trust with her and that would take time.

I'd give her some time – I'd wait a few days and then I'd ask her once more to come out with me for a meal. Maybe if I showed her I would be completely hands-off at Dominion from that day forward, she'd feel better about us seeing each other.

To that end, I send her one last text.

JOSH: *I understand that you're reluctant to become involved with me because I own Dominion Publishing. If you change your mind or even just about the meatballs, you can text me and I'll be here. I really enjoyed meeting you and assure you that I would never use my position to gain any kind of advantage over you or force the issue. It's totally up to you.*

Then, I went back to work, determined to give her some time and space to consider what I'd said. In a couple of days, I'd try again.

A FEW DAYS LATER, after I'd immersed myself in work and tried my best to put Ella into the back of my mind, I decided to pop down to her office and see if I could accidentally run into her on the way to speak with Sharon.

I left my office and took the elevator down to her floor and went to Sharon's office, hoping to find Ella before she left, but I was too late. The office was still open, but Sharon was the only person remaining inside.

I popped in and saw her sitting behind her desk, a stack of files in front of her.

"Hey," I said and entered the office, taking the chair across from her. "How are you doing? We haven't had a chance to really sit down and talk since my father's death."

"I'm fine," she said and closed a file, removing her reading glasses and giving me a smile. "How are you?"

"I'm good. No complaints. Just wanted to see how things were in your neck of the woods. We've been in meetings together but we haven't had the chance to talk alone."

"I'm hugely relieved after finally getting my new assistant."

"Yes, I imagine. I'm glad you found someone to fill the role. Tell me about her. I haven't had a chance to read through any of the HR files." I shrugged, not sure I'd even seen any nor had I taken time to look.

"Oh, Ella? She's really bright, finished a BA in English from Dartmouth College. Wants to do a MFA at Columbia next year. She specialized in editing and creative writing, so she has an eye for both good writing and story. I'm really happy with her. It's a crime that we're getting her for free. I hope we can offer her a paid position when her internship ends."

"New Hampshire? Her last name is Carlson. Why does that ring a bell?"

Sharon raised her eyebrows. "Daddy is none other than the notorious Governor Emmet Carlson."

That shocked me. I sat back and rubbed my chin. "Governor Carlson? I think *The Chronicle* did a piece on him a few years ago. Has a lot of friends in high places who were passing on intel on some biotech stocks. He was never charged, but some of his underlings were."

"That's right. I remember it now. Ella just got out of a bad breakup. Seems there were a few problems with her fiancé." She wagged her eyebrows. "Not that I pry into my staff's personal lives, but given her father's position, stuff gets published. She just had a big breakup and she said she, and I quote, 'wanted to get the heck out of Dodge.'"

"Yeah, I know all about that," I said, referring to my own sorry tale of engagement woe. Sharon knew all about it. I'd asked her to take over soon after Christie and I split and I took some time off. I'd been honest with her, wanting to take a long vacation and try to wash Christie out of my system and Sharon had been only too happy to help me out. It meant a promotion for her, but she'd shown she could handle the added responsibilities.

"How are *you* doing?" she asked, her expression sympathetic.

"I'm good." I stood up, hoping to end that line of questioning immediately. "Well, I'm glad things worked out with the new hire. I just wanted to pop by before I left and make sure you were good. If you have any concerns, just call me. You know my door is always open."

"Thanks," she said and smiled.

I left, hoping I hadn't raised any suspicions on her part about my visit.

Then I took the elevator down to the parking garage and sat in my car, pondering my next move.

If she wouldn't answer my texts, I'd have to run into her at work, which might cause all sorts of issues, but the only alternative was to go to her new place and try to contact her that way. Which sounded way too stalkerish even to me.

I decided to order some flowers and send them to her office tomorrow.

Maybe I could win her over with yet another apology. She wasn't a lightweight, and probably had developed a strong spine after her own failed engagement.

Whatever the case, I wouldn't give up until she and I sat face to face and talked it out.

I checked out an online florist and ordered two dozen violet roses. For the card, I put down the following:

ELLA:

I know we got off to a rocky start, with scraped knees and elbows, and you're worried about who I am, but my offer of the greatest Italian meatballs stands.

Sincerely,

Your Friendly Neighborhood Bicycle Courier Impersonator

THERE REALLY WASN'T anything else appropriate for me to do but make the offer and see if she responded. She had every right to ignore me but I hoped I could convince her that I was sincere. I wanted to give it a good try at least, before either of us wrote off the relationship. I should have probably just put her completely out of my mind, but I couldn't.

CHAPTER FIFTEEN

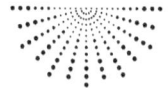

ELLA

I LEFT Josh's office and went back to my own, conflicted about everything. It felt really strange to have to pretend that I didn't just almost sleep with Josh and I knew that if we kept it up, it would be very awkward – and potentially very dangerous – for me to become involved with Josh.

I didn't want to be beholden to him and so I went to Sharon when she returned from her meeting with Josh and told her what happened, asking her to get me a cashier check so I could take possession of my apartment on Monday.

I stood in front of Sharon's desk and held my breath, waiting for her reply.

Her mouth dropped open, but she agreed right away, with no hesitation.

"Of course, I'll help you. Sit down sit down," she said and pointed to the chair across from her desk. "You should have come to me right away, you poor thing. How much do you need?"

I sat down and heaved a huge sigh of relief. It was hard working up the guts to go into Sharon's office and ask for her help. I'd sat in the bathroom and scrunched up a tissue, trying to get up the nerve to go in and ask for her help.

All my anxiety was for nothing.

"My first and last month's rent for the studio is $5400.00. I'll transfer you the money as soon as the bank gets my account reactivated," I said and held up my cell, showing her my banking app, and the balance in my account. "Just give me the email you want me to send it to and it'll be in your bank account once the bank lifts the block, which they do when your bank card is stolen."

She told me and I made a note on my calendar to make sure I sent it after the block was lifted.

"I'll go down to my bank during my break and get you the cashier's check," Sharon said, smiling.

"Thank you so much. You can't know how relieved I am. I was afraid I'd lose the apartment and have to stay in this tiny little Airbnb I have now. I wasn't even sure I could do that, because I had to report my credit card stolen and so I wouldn't be able to use it to pay for any extra days."

"I thought you said everything was fine," Sharon asked. "If I had known..."

"I didn't want to be your problem," I said, my fingernails digging a bit too firmly into my palm, thinking of what Josh had said to me in the elevator. "I wanted to be the solution to your problems. If I asked you to get a cashier's check so I could get my apartment, I'd become your problem which is the opposite of the reason you hired me."

"You shouldn't have worried. I'm just sorry you waited so long. You must have been frantic."

"I was at first," I said, nodding. "But I went to my bank and told them what happened. They walked me through the steps to get new ID, but I couldn't get a cashier's check until I had something tangible to prove who I was and my address. But I wouldn't have anything tangible until I got the mail at my new address with my new card -- in ten days."

"The old catch-22."

"Exactly," I said. "I thought I had someone who could help me, but it turned out to be a flop. You were my last hope."

"Well, I'm glad I can help you." She smiled softly. "Now, go find me some good books. I need something to show the editorial team tomorrow."

"I'll do my best."

I left her office and went to my own, sighing with relief.

When I left the office at six, I hoped I didn't run into Josh. The last thing I needed was to see him and be reminded of what a hunk of man he was, and how much I was going to regret having ethical standards.

Jerkface had been screwing his secretary.

I was determined that I wouldn't become just an office romance to anyone – even someone as gorgeous and powerful as Josh.

THE NEXT MORNING as I left the elevator on my way to my office, I passed a delivery man going into the elevator. When I arrived in my office, I saw a bouquet of flowers on the desk.

I knew immediately who they were from...

I sat at my desk and stared at the flowers. Two dozen of the prettiest violet roses with a spray of baby's breath. I read the card and couldn't help but smile despite my anger.

From your friendly neighborhood Bicycle Courier Impersonator...

It was almost enough to make me take out my cell and text him, accepting the offer of the best Italian meatballs for supper.

But I didn't.

I couldn't get past the boss-employee thing. If he had been just a bicycle courier, and not one of the wealthiest men in the US, I would have been happy to go to his – to his company's -- apartment for some late-night bed-tumbling. But he wasn't just a bicycle courier.

He was my boss.

I sat staring at the flowers, thinking about Josh. He did help me out. He was very generous, and now of course, I realized that it was because he truly could afford to and not only because he had a good heart. My first and last month's rent was probably what he paid a day for his apartment. I'd seen an article about apartments in SoHo that rented for a cool half million a month. That kind of wealth was unthinkable. I couldn't imagine it. I grew up privileged with my father being a successful lawyer before becoming Governor. But Joshua Macintyre Jr? His father had owned Macintyre Broadcasting. It was one of the biggest media empires in the country.

Probably the world.

Frankly, he scared me.

Monday came and I went to pick up keys to my new place in Chelsea and compared to my Airbnb place, it was a palace. Hardwood floors, real exposed brick on one full wall with windows overlooking a small courtyard. It had its own bathroom, which, while tiny, wasn't shared. The kitchenette was cute if really small, but I had a big open space for my bedroom / office.

And it was all mine.

I loved it. I hauled my one suitcase into the space and did my best to make it my own. I had been able to get some cheap bedding and some drapes for the windows. Luckily, the place was furnished with a proper full-sized murphy bed in a nice cabinet and tiny two-seater sofa and coffee table. There was a small table against the wall with two chairs.

Really, it felt like a mansion compared to the Airbnb. I went out that night and bought some groceries, and had my first home-cooked meal in my new apartment.

I was in seventh heaven. Now, if only Josh hadn't been so deceptive about his real identity, I might have been in bed with him and we would be enjoying each other's bodies the way we should have been.

The next week passed pretty slowly, and although I was glad I didn't have to face Josh and be tempted by him, I felt a little sad that he hadn't persisted. But it was probably for the best that I didn't become involved with him. The last thing I needed was to get involved with my boss. Josh was the kind of man I could fall for and who would probably throw me over for someone more beautiful – a better catch than I was.

When Friday night rolled around, I was sitting on my bed, my laptop open, and was reading my Twitter feed when my cell pinged, indicating an income text. I took it out and checked my messages.

Speaking of the devil, the message was from Josh.

JOSH: I'm going to be sitting in the restaurant waiting for an order of the best damn meatballs in all of Manhattan -- perhaps the world – Saturday night. Say, around seven o'clock. If you're interested, I'll be waiting. But I won't wait too long. Nothing worse than cold meatballs! Seriously, Ella. Please meet me there and eat some meatballs with me. We could set some rules governing our relationship if being boss and employee really bothers you. Then, whatever you decide, I'll be happy to accept.

. . .

137

THERE WAS EVEN a pasta emoji at the end of his message. It was so cute with the tiny fork rolling spaghetti that I was almost won over.

Almost.

But if you didn't have standards, what did you have?

I didn't answer him. Instead, I closed my cell and got ready for bed, trying my best to put him and his offer out of my mind. Just when I was starting to feel okay about leaving him out of my life, he had to contact me and ask me out on a dinner date.

I brushed my teeth and got into my pajamas, then snuggled down into my bed in my tiny studio apartment in Chelsea, wishing I had fewer standards and could allow myself to go tomorrow night and sit at a table in the window with Josh, slurping spaghetti and eating the world's best meatballs.

THE NEXT DAY, I went for a long walk around my new neighborhood, hoping to find all the great places to eat and shop in my local area. Of course, all morning, I kept thinking of Josh's offer, and was torn whether to accept. I wanted to. I wanted to find out what could happen between us, but I was worried that I shouldn't. I needed to talk to Steph so I picked up my cell and called. She answered on the third ring.

"What's up, kiddo? How's the Big Apple treating you? Did you get the ID thing sorted out? Did you and Mr. Straining Glutes have dinner?"

"I did get the ID thing sorted out and yes, Mr. Glutes and I did have dinner. But there's a problem..."

I bit my lip and wondered how to phrase my next confession.

"A problem? Do tell..."

"The thing is, Mr. Glutes isn't really a bicycle courier."

"Don't tell me. He's really a hitman for the Russian Mob. I

always told you that you were too trusting of people." She laughed, but I imagined she was only partly kidding.

"No, Steph. Don't laugh. This is serious. He's really," I said and hesitated, hating the words I'd have to tell her.

"He's really what?" she said, her voice impatient. "Quit with the teasing. Who is he?"

"He's my boss." I cringed when I said it, because the thought that I had almost had sex unknowingly with my new boss was the very last thing I should ever have done.

"Your boss? I thought this Sharon lady was your boss."

"She's my supervisor, but he's the boss. He's the big boss. As in, Joshua Macintyre Jr, CEO of Macintyre Broadcasting Corporation."

"MBC? The CEO? Oh, my God, Ella. Seriously?" I heard her typing on a keyboard. "I'm searching now for Joshua Macintyre. Annnnnd..." she said and then I heard a gasp.

"Oh, my God, Ella. He's a freaking hunk. You actually thought he was a bicycle courier? How could you ever imagine that? I mean, Armani model yes, but bicycle courier?"

"He was wearing a bicycle outfit, you know, with the whole tight body suit and slick helmet. What else could I think?"

"Like, maybe he was just riding his bike and he takes riding seriously? He's gorgeous."

"Yes, he is. He's a total babe. And the worst part of it is that we ended up at his apartment and he had my bra off and was just about to take off more when his drunk ex-fiancée walked in and caught us."

"Shut the front door," she said, laughing. "Are you shitting me? This is one of your erotic stories, right?"

"No, I'm not kidding. It really happened. We were all hot and heavy and I looked up and saw this blonde woman standing in the doorway, crying. Needless to say, it spoiled the vibe I was trying to create what with his face between my boobs."

"No kidding. Look, kiddo. When I told you to live it up, I had no idea you'd take me so seriously. He's the actual CEO of MBC? Are you sure he wasn't tricking you or something? You are very naive..."

"No, seriously. He's the big boss in all his impeccable Armani-suited-hunkiness and I saw him actually sitting behind the biggest desk you've ever seen."

"He's the one with the perfect mouth and blue-gray eyes? The sexy longish hair that flops in his eyes? The perfectly trimmed beard? The devastatingly square jaw? And you were kissing that mouth?"

"I was. That mouth was licking my tattoo just when I saw the ex-fiancée gawking at us in the bedroom doorway."

"Oh, my God. Ella. What a story."

"I know, I know. I told him I couldn't see him again."

"What? Why?"

"He's my boss, Steph. I thought you'd understand."

"He's gorgeous! How could you turn that down?"

"I know, right? But he's my boss. Anyway, he texted me with an invitation to go out for supper for the best meatballs in the world and try to set some ground rules, but I turned him down."

"You're turning down meatballs? He wants to lay down ground rules? You mean, finish what you started, right?"

"Yes, but Steph, I can't. It would be what Jerkface did to me."

We both had been hurt by office romances but it seemed the two of us were just interested in being together, and the rest of it didn't matter all that much.

"You're turning down one of the richest hunks in all of the USA?"

"Yes," I said, pouting at the tone of her voice. "He's my boss."

"You've said that three times already and each time, I still don't understand. You met and you like each other. End of story."

"It's hilarious, because I thought he was a bicycle courier. He played along for a while, amused. I even offered to pay for his health care if he needed to see a doctor for stitches. God, I offered to call his boss and provide a letter that he'd hurt himself because of me."

We laughed for a moment and I thought of how truly funny it was.

Once I got under control, I sighed. "He seemed to like me thinking he was just a bicycle courier."

"He's probably used to having dozens of young women offering themselves to him because of his money."

"And his looks," I added.

"Yes. The being a total hunk part doesn't hurt but makes the millions seem even more enticing. He was probably happy that you liked him for himself, rather than his money. You know, poor little rich boy nobody can really see because they have dollar signs in their eyes."

"I suppose so. Thing is, I would have kept seeing him if he was just a bicycle courier."

"You are such a stickler. And that's prejudiced, by the way."

"I even asked him if he knew any Mr. Big types he could introduce me to."

"Oh, my God, that's just too good. He was the actual Mr. Big."

"I know, I know...Why did he have to be my boss?"

"What's he like?"

"He was so nice. Offered to help me. Handed me money and a cell. Took me out for supper and drinks. Sent shivers down my spine before we were rudely interrupted."

"The shivers down your spine part. Spill, sister."

"He kisses good." I smiled, knowing that would drive Steph wild.

"He kisses good? That's all you're giving me? What about the licking the tattoo part?"

"I'll write a story about it. I feel weird telling you."

"Okay, you do that. Write a story. Except, finish it the way you wish it turned out. Maybe title it, 'He Was Just A Bicycle Courier But He Sure Spun My Tires.' Or 'Pulled my chain'. Or Blew My Horn.'"

"You're crazy..."

"You know it. Seriously, Ella. Go out for dinner with him. Have a nice meatball or three. Give him a chance. Jump his damn bones."

"I'll think about it."

"Don't think too long or someone else will come along and be only too happy to take your place, sweetheart."

"Okay, okay. I'll think about it quickly. I gotta go, but thanks for listening."

"Hey, who loves you?" she said with a laugh.

"You do," I replied. "Love you back." Then I hung up, smiling at the thought of her own smile I knew would be plastered across her face.

At around seven, I checked my messages and while I was wishing that Josh had sent me yet another message, thinking that if he had I might have broken down and gone to meet him, a message popped up from Steph.

STEPH: *So I take it you're right now sitting in a nice Italian restaurant in Mid-Town Manhattan across from one of the hunkiest richest publishing magnates in the world, enjoying world-famous meatballs like I said you should?*

I SIGHED.

. . .

ELLA: *Actually, I'm sitting on my bed. There's a frozen dinner in my freezer with my name on it, but I'm not really all that hungry right now...*

STEPH: *Oh, cry me a river. You're in Damn Manhattan, in a studio apartment in Chelsea, with a job in publishing, and a millionaire hunk wanting to lick your tattoo and a whole lot more. Get your ass down to the restaurant and have some damn meatballs, will ya???*

ELLA: *Okay.*

STEPH: *That's better. Dammit! Text me to let me know how it goes. If I don't hear from you, I hope it's because he's busy licking something other than your tattoo. And not his spoon either!*

ELLA: *Okay, okay. I'll go. *Smooch**

STEPH: **cracks whip**

I SMILED and put my cell into my bag and left my apartment.

CHAPTER SIXTEEN

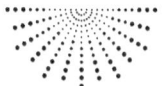

JOSHUA

I SENT the text and waited, hoping Ella was willing to give us a chance. I didn't expect her to show up. In fact, I expected her to ignore me completely. I sat and checked my cell, then watched outside the window at the street, hoping to see her and her long brown hair come bobbing along the street.

Nothing.

I checked my watch and it was already 7:15. If she was coming, she was late, but I had to expect that since she was new in Manhattan and the trains could be delayed during rush hour.

Then I saw her.

She wore a short jean skirt, a sweater and heels and looked casually delicious, her long hair pulled back in a braid that fell over one shoulder. She opened the door to the restaurant and glanced around until her eyes finally met mine.

I think I saw the slightest bit of a smile on her face and that tiny quirk of her lips gave me hope. I stood and held out a chair.

She remained in the entrance, as if she was rethinking her decision to join me. I saw her bite her bottom lip and so I knew she needed some extra enticement. I held up the basket of fresh bread sticks and mouthed, 'They're_fantastic!' and kissed my fingers the way an Italian chef would.

This time, she smiled broadly and I felt a surge of adrenaline go through me.

She approached the table, stopping when she got to the chair I held out for her.

"Ella, thanks for coming," I said and gestured to the chair. "I know you're concerned about being with me because of who I am, but I want you to feel completely comfortable about it. What will it take to make you less concerned?"

"I don't know," she said and sat down.

I pulled out her napkin and draped it on her lap. Then I sat beside her instead of across from her so I was closer. I turned my chair so we faced each other.

"Let's be totally honest with each other from this time forward. You can ask me anything, and I'll tell you the honest truth. Anything you want. Total open book."

"Anything?" she said and sat down.

"Anything."

She smiled, a wicked gleam in her eyes. "What's your favorite porn indulgence?"

That threw me. My eyes widened at her question. "That's pretty... hard to answer, really. I mean, a man sees porn like a glutton sees a smorgasbord. It's hard to choose and pretty much anything is tasty. It's all food. Well, except the illegal stuff, but I don't go there."

She rested her chin on her hand and batted her eyelashes. "Give me one thing that you go back to over and over."

I laughed and leaned back, surprised but charmed by her forthrightness. "I should be like my father and say I don't need to look at porn because I have dozens of women willing to take part in a *pas de deux* with me. He made that argument to me once when he found me watching porn on the internet and I challenged him about what he watched. Except, he said he didn't look at porn because he had my mother, which made me go all *gross*."

"Gross? You thought your mother was gross?"

"No, I mean, I thought my parents having sex was gross. When he found me, I was eleven and thought that married people only had sex to procreate."

She nodded. "A good Catholic, are you?"

"A failed Catholic, actually."

She folded her arms and looked at me pointedly. "Your favorite go-to porn. Chop chop."

"Chop chop?" I said, stalling for time. What did I like that I felt comfortable sharing? "I like watching," I said keeping my voice as low as possible, "when a woman uses a dildo and makes herself orgasm."

She raised her eyebrows. "Voyeur, are you?"

"A bit."

"Why?" she asked, leaning closer. "What do you like about it?"

I tilted my head to the side, considering. "I like to see a woman's desire. Her need. I like to see her fulfilled."

The waitress came to our table to take a drink order, interrupting our little conversation and I hoped that was it with the intimate questions.

"Feel like some Italian red to go along with the meatballs?" I asked.

"Sure," she replied.

I turned to the waitress. "Tell your bartender to pick a red for us. We'll be having the spaghetti and meatballs."

The waitress smiled and left us.

I turned to her, trying to shift the line of questioning from my porn preferences to anything else.

"I'm glad you decided to come," I said and leaned in closer.

"Tell me more about you," she said and picked up one of the breadsticks, her lips closing over the end of it in an all-too suggestive way that made my mind go to her sliding my dick into her mouth instead. Then she bit down-- hard and chewed, smiling.

She knew what she did to me. I smiled to myself. She was playful. And a bit of a tease.

I liked it.

"I'm Joshua Macintyre Jr, oldest brother of five. I'm the one who obeyed all the rules and always asked permission, while my younger siblings broke all the rules and asked for forgiveness," I said with a laugh, because it was true. "I'm the responsible one. The one everyone can count on to do the right thing."

She nodded and her gaze moved over my face. "Why do you think your fiancée cheated on you?"

That set me back a bit. "Wow." I actually physically leaned back in my chair. "Let me think." I bit my bottom lip and narrowed my eyes. "Because she never really loved me but she loved the idea of being the wife of Joshua Macintyre Jr and starting a dynasty between our two families."

"But you loved her for herself," she said and took another bite off the end of her breadstick. "There was nothing shallow in your relationship with her. She was beautiful. Tall, blonde hair, perfect skin from what I could see. Very shapely. Obviously from a wealthy family."

"I thought I loved her," I admitted. "I loved us as a couple. We were a power couple. Two big business families joined, two fortunes united. I could see it all from where I sat. Charity balls, exotic vacations, our children going to the best private schools, Ivy League colleges, inheriting the business or starting their own dynasties. But she was really in love with one of my mid-level managers from a middle-class background." I shrugged, helpless.

"It was true love on their part but she couldn't marry him. He wasn't rich enough. That hurt."

"Yeah, same story on my part," she said and glanced away, her expression still pained.

"I know your pain," I said, hearing the edge of sadness in her voice. "Wounds still fresh?"

"Too fresh," she replied. "Not enough scar tissue yet. Still raw."

"Say no more. I'm in the same boat."

"We're a pair," she said and smiled. "Losers at love."

"Losers at love," I replied and held out my breadstick. We tapped them together and chewed, each of us probably thinking about our cheating exes.

"Hopefully winners at life in general. We need something to make up for it."

"Have you dated anyone since you split?" I asked, interested in her romantic life.

She shook her head. "Nope. I swore off men for a full year."

"You came with me to the apartment..."

"I'm weak."

"So, you're ready to try again?"

"I was," she said softly. "Unfortunately, I ran into a really nice guy who ended up being my boss and I was pretty much ready to throw in the towel for the rest of the year because I promised myself I'd never do an office romance."

I shook my head. "Office romances aren't all that bad..."

She smiled at me, her smile warm. "My BFF told me I was being an idiot. That I was being prejudiced because I would have kept seeing you if you were only a bicycle courier."

"You liked me in spite of thinking I was just a bicycle courier putting myself through college with dreams of buying a newspaper one day."

She leaned back when the waitress brought the bottle of wine and we stopped talking while she uncorked it and poured me a sample. I nodded in approval and we were quiet while she poured us each a glass. Once she was done, I held up my glass.

"To us. Losers at love. Winners at life."

"To us," she replied and we both took a sip.

"What do you think?" I asked when she put her glass down. "Do you approve?"

She shrugged and wagged her eyebrows. "Honestly, I wouldn't know a good wine from vinegar."

I laughed. "Well, this is a good Italian red. Dry and perfect for the world's best meatballs."

We talked for a while about her job and what it entailed. How she'd met Sharon at a conference, hitting it off during their meeting.

"So, tell me what you're writing. I'm a publisher. I might be interested."

She laughed. "Nah, I don't think so. I plan on writing a romantic comedy one day, but right now, I'm in this group of women who are all writing erotica."

"You write erotica?" I said, my body responding to the idea she was a hot little number under the innocent exterior.

"I do." She smiled and took a sip of her wine, her eyes twinkling. She was enjoying teasing me. She had to know what it did to me to think of her writing erotica. Of me reading the erotica she wrote.

"You have to let me read some."

"Not on your life," she said and laughed. "It's for women, not men."

"Come on," I said and pouted. "You can't do that to a guy -- tell him you write erotica and then not let him read it."

"You couldn't handle it," she said.

"What do you mean? Why couldn't I handle it? Is it kinky? I can handle kinky."

"Nuh, uh. Not telling you."

"Dammit, woman. You can't do that. It's totally unfair."

She only smiled in response.

Our food arrived and I waited impatiently for her to try the meatballs, my mind thankfully diverted from thoughts of her writing erotica to her response to the meatballs. She poked one of them with her fork and opened her mouth, wrapping her lips around it. Of course, my mind went there right away and I watched as she bit down and chewed.

"Oh, God," she said, closing her eyes in ecstasy. Which, of course, made my mind go there again.

"You like?"

"Oh, these are the *best*," she said and ate the rest of the meatball, then twirled some spaghetti with tomato marinara sauce. She sat and ate meatball after meatball, pausing only to dip her breadstick into the sauce. "I swear, this is the best I've ever eaten. Not that I've eaten much authentic Italian, but it's definitely the best."

"Told you," I said and drank some wine, smiling. "You can trust me."

She narrowed her eyes. "Will you be mad when I tell you I'm not coming home with you tonight, despite how good the meatballs are?"

I leaned closer and looked in her eyes, trying to put on as sincere an expression as I could.

"Not mad. Sad. I was hoping you'd come back home with me tonight and finish what we started."

She leaned forward. "If you weren't my boss, I would." She smiled and poked her last meatball then took a bite. "I make it a rule not to boink the boss. I thought I'd be nice and tell you in person. Considering both of us have been burned by office romances gone bad, I'd think you'd agree."

I leaned back, resigned to the fact that she was not going to come home with me. She was not going to see where this thing between us was going to go -- on principle. Part of me was upset of course. I wanted her. The prelude to sex we had both played the previous night had been good. Really good.

I wanted her.

The other part of me admired her for sticking to her principles. In contrast, I'd be willing to throw mine out the window for a chance to fuck her brains out.

"Your fortitude is admirable," I said. "On the other hand, I'd throw caution to the wind and gladly take you home with me. Boss or no boss."

She mopped up some of her sauce with a piece of breadstick. "As my grandfather would say, any port in a storm."

I laughed. "Your grandfather was a mariner?"

"Navy. Worked at the Navy Shipyard in Portsmouth, Maine until 1982 when he retired."

"How'd you end up in Concord, New Hampshire?"

"After my father graduated, he moved to Manchester and worked as a lawyer for a few years, he became involved in politics and moved to Concord. That's where I was born."

"My father was in the Navy as an aviator before he started MBC. I was as well. All of us boys served in some capacity."

"That's admirable," she said and her eyes, which were sharp, softened just a bit. "Not many really rich people send their sons and daughters to join the military."

I shrugged. "My father had ethics. He saw wealth as a byproduct of doing what he really loved, rather than an end in itself."

She exhaled and placed her fork on the table. "This was really good," she said and took a sip of her wine. "All of it. The restaurant. The meatballs. The wine."

"The company?" I asked, raising my eyebrows.

"The company, too. I wanted to thank you for helping me out

when you didn't have to. Sharon came through with the first and last month's rent cashier check so you're officially off the hook but I wanted to thank you for the offer. I really needed the cell you lent me. It's been a godsend. I'm going tomorrow to pick up my new iPhone from this tech store. I paid for it online and it should be ready in the morning so I'll return this to you once I get it. I'm also getting a new tablet that can double as a laptop for writing."

"Your homage to Sex and the City?" I said, realizing she was giving me the, *'I like you but I'm not going out with you again'* letdown.

"Something like that," she said with a soft smile. "I can't see you again, though. It's not good to date someone in your office. Especially not the boss. The whole power imbalance thing isn't really healthy."

"You figure you'd have me wrapped around your little finger too easily, do you?" I said and grinned at her, feeling sad that we weren't going to go home together.

She shook her head and smiled. I think I detected a slight bit of regret in her eyes.

"If you change your mind, I'll be only too willing to forgo my ethical stance against office romance."

She laughed. "I thought you were the good brother who always followed the rules and asked permission."

"In most things, yes. In this, I'll throw caution to the wind. So if you decide you want a totally meaningless no-strings attached relationship based on pure mutual pleasure, you know where to find me."

"I do," she said, smiling, her green eyes crinkling in the corners. "But I won't."

"Damn," I said and snapped my fingers. "My offer stands. Take me up on it anytime."

"Well, I better go," she said when the waitress dropped the

bill off. She reached into her bag to retrieve her wallet and I stopped her, my hand on hers.

"Don't worry about the bill," I said. "I made the offer. Let me get this."

"Thanks," she said and stood. "Sharon said you spend most of your time on the paper and so we likely won't see you around the office much."

"No," I said and dropped a few bills on the table. I pulled on my jacket. "I have to attend periodic meetings with my managers at the various offices of MBC, but I'm going to focus on getting the *Chronicle* up and running again. We'll still be in the same office building though."

"Hopefully, we won't run into each other very often."

"Don't say that," I said, opening the door for her. "We can be friendly. We should go out for a meal now and then, so I can see how you're doing and try my hand at seducing you again in the hopes you'll finally succumb."

She laughed. "It's better this way," she said and stuffed her hands in her sweater pockets. "Don't want to tempt each other."

"I've already been more than tempted."

She smiled and then turned away, walking down the street.

"Can I give you a ride home at least?" I called out.

"Not on your life," she said after turning around and walking backwards for a few feet. "You're not going to tempt me."

"Damn," I said and smiled. "A guy's gotta try."

Then she turned around and walked out of my life.

I GOT HOME about fifteen minutes later after parking my vehicle in the parking garage and stopping to pick up a package from the front desk. I really enjoyed my meal with Ella, and wished she wasn't my employee. I had a feeling that if she wasn't, we might be on our way upstairs.

I went to bed alone, my thoughts going to her in her tiny apartment, writing erotica late into the night with her group of women writers, and of course, it made it impossible to sleep without taking care of my raging erection. So instead of sleeping with her the way I had hoped the night would end, it ended instead with me alone in my bed, my cock in hand, wishing it was her.

CHAPTER SEVENTEEN

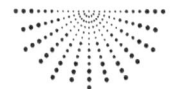

ELLA

I TOOK the subway home and went to my apartment, regretting that I'd turned Josh down.

Still, it was for the best. He was way too gorgeous and way too powerful. There was no way we'd be on equal footing. I'd always be the poor little country mouse next to his city slicker mouse. I wouldn't fit in and so the most we could have would be a purely sexual relationship. As much as I would have liked to sleep with him, I knew it would be a mistake.

I thought about Jerkface and his sexretary and there was no way I was going to be that kind of woman.

Instead, I opened my cell and skyped with Steph.

*ELLA: I just got home from supper with Josh. Best meatballs in the world. *Sigh**

In a moment, she responded.

STEPH: WHAT ARE YOU DOING HOME ALONE YOU SHOULD BE IN HIS BED!!!

ELLA: He's my boss!

STEPH: If you played your cards right, he might end up your husband...

ELLA: In case you forgot, I'm not in the market for a husband. A handsome hunk of a boy-toy, maybe, but a husband? No.

STEPH: HE COULD BE A BOY-TOY!

ELLA: He's my boss.

STEPH: Seriously, I'd do him just for the experience. A notch on your belt, which, I might add, has very few -- like, ONE -- notch on it.

ELLA: Two. You keep forgetting Sidney Johnson.

STEPH: That didn't count. He didn't even get it inside of you, I recall you telling me.

ELLA: It was still sex. And we were still naked.

STEPH: And you were still a virgin afterwards, so no. It doesn't count. You need experience, Ella. Go get you some.

ELLA: *sigh*

STEPH: See? You regret not going home with him. The two of you are going to be filled with regrets. Not a good way to live. You should seize the day. Live life to the fullest.

ELLA: So what you're saying is that I should just forget all my ethics.

STEPH: I'm saying you should JUMP HIM!

ELLA: I think I'm going to write some erotica instead.

STEPH: Oh for God's sake... What's the use of moving to The Big Apple and not taking advantage of the men?

ELLA: I will, once I find one WHO ISN'T MY BOSS...

STEPH: Boss, schmoss. I bet he's good in bed. Now you'll never know.

ELLA: It's too late now anyway. I'm going to say goodbye. I've taken enough abuse for one night...

STEPH: You love me.

ELLA: I do. *Smooch*

STEPH: *Smooches you back*

STEPH: Look, kiddo. If he asks you out again, don't say no. Sleep with him and see where it goes. He's so damn gorgeous, you'd be a fool to let something as trivial as morals and ethics get in the way. ;)

ELLA: And instead let something as trivial as his good looks guide my way?

STEPH: When it comes to sex and pleasure, good looks are important factors in satisfaction.

ELLA: GOOD NIGHT!!!

STEPH: XOXOXO

I SMILED and put my cell away, then opened my Iron Man notebook. Instead of actually going out and enjoying Josh the way I probably should have and could have, I decided to write a new erotic short story. In fact, I decided to write one about Josh, although I'd use a different name.

My pencil from the kiosk was much shorter, but luckily, I thought to sharpen it at work before I left for the day. Otherwise, I'd have to use the dictation app on my cell and I could never get the hang of it.

TEMPT *Me*

THE MAN *in the grey flannel suit was not my Mr. Big but he was a pretty damn good substitute...*

I SAT at my kitchen table and tried to think of a scenario that excited me, and one that would excite my readers. Maybe, an agreement to have sex in the middle of the day, at a ritzy hotel, no words spoken, just get a key, take the elevator up, and go meet a man for sex. Someone you didn't know but who had been vetted by a group you belonged to -- a sex club for people who had needs but those didn't include romance or marriage.

Kind of the way both Josh and I felt after our own heartbreaking bad engagements.

I wrote my story, using Josh as my hero and myself as the heroine -- if you could call my two characters by those titles. I decided on the Ritz-Carlton Hotel across from Central Park. It would fulfil my fantasy of meeting a hot rich man there and having wild sex.

At my usual pace of four pages an hour, it took me about five hours to get the first part of the story done. When I was finished for the night, I closed my notebook and put my pencil away, then had a lukewarm shower, and went to bed with B.O.B.

Just another ordinary but sad night in my otherwise exciting new life in Manhattan.

THE NEXT MORNING, I rushed to work, having slept in past my alarm. I almost didn't make it, but was glad that I was able to slip into my office without running into Sharon, who was in an early meeting. I sat at my desk and pulled the box of manuscripts closer and fished out the first one, opening my notebook and taking out my pencil.

It was then I realized I forgot to remove the story out of the notebook and leave it at home. I pulled out each page and stuffed them into a file on my desk, then I spent the first part of the morning reading manuscripts and queries from various authors, reading the first five pages of book after book, deciding whether to read on later or pass. Sharon didn't want me to read past the first five or six pages, arguing that I would know whether a story gripped me in that short time. It made me feel bad for all the authors who put so much care and attention to their beloved manuscripts, only to have me reject it after the first five or ten pages, but that's what Sharon wanted. Unsolicited manuscripts were rarely accepted by the publisher. Most of the books published came via an agent or one of the editors already working in the publishing house.

By the time my ten thirty rolled around, I was ready for a break, my eyes watery after reading page after page, scratching down notes in my notebook about the ones I liked. There were a couple, and I felt they needed to be read fully, but I'd consult with Sharon first.

It was time for me to go and get my new laptop and cell from the local electronics store, so I grabbed my coat and bag and told Samantha at the front reception that I'd be gone for half an hour but would take a shorter lunch break.

"Going to get my new cell," I said as I pushed the elevator button.

"Have a good one."

I went down the elevator to the main floor and out into the glorious autumn day in Manhattan. Around me were the sounds of the street -- pedestrians walking, talking and horns blaring in the busy traffic, which always seemed to be clogged up. In the distance, a siren wailed. I glanced around and was glad to be so lucky to be here.

I made my way to the electronics shop and picked up my new iPhone 8 Plus, and after getting it activated and my data transferred, I picked up an iPad with a detachable keyboard. It was a lot cheaper than an actual laptop. After I was finished, I grabbed a coffee and went back to the office. I had a meeting with Sharon and so I had to rush the last few blocks so I wouldn't be late.

When I arrived in my office, Sharon popped her head in.

"Meet me in the boardroom. Bring your stuff and we can talk about what you've found for me."

"I will," I said and gave her a smile, trying not to appear too flustered. I sat behind my desk and exhaled, excited to meet with her and talk about the manuscripts. I gathered up the pile that I'd marked "Further Consideration" and grabbed my notebook, because I hadn't had the time to set up my new iPad, which would take maybe fifteen or twenty minutes. It was then that I noticed my red file with the erotic story I'd removed from my notebook was missing. I checked under the box, and under a pile of rejected manuscripts, but it wasn't there.

Where the hell was it?

It was a red file and I remembered putting it off to the side of my desk, away from the manuscripts so they wouldn't get mixed up.

Crap!

I checked under the desk on the off chance that I'd knocked it off and didn't notice, but the floor was bare. Nothing.

I went out of the office to the reception area.

"Have you seen a red file folder anywhere? I can't find it. It was on my desk when I left for my meeting with Sharon and now it's gone."

Theresa shook her head. "No, I haven't but Mr. Macintyre popped in when you were out, looking for you. I asked if he wanted me to let you know he'd been by, but he said no. He'd call you later."

"He was in my office?" I asked, a sinking feeling inside.

"Yes, he just popped in for a moment."

I swallowed hard. "Did he have a red file folder with him when he left?"

She shrugged and made a face. "Not that I remember, but he did have a bunch of files with him when he stopped by."

Oh, *God*...

162

Had Josh found my file folder with the erotic story ABOUT HIM?

There was no way he wouldn't see that he was the hero. Rich. Handsome with blue-gray eyes. Brown hair, a bit longish. A well-trimmed beard. Tall. Built. Even a newspaper magnate.

I cringed internally when I thought about it. Oh, God...

I felt momentarily sick and went back to my office, sitting at my desk, not knowing what to do or how to handle it.

I made one more attempt to find the red file folder before I completely gave up hope, but it wasn't anywhere to be found. Then I thought that, maybe, I'd accidentally brought it with me to the boardroom and traced my steps back there.

Nope.

I went back to my office and sat behind my desk, staring blankly at my files, trying to decide what to do. I was going to do nothing. I wasn't going to contact Josh and ask if he had it. If he contacted me, I'd act as if it meant nothing. I'd laugh and say I was using him to make money, because I could actually sell my stories for a few bucks on Amazon.

I would *not* let it get to me.

Crap!

I texted Steph.

ELLA: You'll never guess what just happened!

STEPH: You won the lottery and are inviting me on a world cruise? Prince Something of Somesuch Country proposed and you're finally going to realize your dream to be a princess? The Nobel Prize Committee just awarded you the Nobel Prize for Literature? Do tell...

ELLA: I wrote an erotic story featuring Mr. Straining Glutes and me in a tryst at a hotel. I had it in a red file folder on my desk. While I was out at a meeting, he dropped by my office and found the file and took it!!! Hasn't said a word but he's the only one who could have it. I don't know what to do.

STEPH: *Oh, now you're in for it! He'll probably pester you until the two of you act it out. I can see it all now -- you'll bang each other's brains out and decide you can't stand to be apart and will get married and have five kids.*

ELLA: *Steph! This is serious! I'm mortified...*

STEPH: *Seriously, kiddo. He'll probably have to make a trip to the executive washroom to rub one out after reading it. Your erotica is good and I mean gooooood. Chill out. He's hot as a firecracker and now he won't be able to get you and your story out of his mind. Betcha a million bucks.*

ELLA: *You don't have a million bucks.*

STEPH: *But if I did, I'd bet it.*

ELLA: *What should I do?*

STEPH: *Do nothing. Let him come to you. Act nonchalant. Tell him that you were searching around for a story to make a few extra bucks and threw it together at the last minute, but you're not sure it's hot enough to sell. It might need editing. Act like it's purely a business decision. He'll be totally impressed and totally captivated and will want you even more than before.*

ELLA: *He's, like, a billionaire, Steph. He could have any woman he wanted. Models, starlets, debutantes.*

STEPH: *He'll want you. Trust me on this. Now, just go do your job and text me if anything happens. XOXOXOX*

ELLA: *Okay... *sigh**

I DID what Steph suggested and totally ignored the panic welling up inside me. I could do nothing about the fact that Josh had found my erotic story. He had it and so now, the ball was in his court. It would be up to him whether he'd let me know he had it.

164

I tried to spend the rest of my day not thinking about Josh reading my story, but it was damn near impossible. I went to my meeting with Sharon and at least that distracted me for a while. At about five thirty, I packed up my things and took the elevator down to the main floor, hoping beyond hope that I wouldn't run into Josh on the way out of the building. I heaved a sigh of relief when I made it past the security desk with no incident and walked down the street to the subway stop.

Then I got on my train and went home, thankful that the confrontation that I knew would eventually happen was postponed for at least another day.

ABOUT NINE O'CLOCK that night I got a text from Steph.

STEPH: Nothing yet?

ELLA: No, thank God.

STEPH: Strange. I would have thought he'd make a point of dropping by to let you know he'd read your story.

ELLA: Believe me, I am just as happy that he hasn't. I don't need any drama.

STEPH: You wait and see. I know I'm right about this. He'll say or do something to acknowledge it.

ELLA: I just want it all to go away.

STEPH: Text me as soon as he does something. This time tomorrow, I'll bet he's asked you out for dinner or drinks. Maybe you'll be boinking him in the executive bathroom after he confronts you with the story.

ELLA: I don't want to boink him in the executive bathroom!

STEPH: Where do you want to boink him?

ELLA: In my story, we were at the Ritz-Carlton. The room had a view of Central Park.

STEPH: Maybe you'll boink him there. It's possible. Wherever he wants to boink you, take it!
ELLA: You are so bad...
STEPH: You love me.
ELLA: You know it.

I WOKE up the next morning, a sense of dread filling me at having to face Josh at work the next day. I had to return his cell, and would see if there was any way to do so when he wasn't there. Maybe I could leave the cell at the front desk to give to Josh when he arrived for the day.

That was my plan, at least.

I went through my usual routine and made it to the office in record time. I was even able to stop and pick up my coffee, having time to spare. Once I was there, I entered the building, showed my ID and dropped the cell off with the security guard on the front desk, asking if he could return it to Josh when he came to the desk to sign in.

"If you want, I can have it delivered to his office," the guard said. "We take the packages that arrive up each day and I could do it then."

"Thanks," I said and reached into my bag to remove a five-dollar bill. "Let me give you something for your troubles."

The guard waved it away "No charge," he said. "Next time you're out, bring me a coffee with two sugars and say we're square."

"Oh, thank you," I gushed. "You're so sweet."

"That's what my wife says," he replied with a grin.

I left the front desk and I took the elevator up to my office, wondering about Josh and what he really thought about my story. I liked it. It was a fantasy of mine -- meeting a strange but gorgeous man for hot sex in the middle of the day at a ritzy hotel.

166

No words spoken -- just enter the room, and go at it. Of course, the man would be totally alpha, a hunk, and know precisely what to do to make my heart beat faster, my body respond and my orgasm -- or three -- be mind-blowing.

My body warmed to the thought of Josh waiting at a hotel room for me and I had to take in a deep breath and try to shove the thoughts out of my mind.

When the elevator arrived, I was almost ready for my day. I stopped to say hello to Sharon on my way inside.

"How are you doing?" she asked, glancing up from a pile of files on her desk. "Everything okay on the financial front?"

"Yes," I said and nodded. "I picked up my keys on Monday. My old place was so small so my new place feels like a mansion by comparison. It's nice to have my own bathroom and a real kitchen."

"Good, good," she said. "There's a new box of manuscripts in your office."

Before I could respond, her phone rang, so she gave me a smile and mouthed *I have to take this*, so I left her to her phone call, walking down the hallway, feeling eager to get started.

I went into my office and plopped myself down behind my desk, tucking my bag into the bottom drawer and placing my coffee cup on the desktop beside my laptop.

It was then that I saw the small black plastic hotel room keycard. It was unmistakable.

A hotel room key to the Ritz-Carlton New York - Central Park. 50 Central Park West.

Adrenaline coursed through me and I had to actually catch my breath. I picked up the keycard and turned it over. Inside was the room number. I googled the room number and saw it was a room on the 9th floor overlooking Central Park. There was a small yellow sticky on the back of the envelope holding the keycard.

167

It read three thirty that afternoon.

Oh, my *God...*

Of course, the first thing I did was text Steph.

ELLA: OMG he left a key card to the Ritz-Carlton Central Park on my desk. I'm supposed to meet him at three thirty today...

STEPH: Told ya! You go, girl! That story must have really impressed him.

ELLA: I don't know what to do.

STEPH: What? ARE YOU CRAZY? Go! Enjoy. You deserve it.

ELLA: I've told you how I feel about office romances.

STEPH: Pffft. That was then. This is now. This is your fantasy, kiddo. He wants to fulfill your fantasy. How could you turn that down? Go and get some for all us single ladies.

ELLA: What he must think of me...

STEPH: He probably can't stop thinking of you and had to jerk off several times after he read your story.

ELLA: You have such a filthy imagination.

STEPH: No, I have three brothers and lived with a guy for three months once.

STEPH: DO IT! You know you want to...

STEPH: Write me back with all the deets when you're able.

ELLA: Okay. If I go. And I'm not 100 percent sure that I will.

STEPH: You'll regret it the rest of your life if you don't. GO.

ELLA: Later. XOXOX

STEPH: XOXOXOMG

I SMILED AND LEANED BACK, a most definite ache in my core at the thought that Josh would be waiting for me at the hotel room.

He must have really liked my story...

CHAPTER EIGHTEEN

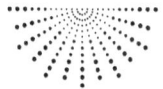

JOSHUA

I WASN'T GOING to accept no for an answer.

I wouldn't be a dick about it, but I wouldn't just give up. I'd keep running into her, accidentally on purpose, and I'd be as charming and as gallant as I could possibly muster. I enjoyed her too much to give up without a fight. We had definite chemistry. Our brief interlude at the apartment was testament to that fact. We were both recovering from a bad relationship and needed each other as solace. That was how I saw it, anyway. Now I just had to find a way to convince her to my way of thinking.

The whole boss-employee thing was an inconvenience, but I was totally a hand's-off kind of boss so it wasn't like we'd be working together on a regular basis. In fact, I had very little to do with the book publishing arm, and focused my efforts on Macintyre Broadcasting Corporation and its print news division.

My cell rang and I checked the caller ID. It was Marcella. No doubt with my first 'date', but in truth, I was in no mood to meet one of her carefully-selected candidates for the position of my life partner.

I was too focused on convincing Ella that she really did want to boink me, as she called it.

"Hello, Marcella. How are you?"

"I'm fine. I have a few candidates for you to review. Can I drop off their CVs and photos? I also have a couple of videos you might like to watch. We can discuss setting up some meetings, too."

"Already?" I said, surprised she had found candidates so quickly.

"You said you wanted to move fast, so I pulled in all my markers. I think several of the first crop of ladies are quite prime real estate."

"Oh, yes?" I said, imagining a group of haughty debutante types with moneyed families and dreams of marrying a richer man than they were. "Come on up. I don't have much time but I can squeeze you in right after my nine-thirty meeting. Say, ten o'clock?"

"I'll be there."

I ended the call and leaned back, not really wanting to face the whole 'finding a wife' project just yet, but I had agreed that Marcella should do her magic and so I had to follow through.

What I really wanted was to go out with Ella and finish what we started. I didn't get the chance to really lick her tattoo the way I had wanted as soon as I learned of its existence. It had driven me crazy since she told me about it and I saw her breasts so up close and personal without being able to really enjoy them.

Before Marcella arrived, I had a meeting with one of the guys in finance about the cost of renovations, and luckily, we were done early. I decided to pop down to Ella's office and see if she'd give in and meet me for lunch. The receptionist was gone from her desk, so I went to Ella's office and popped my head inside. The room was empty, and so I thought I'd leave her a sticky note, asking her to give me another chance and meet for lunch.

I went to her desk and searched around for a pencil and sticky notes, but couldn't find anything. Then I remembered our lack of supplies because of the renovations and new offices. Of course, she probably was using her notebook. The Iron Man notebook that I wanted for myself.

I smiled and opened a drawer but found nothing I could use to write a note. There was one file folder on her desk -- a red file folder -- so I opened it up to see if there was any spare paper, but it was some hand-written notes torn out of a spiral notebook -- most likely the Iron Man notebook she was forced to use.

Only, they weren't coverage notes, but were instead pages of a short erotic story.

Holy hell...

A very hot short erotic story...

I picked up the file and paged through it, and immediately, I realized that the story was written about me. Billionaire (wrong -- not quite) newspaper mogul, tall, built, brown hair and blue-gray eyes, well-trimmed beard. She meets him at the Ritz-Carlton for hot sex. No words are spoken. Just fucking and lots of orgasms. Then, they kiss and go their separate ways. No strings.

While I was getting hot under the collar reading the story, I heard the receptionist, return to the office, her laugher audible from the hallway. I closed the file and tucked it under my arm, then made my way out of Ella's office. I had to read the entire story.

I *had* to.

"Hello, Mr. Macintyre," she said when she saw me. "How are you today?"

"I'm very well, thank you," I said. "Just looking for Ella Carlson."

"She's in a meeting with Sharon, but she should be done by eleven if you want me to have her call you."

"Thanks, that's okay. I'll call her."

I smiled and left the office, the very hot erotic short story tucked under my arm possessively.

Needless to say, I spent some time in my private washroom, taking care of business before my next meeting...

LATER, Keith dropped into my office, while I was busy re-reading Ella's story.

"Hey, what's up?" he asked, and sat at the chair across from my desk. "I haven't heard from you all day."

"I'm busy," I said and closed the file.

"Too busy for your best friend?" he asked, grinning because he knew he could always pop into my office and as long as I wasn't on the phone or in a meeting, I'd make time for him.

"Never too busy for you," I said and pushed the file off to the side of my desk. The last thing I'd want was for him to read Ella's story. No way. That was for me to savor.

"What you got there?" he said, pointing to the file. "A new hire? New business proposal?"

"No, just some notes I made at a meeting. What's up with you?" I asked, hoping to divert his attention from the file.

We talked about his latest project and then he admonished me for not going out with him for a long time and I promised we'd go out one night soon.

Then, he left me alone with the file.

I had to open it once more and read the story again.

THE MAN *in the grey flannel suit was not my Mr. Big but he was a pretty damn good substitute...*

. . .

BEFORE I COULD GET MORE than a paragraph in, Marcella showed up and I had to close the story once more and try to ignore the ache in my groin.

"Here you are, Joshua," she said and placed five files on my desk. I moved the red file into my briefcase, and then instead of taking matters into my own hand as I had planned, I tried to turn my attention back to the matter at hand. Finding a suitable wife and mother of my future children.

It was not at all what I wanted to focus on at that moment.

"What have you got for me, Marcella?" I asked, trying to be positive, considering I was paying her handsomely to headhunt a wife for me. "Someone good, I hope."

"Some very good candidates. Any man would be very lucky to have such women as their wife. First up, is Dana Rae-McPherson, daughter of John McPherson and Lisa Rae, who you will remember is the heir to the Rae fortune in shipping. She's twenty-eight, has a BA from Brown in Communications, and currently runs her own media company with fifteen staff. She's also very attractive, as you can see from the photo."

I opened the file and examined the image. Yes, I'd seen Dana before, having met her at a charity function with my father, but I had never even thought twice about her. She was quite brash, with a big personality and a cutting wit. She took over any room she entered and you could almost feel her assessing everyone in the room as to whether they would benefit her or not.

She was not my type, although she certainly ticked all my boxes.

Except the chemistry box.

I'd never even considered her as a sex partner, let alone a life partner.

"Sorry," I said and closed the file, handing it back to Marcella. "I already know her and am not interested."

Marcella took the file back and appeared a bit taken aback by my fast refusal.

"May I ask why?"

"No chemistry. When we first met, she rubbed me the wrong way and having met her several times, my opinion hasn't changed."

"Can I ask what it is about her that you don't like?"

I shrugged. "She's not nice."

"Not nice?" Marcella frowned. "What do you mean, not nice?"

"I mean, she's not a nice person. She's cold and calculating. Like she's always sizing everyone up. Judging. And she isn't warm at all."

Marcella nodded. "I understand. That's good to know. You want warmth of personality. Someone who is nice." She sifted through the files and handed me another one.

I opened it and saw the picture.

The woman was attractive, with fair hair and skin and blue eyes.

"This is Theresa Rutherford. Daughter of Pat and Elaine Rutherford, of Baylor Industries. She has a BA in Music and is a flute instructor as well as a performer in a small quartet. She is a volunteer on the Humane Society International board of directors and does a lot of charity work in addition to her teaching. She's thirty and loves to travel."

I read over her resume but she seemed bloodless. Pleasant but not someone I felt I wanted to get to know better. In fact, I had the sense she'd be boring. She had no spice to her. Flute? She was a flautist. She taught the flute and gave money for animal welfare. I could have yawned as I read her resume.

"A little too nice, maybe."

Marcella raised her eyebrows but sorted through her files and handed me another.

"Alicia Barnes, daughter of Jack and Nancy Barnes, on the Fortune 500. Bachelor of Commerce, has her own fashion line. Attractive and smart."

I took the file and flipped through the pages. She was attractive, but fashion wasn't something I was interested in. Frankly, I found it frivolous. A lot of to-do about nothing. Painfully self-absorbed.

"Not interested."

Marcella exhaled in frustration. "Take a look at these two. Maybe you can review them all and send me an email when you decide what you really want to see."

What I really want to see? At that moment, I really wanted to see Ella naked -- that's what I really wanted to see. Naked and on the huge bed in one of the Ritz-Carlton's best suites overlooking Central Park with her legs spread wide, while I pumped hard into her willing body.

I flipped through the other two files, but neither one caught my fancy.

"I'm sorry, Marcella. These are all great candidates," I said, realizing I had to keep on her good side. "They just don't do it for me at the moment. You might as well take all the files with you."

"Fair enough. I can go back to the well and find more suitable candidates."

"I appreciate all you do for me."

She gathered up her files and left the room, and while she gave me a smile on the way out, I could tell she was frustrated.

So was I.

Sexually frustrated and wanting to re-read Ella's story and then make a quick trip to the executive washroom.

Which I did.

. . .

I CAN'T KEEP DOING *this...*

Of course, I could and would. I was a man, after all. What I meant when talking to myself after I zipped up my slacks and washed my hands, was that I had to do something to force the issue with Ella one way or the other so I could move on.

Until I had her in my bed, or she told me to fuck off forever, I wouldn't be happy. I needed to finish what we started and so as I beat off in total frustration, I had the image of me with her ankles around my neck while I pumped my cock into her wet pussy on a plush king-sized bed at the Ritz-Carlton.

I needed to see that scene come to fruition, if it was at all possible.

When I got back to my desk in my office and had a sip of my now-cold coffee, I took in a deep breath and googled the hotel.

After I checked over the various options, I settled on one of the rooms with a view of Central Park. With a few keystrokes on my keyboard, I reserved a room and all I had to do was pick up the keys and the rest would be history. I reserved it for two full days so I could drop by on my way home and pick up the keys, and then I'd get to work early in the morning, before anyone else was there, and leave the key on Ella's desk.

If she wanted to come and have the fantasy she wrote about, I'd be there waiting. If she didn't show up, there was always my hand. I'd expended quite an effort on my dick since I met her and I could survive if she rejected my offer.

But I hoped she'd bite at the chance to live out her fantasy.

The fact that I starred in her fantasy fuck was threatening to make me hard once more, so I closed her file, shoved it off to the side of my desk, and decided to try to get some work done instead.

. . .

FOR THE REST of the day, I tried to immerse myself in my work and finally, when my day was over at close to seven o'clock at night, I dropped by the Ritz-Carlton and picked up my room keys. I went up to the room to check it out and was happy that I'd gone through with it. I'd order some fresh flowers and some champagne for us, the way the male character in the story had, and tomorrow, I'd be waiting by the window for her to show up.

We'd fuck our brains out for an hour, and then, both of us would return to work for the rest of the day and no one would be the wiser.

Hopefully, I could convince her to return after work and spend the rest of the night with me. We'd have another round of fucking, and then room service, a hot tub bath, and more fucking before going to sleep on the luxurious bed, the curtains open to show the gorgeous skyline.

That was my plan.

As I went to bed that night, after yet another pitiful round of spanking the monkey while I imagined us going at it in the hotel room, I fell into my bed and slept like a baby.

I'd find out soon enough if my offer was enticing enough to overcome Ella's reluctance.

CHAPTER NINETEEN

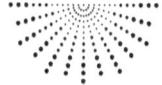

ELLA

I HAD TO MAKE A DECISION.

I paced my office, the box of manuscripts unopened on my desk. A new box had come in overnight and I had yet to finish the box I'd received from Sharon the previous day. I had no idea how many authors were out there, looking for a chance to see their book in print. They'd have to wait for I had to finish up the current crop and write up some cover for the ones I had selected to discuss with Sharon. Several dozen manuscripts lay on top of my desk. Among them were my favorite out of all the manuscripts I'd read since starting but I was only supposed to bring five.

Of course, the decision wasn't about which manuscripts to choose for my meeting in fifteen minutes.

It was whether I could afford to take an hour off to go to the Ritz-Carlton and meet with my boss for a mind-blowing fuck on a huge king-sized bed.

My body was uncomfortably warm and swollen as I stood in front of the desk and held the room key in my hand. I had to get the image of a naked Josh standing over me, his erect cock sliding in and out of my body if I hoped to speak anything more than gibberish to Sharon in the meeting I was going to in ten minutes. I put the room key into my bag and then sat back down and opened the first manuscript, going over my notes in the hopes of distracting myself from my thoughts of Josh.

Finally, my cell alarm beeped and I had to leave to go to Sharon's office. I pulled the manuscripts into one file and brought my notes along with me. For the next two hours until lunch, I sat with Sharon, drinking coffee and talking about each manuscript and why I thought they were worth considering.

Sharon seemed pleased with my choices and promised to look at each one on her own and make a decision. As I was getting ready to leave, I stopped in the doorway.

"Is it okay if I take an hour off this afternoon? I have something to pick up downtown and I'll need time. I'll work through my lunch so I won't miss any time."

"Take the rest of the afternoon off after three if you need it. You've been staying late so you're probably way ahead of the eight ball anyway. I'll see you tomorrow."

"Thanks," I said, relieved that I wouldn't have to rush back to the office after... If I decided to go, that is.

I still hadn't decided whether to go.

I GOT BACK to my office and sat down behind my desk, and while it was now lunch time, I wasn't hungry. In fact, I felt like I needed a stiff drink. I had to work up my nerve to decide one way or the other whether to go.

· · ·

ELLA: *What should I do?*

STEPH: *GO! GO DAMMIT!*

ELLA: **sigh* My boss gave me the afternoon off after three, so if I want, I don't have to rush back. If I don't go to the hotel I think I may go and get a tub of ice cream and eat the whole thing alone in my tiny apartment in Chelsea.*

STEPH: *Going to the hotel will work off calories so if you want, go spend the night with him, and then get a tub of ice cream and eat it off his body.*

ELLA: *You're crazy!*

STEPH: *I'm hungry and haven't gone to lunch yet. I also need a man. A man or a tub of Dutch chocolate ice cream. The really good stuff. Preferably both at the same time.*

ELLA: *Okay, I'm going to go.*

STEPH: *FINALLY... good choice. You won't regret it. People regret not doing something.*

ELLA: *They also regret doing stupid things. What if this is stupid?*

STEPH: *You're attracted to him. He's attracted to you. You're both young and attractive. I don't see the issue.*

ELLA: *Other than he's my boss...*

STEPH: *Small detail.*

ELLA: *Rather important detail.*

STEPH: *Go, see how it feels to be with him. If you like it and he likes it, keep it up. If not, move on. It's simple. Only a fool would make it more difficult.*

ELLA: *Okay.*

STEPH: *Text me when you can. I'll be sitting here in my jammies eating Dutch chocolate ice cream and wishing I was in your shoes.*

ELLA: *I will.*

STEPH: *Who loves you?*

ELLA: *XOXOXOX*

. . .

I SAT BACK and smiled to myself. Steph could always talk me down from a bad choice and she'd never steered me wrong before. She didn't really like Jerkface and had always suggested I date other men before I got married -- so I'd know for sure I had picked the right guy for my husband. She was probably right about Josh, too.

I went to the office kitchen and took out my lunch, which I had picked up on the way to work. I sat at my desk and worked through lunch, noshing on a pastrami sandwich on rye but did not indulge in the side of garlic pickle, not wanting to ruin my chances with Josh. When three o'clock came around, I packed up my things, reached into my bag to find the small black hotel room key with the Ritz-Carlton logo on it, and left the office. The Ritz-Carlton wasn't very far away. I'd go to one of the hotel's public restrooms and brush my teeth, freshen up before I went up to the room.

My stomach was all in knots as I arrived at the front of the hotel. I stopped and looked up and down the street, taking in the experience of actually being there. Across the street from the hotel was Central Park and directly across from the entry was a bronze statue of Jose de San Martin. When I walked up to the front doors, I saw two black-suited doormen in top hats, who opened the doors when I approached.

"Good afternoon, Miss," one of them said. "Welcome to the Ritz-Carlton."

"Thank you," I said and entered the plush interior. I walked around the entrance and tried to brand it all into my memory so I'd never forget it, no matter what happened with Josh. I smiled at the front desk clerks and made my way to the public washroom beside the bar, where I spent about ten minutes freshening up. My hands were actually shaking just a bit at the prospect of going up to the room, wondering if Josh was already there.

I left the room and went to the reception area, taking one of the plush seats and checking my cell.

ELLA: *I'm here, in the lobby. I'm so nervous!*

STEPH: *You're almost there. YOU GO GIRL!*

ELLA: *Wish me luck.*

STEPH: *You don't need it.*

STEPH: *XOXOX*

ELLA: *Back at you. XOXO*

I took in a deep breath and got up from my seat, smoothing my dress and making my way to the bank of elevators, deciding to act as if I belonged there, although I felt like a fish out of water. While I had been raised in a comfortable upper-middle class lifestyle, this was luxury beyond my experience. I was in awe as I waited for the elevator. Everything was marble and gold, wainscoting and dark cherry wood with gilded fixtures.

The elevator opened to the seventh floor and I was impressed by the beautiful furniture and decor as I walked down the hallway, following the arrows to the room. I stood outside and closed my eyes for a moment, gathering my nerve. Taking in a deep breath, I slid my keycard into the slot and opened the door. Inside, the room was just as fantastic as the hotel lobby - all cream wainscoting with gilded trim, with dark cherry wood furniture.

There, standing in front of the window beside the edge of the bed, was Josh. His jacket was open and he looked like a million dollars. He fit right in with the hotel, rich, cultured. Perfect.

I stopped and stared, the door closing with a click behind me.

He held out his hand to me, and that was it. All reluctance, all hesitation, was gone. I went to him, taking his hand, and when we touched, a jolt of desire sped through my body. This was really going to happen.

I'd been intimate with him before, so it wasn't that. It was that

I didn't know who he was that night. I wasn't intimidated, but now I was.

Now he was my boss and he was Joshua Macintyre Jr, one of the heirs of the Macintyre fortune, and on top of everything else about him, he was gorgeous.

On the table was a huge bouquet of purple roses. Beside it, a bottle of Moet and Chandon chilled in an ice bucket.

He was making my fantasy come true, and I was already wet with anticipation, my breath coming fast and shallow.

Like I'd written in my story, he didn't speak, just pulled me close and kissed me, passionate right from the start. He pressed his body against mine and I could feel his erection hard against my belly. I closed my eyes and just let everything happen, turning off the little angel in my head that always judged me.

I didn't care that he was my boss or was one of the richest men in America. I only knew that we wanted each other and that our bodies felt perfect together. His hands expertly removed my clothes and soon, I was naked, standing in front of him as he sat on the side of the bed.

He pulled me between his thighs and kissed me, his hands moving over my body, squeezing and stroking me, before burying his face between my breasts. Finally, he kissed and licked my tiny tattoo the way he said he wanted before we were so rudely interrupted. I gripped his shoulders and bit my lip while he sucked a nipple, the sensations making me squirm with delight. He roughly spread my thighs and slid his hand between them, his palm cupping my sex and pressing firmly while his thumb found my clit and circled it slowly, making me move against him hungrily. The pressure was enough to build my desire and I couldn't stop pressing myself against him, my eyes closing in delight as he moved to the other breast and his lips and tongue tugged at my nipple.

When I was groaning with need, he stood and turned me

around, pushing me back on to the bed. He loomed over me and kissed me again, then began undressing, roughly removing his clothing, throwing them on the chair at the side of the room. When he was finally naked, his beautiful cock long and thick and ready, I sat up and pulled him closer, my hands on his hips, wanting to take him into my mouth and taste him. I took his thick cock into my fist and lapped the head, glancing up at him to catch his eye, wanting to watch him watch me while I took the head into my mouth. I knew it would please him.

Then I stroked his shaft while I tongued the head of his cock, swirling my tongue around the rim before pulling the head into my mouth and moving on it as far as I could take him. I kept up the rhythm as long as he let me and he began pumping a bit into my mouth, one hand on my head to guide me.

Finally, he pulled out of my mouth and lifted me up for a kiss before pushing me back on to the bed again. He leaned over me and ran his tongue down my neck to my breast, lavishing attention on each before moving lower while he spread my thighs once more.

When he claimed me with his mouth, I cried out loud, for I was so ready, I knew it wouldn't take long before I came. While he licked and sucked my sex, I writhed beneath him, my eyes squeezed shut, focusing on the sensations.

"I'm going to," I said, breathless, the pleasure rising, sending me close to the edge.

But he leaned up and pressed his finger against my lips to stop me from speaking. I'd forgotten my fantasy meant that no words would be spoken, and nodded in understanding. He wanted to follow my fantasy to the letter, which meant I was in for another orgasm while he fucked me.

He moved back down between my thighs and his mouth found me once more, slowly bringing me back to the edge once more. When he slipped two fingers inside of me, that coupled

185

with the pressure from his tongue sent me over, my orgasm sending shudders of ecstasy through my body from my core down my legs and up into my chest. My body spasmed around his fingers and finally, I had to stop him for my flesh was too sensitive.

I gasped because of the overwhelming sensation, pressing against his shoulders.

He rose up and leaned over me, staring down into my eyes, then he kissed me, his hand sliding to my breasts once more. Finally, he stood and reached into his jacket pocket, retrieving a condom and opening the package and sliding it over his erection.

He pulled me to the edge of the bed, and turned me around just like in my story, leaning over me from behind, his erection sliding against my pussy. He took my hands in his and leaned over me, his face beside me. I was so wet from his mouth and my orgasm that soon, the friction began to feel good again and I started to move with him. He let go of one of my hands and reached down, guiding his erection into my body and it felt so good, I couldn't help but groan. While he thrust inside of me, slowly, deliberately, he played with my clit, his hand slipping down between my thighs.

I was still so aroused from my first orgasm that in only moments, I was ready again and began moving with him, pressing against his fingers greedily. I tried not to say a word but the pleasure grew to an incredible peak and with him inside of me, I orgasmed hard, the pleasure almost blinding me.

"Ohhhh..."

He slammed into me, thrusting harder and faster and I knew he was almost there as well. I felt his cock harden and then he orgasmed, his thrusts slowing while he groaned, grunting through his ejaculation. Then he collapsed against me, his arms on either side of my shoulders, his face next to mine.

Then, like in my story, he left the bed and went to the bathroom to dispose of the condom and wash up while I crawled under the coverlet. He returned to the side of the bed and dressed without a word while I lay on the bed recovering, my body warm and satisfied.

He leaned down once he was fully dressed and kissed me, then left the hotel room.

That was it.

He'd found my story that expressed my fantasy fuck with him, and then he fulfilled it.

I got up and went to the bathroom to wash up, smiling to myself. He left a note on the desk:

ELLA - THE ROOM *is yours for the night. Order in room service and enjoy your stay.*
Josh

I CRAWLED BACK under the covers and lay in silence for a few moments, wondering whether what happened between us would be a one-time thing or the start of something more.

I felt a little guilty, like I was a hooker or a call girl, but this was my fantasy, not his. He just happened to be generous enough to want to fulfill it.

Then I shut off my stupid brain and grabbed the hotel menu off the desk to see what I could order from room service for my dinner. The options were beyond what I imagined and I selected a filet with all the sides and a cheesecake for dessert.

Then, while I waited for room service to arrive, I grabbed the channel changer and turned on the movie channel, determined to do nothing for the rest of the day.

I'd deal with reality tomorrow.

CHAPTER TWENTY

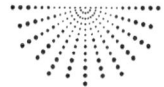

JOSHUA

I LEFT THE HOTEL ROOM, smiling to myself as I went down the elevator.

The sex was very good. It was almost too good, frankly. I'd been with many women over the years, but I'd never had insight into their fantasies the way I had when I found Ella's story. She wanted me to be her Mr. Big, to fulfil her desire to be taken and pleasured without any awkward maneuvering or empty words. Just mutual want and need.

No words required.

I was pleased to be the one to fulfil those desires.

In fact, her fantasy was pretty much close to mine -- a beautiful sexually needy woman meets me at a hotel room for pure pleasure. No words spoken because none are needed.

Of course, in my fantasy, the fucking went on all night and into the next day, never leaving the room for anything but a swim in the ocean, but this was Ella's fantasy and it was one really great fuck with two great orgasms and then she got to stay in a beautiful luxury room overlooking Central Park.

As I left the hotel, walking down the street to the office, I pondered whether to reserve the hotel room for one more night so I could go back and spend the night with her. We could order room service together and spend twenty-four hours fucking each other's brains out, thus fulfilling my fantasy.

However, my fantasy took place in Bali or somewhere exotic, with a beach-front room that we could walk out to when we felt like some sun or a splash in the crystal clear ocean.

If anything more happened with Ella, I might consider booking a couple of first-class seats to Bali for just that -- fulfilling my fantasy of escaping the city and spending a weekend alone, just me and my lover, eating and drinking and fucking and surfing and swimming together with no worries, no business, no emails. Just the two of us, some books, maybe watch some movies on the big screen television.

That seemed like a fantasy I could fulfil with Ella.

For the past five years, I'd been so busy building up my business that I hadn't really looked up from my desk except to plan my marriage and life with Christie. When that fell through, I'd immersed myself in work to the detriment of every other part of my life.

Now, I felt I deserved an escape.

Ella was like me -- down on romance and marriage. She wanted just great sex and to work on her career. Maybe, while I was trying to get the paper up and running and she was getting experience in the publishing business before starting her MFA at Columbia, we could be each other's escapes.

When I got to my apartment back at the office building, I had a quick shower and ordered in some Pho from a local restaurant that delivered. While I waited for it to arrive, I sat down at my desk and turned on my laptop, filled with an unusual energy, wanting to do something. On a whim, I bought a couple of tickets to Bali, leaving on Thursday. It was for a long weekend, Thursday through Tuesday, but it would be enough. Once the payment went through, I printed off the tickets and boarding passes and ordered a dozen roses to be delivered to Ella's office. I'd leave the ticket on her desk with a note that I wrote and enclosed in the envelope.

I FULFILLED one of your fantasies. Here's mine. Meet me at the Emirates Airlines lounge before the flight and we can have a drink before boarding. You can use the sex-drenched weekend fulfilling my fantasies as fodder for your fledgling career as a bestselling chick-lit author.

Yours, Josh

I HOPED she'd accept and that I wouldn't be left waiting in the lounge alone until the first boarding call. If she didn't show, I'd cancel the tickets and reschedule until she agreed but I hoped she'd have been happy enough with our little hotel room tryst to try for another bout -- this time for a whole weekend.

And there would be talking.

Three glorious days at an all-inclusive luxury beach-front hotel in the honeymoon suite with its own private pool and a beach front room.

Call me crazy, but at that moment, I was infected by a desire to escape to Bali with Ella and spend the time luxuriating in bed with her, walking the beach with her, and swimming naked in our own private pool.

It cost a cool thirty grand but that was nothing considering I hadn't had a vacation for years. I'd had my nose to the proverbial grindstone for too long and the little fantasy stay with Ella at the

Ritz-Carlton made me realize how little real relaxation I'd had -- or enjoyment for that matter -- in too long.

I ate my Pho and read over my plans, and then dressed in my jeans and a t-shirt, I slipped into the elevator and dropped the envelope into Ella's office. I walked through the empty offices and thought about my accidental but very happy meeting Ella that day outside the building.

Skinned elbows and knees had never turned out to be so fortuitous.

THE NEXT MORNING, after my usual bike ride around Central Park, I went back to my apartment in the building and had a shower, then got ready for the day. Excitement grew in my gut that Ella would soon arrive at her office and hopefully, the flowers would have already arrived. She'd find the tickets and offer on her desk beside the flowers.

Then, I hoped that she'd accept and in a week, I would be waiting at the lounge, hoping to see her walk through the doors.

I arrived back at my apartment and after showering and getting dressed, I took the elevator to my office, eager to get to work.

When I arrived, I picked up my messages from my assistant and sat down behind my desk.

The first was from Marcella. I called her up, my sense of well-being falling a bit at the prospect of a date with one of her matches.

"What's up, Marcella? How's the headhunting business?"

"I have a couple of matches I think you'll really like. I'll drop by later this morning with their files, if you'd like. We can arrange meetings this weekend if any of them catch your eye."

I kicked myself. I should have let Marcella know that I'd put the wife-hunting on hold for a few weeks. I had too much going on at the moment with the paper and now, if Ella and I went to Bali, I'd be away for the weekend and wouldn't have any time for a meeting.

"This next two weeks aren't all that good, Marcella. Sorry, but can we re-schedule until say, two weeks from now?"

"Sure," she said, sounding hesitant. "What happened? You seemed to want to get going immediately. What changed?"

"Nothing, just really busy with getting the renovation complete and ramping up with the newspaper."

"Okay. I'll pencil you in two weeks from now and hopefully, the weekend will be a go."

"I'm sure it will be."

I ended the call and turned back to my computer screen. I had an image of the hotel we'd be staying on my desktop and was imagining the warmth of the sun, the clear blue water and the sound of the surf outside our hotel room.

It was totally crazy of me to be fantasizing about a getaway to Bali when I should have been focused on my business, but at that moment, it was all I could think of. I checked my watch. Ella was scheduled to arrive at her desk any moment and I hoped she'd be pleased with the tickets and flowers. I wanted to go down to her office and watch her reaction, hoping she'd be really excited about it, but I held back. I wanted my fantasy to go the way I hoped it would -- with me at the airport and her showing up, ready for a dirty weekend alone with me at an all-inclusive resort.

I SPENT the rest of the morning trying to keep my mind off Ella's response to my offer, and instead, focused on the issues that had come up during the past week at the *Chronicle*. I had several meetings and wasn't able to even take a breather to think about Ella, and so at the end of the day, I realized that it was already six o'clock and I hadn't had the chance to sneak down to her office.

Once everyone was gone from my office, I closed up and made my way down the elevator, deciding to check her desk and see if she'd done anything about the offer. I used my keycard to get inside and found Sharon still working away at her desk.

"You're here late," I said, and tried to think up an excuse for why I was in the office. "I thought I'd stop by and see if there was any mail for me."

"We sent it up earlier," she said and frowned. "I'm pretty sure the mail clerk was already here. Didn't you receive your mail?"

"I was in meetings all afternoon. I'll check again tomorrow. Don't worry about it. How's Ella working out?"

Sharon leaned back and exhaled. "I'm so glad she's here. I'm just overwhelmed with work and she's helping me get caught up, bit by bit. I have a huge deadline on Monday, and I asked her to work through the weekend to get things cleared up. You know we have that meeting on Monday afternoon to discuss the Spring release schedule."

"Oh, right. It slipped my mind."

"I have Ella working on a presentation that I'll give to the sales department on why we've chosen a slate of books to purchase."

"I'm glad you have Ella to help. You should give her a few days off to compensate."

"I'm glad I have her, too. Believe me, if she wasn't here, there's no way I'd finish this by Monday. But you're right -- I should give her a few days off this week. I'll need her here for follow-up on Tuesday and Wednesday but she could have a long weekend."

"That sounds like a great idea and very fair, considering she isn't being paid."

"I know," Sharon said and raised her eyebrows. "I'm so lucky to have her."

"Okay, then," I said and glanced around. "If there's nothing else, I'll leave you to it. And thanks again, Sharon, for your hard work and dedication. I appreciate it."

"You know I love this work. There's nothing else I'd rather do."

I left her and popped my head into Ella's office on my way out. Her desk was piled with files and I saw the flowers on the desk beside her phone. The envelope with the tickets was gone, so she must have taken them home with her.

I'd have to change the date of the trip -- I didn't want to make Ella choose between her job and a hot weekend with me.

I took the elevator up to the apartment and sat down at my desk, signing into my account and changing the dates of the trip to Bali. I was lucky -- there were still seats and rooms available for the new dates and so I printed off the tickets and boarding passes once more.

I wrote a short note to her, explaining.

Ella, I understand Sharon needs you to work this weekend to get the presentation ready for the meeting on Monday. I've changed the dates for the trip to Bali to reflect this. I hope I'll see you next Thursday at the Emirates lounge. I hope you show up and help fulfill one of my fantasies.

Then, I waited until I was sure Sharon would be gone and slipped down to the office, leaving the new boarding pass and tickets on Ella's desk. I smiled to myself as I went back up to my apartment. I would have preferred to go to Bali that Thursday rather than waiting but it couldn't be helped.

I went to sleep that night and imagined my time with Ella at the resort in Bali. I hoped she'd show up next Thursday. If she didn't, I'd have to change the tickets again and find a way to convince her that coming with me was what she really wanted to do. In the meantime, I lay in my bed in the darkness, my hard cock in my hand, and remembered my hour of forbidden delights with Ella at the Ritz-Carlton.

. . .

THE NEXT MORNING, after my usual routine, I showed up to my office and was hit right away with meeting after meeting with editors and my business manager, trying to get everything in place for the relaunch of the paper. On my way down to the thirty-second floor where the offices of my new paper were located, Ella got on the elevator and the expression on her face when she saw me was priceless. Her eyes widened and I saw her choking back a smile as she stood in front of the control panel and selected her floor. There were three other people in the elevator at the time who were on their way down to the lobby, so there was no way I could talk to her. She stood with her back to me, and I admired her sleek red-brown hair and her shapely butt under a navy blue dress that hugged her body.

Damn... I wished she was mine so I could grab her hand and take her with me up to the apartment for a bit of afternoon delight. Maybe take her to my office and lay her back on my desk and fuck her in front of the Manhattan skyline seen through my office window.

But she wasn't and so I couldn't.

"How's the paper coming along?" a voice asked and I snapped out of my reverie of fucking Ella and turned to the man beside me. It was Clint Jones from the ad agency a floor below the offices of the *Chronicle*. We'd met several times at various business functions.

"Oh, Clint. Didn't see you there. Everything's going fine. Just getting things off the ground in the next few months, if all goes well."

The elevator stopped at Ella's floor and I was sad to see her get off. Then, I was hit with a flash of inspiration.

"Talk later," I said to Clint and followed Ella off the elevator. She walked down the hallway, not saying anything to me, but as she rounded the corner to the other hallway, I saw her smile, her dimples clearly visible.

I grabbed her arm and stopped her, glancing along the hallway to make sure no one was looking. Then I pressed her against the wall and shoved my erection against her, kissing her roughly.

She kissed me back with definite abandon.

When the kiss broke, I ran my fingers along her cheek.

"Ella," I said with a stifled moan. "What you do to me..."

"I don't know what you're talking about, Mr. Macintyre. Whatever could you mean?"

"What is it about elevators?" I said and ground my hips against hers.

"Mr. Macintyre, you're taking far too many liberties with one of your staff," she said in a breathy-yet-saucy voice with a hint of a sultry Southern accent.

"This particular staff member recently had my cock in her mouth, so if I were her, I wouldn't be acting all prim and proper."

She smiled and glanced up at me, both dimples showing, batting her eyelashes seductively.

"Such language at the workplace could get a boss in trouble, even if he is the owner."

"Such language is probably making a certain staff member *hot*," I said, and kissed her again.

Then, before anyone came down the hallway and caught us, I left her where she stood and quickly made it back to the elevator. I pressed the down button so I could get back on my way and not be late for my meeting. I had a silly smile on my face and my semi-erect cock was only now starting to deflate.

By the time I arrived at my destination, I was sure it would be at a near normal state of tumescence.

Whether I made it through the rest of the day without resorting to my private executive washroom was a whole other thing.

CHAPTER TWENTY-ONE

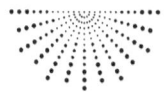

Ella

He left me standing in the hallway, my body practically vibrating with desire for him, my flesh swollen.

He had an evil smile on his face as he left me, knowing full well how I would be feeling. It was fair game, considering he had a delicious-feeling erection. Had just the sight of me in the elevator done that to him?

If so, it gave me a real thrill and made me want him even more.

I went to my office and sat behind my desk, the file folder that contained several new manuscripts from the mailroom tucked beneath my arm. I placed it on my desk and tried to catch my breath, needing a few moments to collect myself and recover from the feel of Josh's body pressed against mine, his kiss and his words.

My hour with him at the Ritz-Carlton had left me wanting more time with him, and now, with the offer of a trip to Bali the following weekend, I was happy that I would get it. The idea that I would be fulfilling his fantasy of a fuck-filled weekend at a tropical resort where he didn't have to worry at all about his businesses made me exceptionally aroused.

Although I had a rule about office romances, given my experience with Jerkface, Josh was so high up there in the corporate ladder, he didn't really feel like my boss.

Not really.

At least, that was the way I justified -- okay, how I rationalized running away to an exotic tropical resort to have sex with him.

I squirmed a bit in my chair, my flesh still swollen. I would have liked to go into the staff washroom and masturbate, but there was no way I would because it was too busy. I'd have to suffer until I could get home. Later tonight, when I was alone in my tiny apartment, I'd have a date with B.O.B. He'd have to do. Only thing was, B.O.B. didn't have a mouth or tongue that had given me so much pleasure the other day.

JOSH: Damn, woman. I have this problem I wish you could come to my office and take care of.

ELLA: Sorry, but I have ten minutes to get my coverage of this book done before my meeting with Sharon. Believe me, I'm suffering, too. You could come and visit me and we could find a broom closet, or we could meet at your apartment during my coffee break...

I smiled and sent the text, wondering if he'd take me up on the offer.

. . .

JOSH: Oh, God... I can't or believe me, I'd be there under your desk, my tongue on your...

I WAITED for the text to finish but it didn't. I glanced at my computer screen and then at the manuscript on my table top, and then finally, back at my cell, but he hadn't finished his thought.

ELLA: ...waiting with bated breath for the body part you were going to name...

NOTHING. I waited and waited but that was it. I finished my work and then left for my meeting with Sharon. For the next hour, I sat there trying to pretend I was listening to Sharon talk, all the while imagining meeting Josh for a quickie, but sadly, each chance I had to check, he never wrote back to tell me if and when and what part he was going to lick, although I had a pretty good idea.

Finally, after I finished up for the day and reluctantly left the office, I heard a ding on my cell while I was sitting on the subway back home.

JOSH: So sorry. On your hard little...

I WAITED BUT NOTHING.

. . .

ELLA: !!!?

ELLA: Are you doing this purposely to drive me insane?

THEN HE MADE me wait again for fifteen minutes.

JOSH: Actually, I was in a meeting and thought I could finish the statement but I was asked a question and had to take over and lead the meeting. Then I was in constant meetings for the rest of the afternoon. But in my mind, I was fucking your brains out in front of my picture window overlooking the city.

I KNEW he was purposely making me suffer by ending his texts where he did, so I decided to make him wait.

ELLA: That's too bad because I was so frustrated that I had to...

HA! Let him suffer the way I had. I didn't believe for a moment that he couldn't have finished that text. It made me smile, because I liked the fact he was thinking of ways to make me aroused and needy. I liked the idea of finding a man who wanted to spend his time thinking of ways to drive me wild with desire.

I got off at my subway stop, deliberately not checking my cell to see his response. I stopped at the local sandwich shop close to my apartment and picked up a pastrami on rye with a pickle for my supper and a take-out container of chicken soup. Then I walked up the stairs to my apartment and entered the space, glad that I finally had enough room to at least have a tiny table and chair near an actual window.

I sat at the table and watched the street below, which was busy with pedestrians as the six o'clock crowd walked home from work. I dug into my sandwich and took a slurp of soup when my cell dinged for a third time.

JOSH: You had to what? Don't leave me hanging...

JOSH: ???

JOSH: I see what you did there. Honestly, Ella, I was not doing that on purpose. I truly was in a meeting, surrounded by my staff and I had to stop in the middle of a text. Besides, I figured it would fill your head full of ideas about where you would like my tongue to go...

I SMILED. Yeah, right... Like I believe that the ellipses weren't strategic. Hell, I was more convinced than ever that they were tactical rather than accidental. And now, he'd done it again by mentioning his tongue and where I wanted it to go. Now, I couldn't help but remember our hour in the Ritz-Carlton and where it was so located on my body and what it was so expertly doing.

I TEXTED him back after about ten minutes.

ELLA: Sorry. I was just in the bathtub, having a nice long soak. Now, I'm just sitting here, wrapped in my little towel, wondering what I'll write tonight. Something racy. Maybe about the hot business mogul who enjoys teasing his lover until she can't stand it anymore. He might tie her hands to the bed posts with silk scarves and blindfold her and then drive her crazy with sensation... Something along those lines.

I WAITED to see what he'd say in response. After a few moments, my cell dinged and I checked what he'd written.

JOSH: Kinky little thing, are you? I like it. If you need help figuring out positions and the steps involved in a scene like that, I'd be willing to come over and assist.

I LAUGHED and replied to him. I was smiling as I wrote my text, my body warming to the thought of that exact scene with Josh in control over me.

ELLA: I'm just thinking of what my audience would like to read. Besides, I have a very good imagination. I have a short timeline for this particular story, so I'm afraid I can't entertain you tonight. As a newspaper man, I'm sure you know all about those pesky deadlines!

I WAITED to see how he'd respond, wondering if he'd give up or keep trying to get me to invite him over.

· · ·

204

JOSH: Well, if you need more inspiration for your stories, there's a nice four poster bed in the room I booked in that all-inclusive resort in Bali that could handle some scarves used as restraints. There's also a private outdoor pool in the yard and the beach is only steps away. Much potential for interesting erotic storylines.

I HAD ALREADY IMAGINED it in my mind's eye after I found the new tickets on my desk earlier. He really wanted me to go to Bali with him and fulfil his fantasy weekend of sun, sex and surf. I wasn't sure if I should encourage him any further than we had already gone.

You'd think that the two of us would know not to get too close to each other. It was a mistake to get involved with a superior, even if he was sex on legs.

But still...

I deliberately didn't respond to his comment about Bali, not sure I would go, even if I really wanted to. I'd wait and see how things went over the next few days before I committed.

ELLA: Gotta say goodbye. Story isn't writing itself. Sleep tight. Don't think too much of me writing my erotic story, or what my mogul is doing to his helpless lover, tied up and blindfolded, waiting for him to do with her as he desires...

JOSH: Not a hope in hell of that now...

I LAUGHED and put my phone in my bag, not wanting to see what he might say next to distract me. I really did have a deadline and needed to finish a short story I'd written for an anthology my writer friend Samantha was putting together. And so, for the next two hours, instead of entertaining a real live hot man in my tiny studio apartment, or in his much more luxurious one on Fifth Avenue, I wrote about a fantasy lover who very much resembled the genuine article.

Then, just to be a real tease, I sent Josh a text with the first couple of lines of my story, hoping to make him want me even more.

ELLA: I thought I'd send you the first paragraph of my new story for the collection. It's called "The Room".

ELLA: When you go through that doorway into the room, you're mine. Outside the four walls, on the beach, in the restaurant, or when we visit the town, you're your own person, but when we're alone inside the room, you'll do what I tell you, when I tell you. I'll own you. Every inch of you. Don't worry. I promise you that the room is all about pleasure -- for both of us. If you're good, you'll have more orgasms than you've ever had in your life over the course of the weekend. If you're bad, you'll have even more...

I SMILED as I sent it off, wondering how he'd respond. In a moment, I got a new text.

JOSH: Oh, God...

JOSH: I guess I can forget falling asleep any time soon. You are very bad. Very bad. You need to spend some time in the room.

. . .

I LAUGHED and a thrill went through my body at the thought he was sitting alone in his apartment, his cock hard, wishing he had me there so we could pleasure each other.

ELLA: Gotta go. Got a story to write! Sweet dreams.

JOSH: If and when I ever get you alone again, I'm going to make you...

HE DELIBERATELY LEFT the sentence unfinished. Bastard! I guess two could play that game.

I didn't bite this time and respond or ask for more. Instead, I put my phone away and went back to writing the story, still not sure I'd actually go to Bali with Josh, despite how much my body told me that I wanted to. My mind kept saying don't. My heart was still afraid of getting too close to a new man, especially one who was my boss.

I'd decide when the time came.

FOR THE NEXT hour and a half, I wrote my story, easily producing another twenty-five hundred words of my fantasies of being alone with a very dominant Josh at a very expensive all-inclusive resort in Bali. I was tempted to send him the rest of the story so he knew my fantasies were about the possibility of a weekend alone with him, but it was his fantasy. I wanted to know what he desired. How his mind worked when it came to living out one of his fantasies.

What would he be like? Would he be all alpha and dominant, like I fantasized? Or would he want the roles to be reversed, with me on top? I had no idea, seeing as the two times I'd been with him, we either didn't have time or we were living out my fantasy.

Would he be kinky or controlling?

When I went to bed, I lay in the darkness and tried to imagine what he'd be like if he had total control over me.

It made it very hard to fall asleep...

THE NEXT DAY, I got up bright and early and went through my usual routine. Today, I'd work late, helping Sharon get ready for her big meeting with her editors on Tuesday. I was so busy, writing coverage for several of the novels I'd selected so Sharon could pick her favorites and develop a plan for them that I barely had time to think about Josh and the following weekend.

On my way down in the elevator, I saw him once again as he was going down from one floor to another.

"Ms. Carlson," he said as I stepped on and stood in front of the control panel.

"Mr. Macintyre," I replied and smiled to myself. He was on the other side of the elevator and there were two people in between us, so there was no way he could do anything to me in the short time I had between floors. I was disappointed, for I would have liked some interaction with him, but sadly, my floor arrived and I left the elevator, feeling his eyes on me the whole time.

I sighed as I went to the mail room and picked up the mail, stopping in the photocopier room to make a copy of my coverage letter for my own files. Before I could leave, the door to the room opened and in came my boss.

"Mr. Macintyre," I said as I took the copy from the machine.

"What brings you to the photocopier room? I thought you had staff to do administrative work for you."

"Stop talking," he said and closed the door. Then he pushed me against the wall, his body pressed against mine. He kissed me, his hand groping my body, squeezing a breast. When the kiss ended, he pulled back and met my eyes. "God, I can't stop thinking of you. Are you going to come or not?"

I bit my bottom lip, trying not to smile.

"Mr. Macintyre, given both our histories with office romances, I'd think it would be a very bad, inadvisable thing."

"This isn't an office romance," he said, his voice filled with a combination of frustration and humor.

"What is it, then?" I said and cocked my head to one side. "Just so I know."

He smiled. "It's pure."

"Pure?" I asked, confused.

"Pure unadulterated lust. Nothing more. Nothing less. I think that's a good thing. Neither of us wants to make the same mistake again, so we won't."

"I certainly don't want to make the same mistake again," I replied.

Then he leaned down and kissed my neck before squeezing my breast and kissing the flesh that swelled under his hand. He made a point to lick my tattoo and it sent a thrill right to my core.

"Then we won't," he replied, his voice husky. "So are you coming?"

He leaned against the wall, his arm beside my head and waited for my answer. I stared into his blue-gray eyes and tried to read him. He obviously wanted me to go to Bali.

"I thought you were going to California next week."

"I changed my plans."

"That seems rather unprofessional. Changing business plans for a dirty long weekend."

"My doctor says it's important for mental health to take regular vacations. I haven't had a real vacation for a long time. Years, in fact."

I smiled. "Me, neither."

"All the more reason for you to come," he replied. He leaned closer and kissed me softly. "I promise you won't regret it. We'll be completely professional while we're at work, and completely unprofessional in private."

"You haven't shown very professional behavior with me recently, kissing me in photocopier rooms and hallways..."

"I needed to clarify what was happening between us."

I stared into his eyes, trying to see if he was being honest. If he was going to be my Mr. Big, I didn't want it to interfere with my work.

"I need this internship, Josh. I don't want anything to hurt my position here."

"It won't. I'm going to appoint Keith as manager of Macintyre Publishing. I'll no longer have a role here. I'm focused on the *Chronicle* anyway. That's all I really care about and it would lift a load off my shoulders to no longer have any management function with the book publishing side. So technically, I wouldn't be your boss at all."

I nodded, thinking that might solve our problem.

"So, is that a yes?" he asked, impatient.

"I'll think about it."

Then he kissed me again and turned away, opening the door, checking the hallway before he left.

I stood alone in the room and tried to catch my breath. I wanted to go to Bali with Josh. It would be the first real vacation for my own personal enjoyment I'd taken in years. I decided that I would wait and make a decision at the last minute, based on how I felt, but part of me wanted to go so badly, fantasizing already what it would be like.

I just hoped if I did go, I wasn't making a big mistake.

CHAPTER TWENTY-TWO

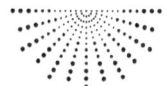

Joshua

I spent the rest of the day trying to recover from my meeting with Ella in the photocopier room.

Damn, that woman was becoming too much of an obsession. I couldn't get her out of my mind, wanting her every moment of the day. Hoping that she would agree to come to Bali with me and let me live out my own fantasy of time away from everything with a woman who was mine to enjoy as I wanted.

The truth was that I would have been happy to start a sexual relationship with Ella and not care about the fact she was technically an employee, although unpaid, of my company. I wasn't cheating on anyone so it wasn't like what we were doing was a betrayal.

I called down to Jerome, who took care of my travel arrangements and rescheduled my trip to California. It could wait another week or even two. Work was ongoing at the new office of

MBC, and my trip there was more to check on progress. Nothing was written in stone about the timing.

BEFORE MY NEXT MEETING, I got a text from Marcella, asking me to call her.

I did, dialing her number and leaning back in my chair, wondering what she wanted to talk about, considering we had a meeting already scheduled.

"Hello, Marcella, what can I do for you? I thought we already had a meeting planned."

"I'm hoping you can come to a charity event I'm hosting. There will be a few of my candidates at the event and you could mix and mingle with them, meet them and feel them out."

I rubbed my forehead. Going to a charity event to meet some of Marcella's picks for me was the very last thing I wanted. I only wanted Ella.

"Sorry, but no can do. I'm totally swamped with work for the next two weeks."

"I didn't tell you what day it was..."

"I don't have any days open," I said, really wanting to avoid it at all costs.

"It would just be for half an hour or an hour. Surely you could spare some time on Tuesday?"

"Nope. I'm really booked right up."

I heard her sigh on the other end. It was then I realized that my heart was just not into the whole matchmaker thing.

"Look, Marcella. This isn't going to work out. I really can't wrap my head around this right now. I don't want to approach this like it's a business decision, so please, give my regards to your candidates and tell them I wish them best of luck in the future but I just can't go through with it."

"May I ask what made you change your mind?"

I sighed. "I met someone who made me realize that it's not the pedigree or the resume that matters in this. It's the person. It's the chemistry. Trying to treat it like some kind of computer algorithm just seems bloodless and emotionless to me. I need to feel that chemistry first before anything else."

"Okay, Joshua. If you change your mind, you just have to give me a call. There will always be dozens of young appropriate women who are more than happy to meet you."

"Thanks for your vote of confidence," I said and I meant it. "Best of luck and if I do change my mind, I'll let you know."

I hung up, glad to get that out of the way. It really didn't appeal to me and never really had, other than the fact it would make it easier for me to meet women, but meeting Ella made me realize you couldn't force chemistry.

You either had it or you didn't.

Next, I called David to let him know I wouldn't be coming until the following week.

"What's up? You were really looking forward to this trip."

"I had something personal come up and will be taking a trip to Bali. It was short notice but I need to rearrange things to accommodate it."

"Personal? What? You're going to Bali instead? Is it a conference or something?"

"No," I said, cringing internally that I didn't have a good excuse.

"Is it business?" he asked.

"No," I replied. "It's just personal. Let's leave it at that."

"It's a woman," he said, his voice satisfied. "Tell me the truth, bro. You don't cancel a business trip and go to Bali for any other reason.

I laughed, because of course David would think it was a woman. "Yes," I admitted. "It's a woman."

"Hey, great. Bring her here, let me meet her."

"No, it's not like that," I said. "It's certainly not at that stage."

"It's at the take her to Bali and cancel a long-planned business trip stage, though."

"I know, I know. But honestly, it isn't like that."

"This is really sudden," David said, his voice sounding hesitant. "You were all down on relationships just a few weeks ago when we read the will."

"I know. Life moves fast. Sometimes, shit happens."

"That it does. Tell me that she's just a good fuck and you're not in love or anything."

"I'm not in love or anything. She's more than just a good fuck."

"Uh, oh. I don't like the sounds of that. You've been working like a dog getting everything in place for the opening of the new office in LA. The fact that you're willing to reschedule at the last moment is pretty telling."

"Let's just say we have an interesting relationship. Neither of us wants anything committed. We both were burned by cheating partners. We're only interested in something physical."

"That's what everyone always says, but then they fall in love. I've seen it happen way too often to know better."

"What about you?" I said, for David had many sexual partners and had yet to stick with one partner for longer than a weekend. "You have lots of sexual relationships. You've never fallen in love. Why can't the rest of us do the same?"

"Because you're not like me. You're the deep serious type. You don't do shallow. You've never done shallow. It's either one night or marriage with you."

"Well, maybe I'll try a shallow meaningless sexual relationship with someone else who wants the same thing."

"I give you six months before you're proposing."

I laughed out loud. "Not likely. In six months, I'll be with someone else."

"Yeah, right. I know you, brother. It's not in you. But you'll do what you want. Just remember who let you cry on his shoulder for a week after your last romantic fiasco."

"I'll never forget and you'll never let me," I replied, thinking of how I actually did cry on his shoulder one drunken night when I explained everything to him -- the whole mess. Me coming home early one day and finding Christie in our bed with her boss.

"Damn straight I won't."

"Look, I appreciate your concern, but I've decided to take a page out of your own book and try just a casual sexual relationship with this woman and we both want to go away and spend some time alone."

"I get it. I'm happy for you. It's time for you to move on from Christie. Get her out of your system. You'll know you're truly ready to move on when she stops being the reason you do or don't do things."

"Thanks for the relationship advice," I said with a smile. "I'll be out there in two weeks, tops."

"Bring this woman. What's her name, by the way? I need to know who'll be my first sister-in-law."

"David!" I said angrily, frustrated that he couldn't just accept that my relationship with Ella was just casual. "It's not what you're thinking."

"Okay, okay. Bring her along anyway. I mean, if it's nothing serious, why not?"

"I'll text you with my new itinerary once the plans are finalized."

"Love you, bro."

"Love you back."

Then I hung up, shaking my head at him. Of all the men to give me relationship advice, he was the last on my list. I knew he meant well, but he really couldn't keep it in his pants and didn't need to. My only concern for him was always STDs but he'd been able to keep clean over the years, despite the extravagant and debauched lifestyle he led.

But even someone as jaded and freewheeling as David had to come down to earth someday, and have a meaningful life with a wife and kids. He didn't have the same financial incentives as the rest of us did, given his income from the band, but even he had to grow tired of the lifestyle on the road with the endless trips and concerts.

He'd succumb someday, but I doubted that day would come any time soon.

THAT NIGHT, after a long day spent putting out business fires and trying to keep my head above water with business matters, I went to the penthouse apartment and ordered in dinner from a local restaurant. I had a shower and sat in my underwear in front of the television and ate my food, watching a game on the flatscreen.

It hit me all of a sudden how much of a loner I had become after Christie and I split. Other than a drink with the guys at work once a week, I really did nothing much else other than work. Before my father died, I'd spent so much of my evenings and weekends during the past six months visiting with him at his house, and at the end, in the hospital by his bedside.

I didn't have time for a social life, although I had slept with a couple of women I'd met at a bar with my friends once or twice after Christie and I split. But nothing more. And nothing like the life I led with Christie before we ended it. We were busy with other couples we both knew, attending gallery openings, charity events, dinner parties.

Now, that was all gone and I really was alone.

I took out my cell and texted Ella.

. . .

JOSH: I've never spent much time in the photocopier room up till now, but it's become one of my favorite places.

I WAITED FOR HER RESPONSE, expecting something impertinent. Soon, I saw the little dots and knew she was writing me back.

The dots hung there for a long time, and I figured she had some smart retort to my text message. As the dots hung there and I waited in anticipation, I wondered what she'd say in reply. Something about how she'd been delayed and that I should really stay out of the photocopier room in the future if I wanted her to do her job. Whatever her response, I was smiling to myself, eager to read her text.

When the response came, I was underwhelmed

ELLA: I imagine.

THAT WAS IT. All that time and she sends two words? I realized she had deleted the longer text she had actually written, having thought better of it. I knew she'd feel unsure of whether to respond at all, because I was her boss.

JOSH: I told you I'd remove myself as manager of Macintyre Publishing so we wouldn't be boss/employee.
ELLA: I know. Not sure if that really addresses the issue.
JOSH: Which is? The only issue I see is whether you're coming on Thursday.

ELLA: Not sure.

JOSH: You're sure to enjoy yourself. I happen to know you have the time off. What's stopping you? I've been clear that there are no strings attached. Just us and pure pleasure for four days. Isn't this what you wanted when you moved to Manhattan? To meet your own Mr. Big and use the experiences to write your best-selling chick-lit novel?

ELLA: Plot twist. In the movie, she marries Mr. Big.

JOSH: Are you marrying me?

ELLA: I'm never getting married.

JOSH: Then, it's settled. No marriage for you. Just pleasure. And great conversation.

ELLA: Like I say, we'll see. Try and enjoy the suspense.

JOSH: I hate suspense. I like to know what to expect.

ELLA: If I come to Bali, you can expect four days of sun, sex and satisfaction. How's that?

JOSH: Sounds like a plan.

I PUT my cell away but felt unsettled after my conversation with Ella. It seemed like she didn't want a committed relationship -- ever-- but at the same time, she didn't really seem to want a casual one fueled primarily by mutual lust. Was she afraid of falling in love? Maybe she didn't trust herself not to.

Whoever Jerkface was, he must have hurt her deeply to be so reticent about another meaningful relationship and yet afraid of a meaningless one. I could understand that sentiment, but I knew I couldn't be happy without sex in my life. If it had to be only casual, that would be fine with me until I did meet a perfect woman and get married. While I waited for that to happen, I saw no reason why Ella and I shouldn't be able to enjoy each other physically, even if we didn't become emotionally involved.

I tried to shove those uncomfortable questions out of my

mind and focus on the game. I was even able to enjoy it for a while, but the game turned out to be way too one sided and my team was losing so I lost interest and turned to the news. That was even less satisfying and frustrating, so I decided to go to bed.

Sleep was a long time coming, and I only fell asleep after another sad bout of solitary masturbation with images of Ella in my mind's eye. In truth, Ella should have been there with me, enjoying a second orgasm of the night. She was young, intelligent, and beautiful and she was attracted to me and I to her. We would have been fucking our brains out, if all had been right with the world.

But of course, it wasn't.

THE NEXT MORNING, I went through my usual routine of getting up and cycling after which I would take a shower and grab a cup of coffee on my way to the office. I should have spent the day at the office in the financial district, but I wanted to finish up some work at the new building. As I rode through the park, I thought back to my first meeting with Ella, and smiled to myself at how sweet she had been, offering to help pay for my medical costs, in case I didn't have good insurance as a lowly bicycle courier.

My knees and elbows were all healed up, but that event had left a mark on me. I enjoyed the fact that she didn't know me as *the* Joshua Macintyre, Jr. I was just a guy to her — someone she was attracted to. When she found out who I was, and that I was her boss, she was hesitant. If I had remained that bicycle courier, we would have probably been fuck buddies by now, but that changed everything and I had to work my ass off just to get her to give me a chance.

So I was really happy to see her rushing along the sidewalk to the building entrance.

221

"Hey, lady, watch where you're walking!" I called out when I got up beside her.

She jumped at the sound of my voice, then when she got sight of me, I saw relief on her face when she recognized me.

"Oh, it's you," she said and held her hand over her heart. Then she smiled. "You trying for another set of scraped knees and elbows?"

"Every day at this time," I said in reply. "I'm extra careful now and use the bike lanes whenever I can, just in case the tourists don't obey the rules of the road."

"You weren't obeying them that day, if I recall."

"Neither of us were obeying the rules. You have to know that they block the bike lanes with construction equipment and other obstacles so sometimes, we bicycle couriers have to improvise."

She nodded and stopped at the sidewalk that angled up to the front door of the building.

"Maybe if we can't follow rules, we should avoid each other. You know. One of us has to be responsible."

"Don't say that," I said. "We can be grownups. We're both gainfully employed."

"Well, not really..." she said with a grin. "I am unpaid..."

"Okay, we both went to college and got degrees. So there's that."

"Yes. But we both have made bad decisions when it comes to romance."

"And that's why this won't be a romance. Just pure unadulterated pleasure."

She glanced around and then turned back to me. "You keep saying that like you're trying to convince yourself."

"I know it's true," I replied. "I'm just trying to convince you."

She smiled. "I have a job to get to."

"Think about it," I said and removed my helmet and glasses and ran a hand through my hair. "You should come with me. It'll be memorable. You'll be able to include real details in your stories."

She tapped her head. "I have it all up here. Stuff I haven't actually done, I can research online."

"Nothing like the real thing," I said as I walked with her to the front door, and into the building where we waited for the elevator. Luckily, we were the only people waiting and when the elevator doors closed, I was pleased to be alone with her. I rested the bike against the wall and moved closer to her, leaning against the wall beside her.

"Have dinner with me tonight. Last night, I sat alone in my apartment and ate some takeout food in my underwear. It was pathetic."

She laughed and glanced at me. "That does sound pretty pathetic, but actually, I did the same. Except, I was wearing my nightgown."

"We should at least do it together," I said. "Then it wouldn't be so pathetic."

The elevator doors opened and it was time for her to get off.

"This is me," she said and started to leave.

I grabbed her arm. "Come have dinner with me tonight. If you want, we could go somewhere nice, or stay in and sit in our pajamas. There's a Knicks game on."

"I'm currently watching Mr. Mercedes on Superchannel."

"We could watch that, too."

She left the elevator without responding.

"Text me," I called out as the elevator doors closed.

She smiled. "I can't. Working late. Then I need to go right to bed so I can get up early and go at it again. Work work work until Sharon's presentation on Tuesday."

"If you change your mind, you know where to find me."

Her smile suggested that she was definitely deciding that she didn't want to get mixed up with me, no matter how much I promised her it would be just casual. I went the rest of the way up to my apartment, ruminating on what I really wanted from her. I enjoyed her wit and her beauty, plus she was hot in bed.

Maybe it wasn't a good thing for me to become involved with her.

I wasn't going to let that stop me.

CHAPTER TWENTY-THREE

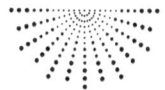

ELLA

DAMMIT.

He wasn't going to let up. He took every chance he could to contact me, whether by text or email or in person.

The problem was, I was beginning to look forward to it, despite all my best intentions. It was so tempting to just let myself fall for him, but everything was happening far too quickly.

He was just so easy to be with. Fun. I enjoyed his sense of humor and of course, his obvious interest in me was flattering to my ego, which was still bruised.

Josh was wealthy, handsome, and successful. Any woman would be more than happy to receive his attention.

Except me. I feared it.

He could have me twisted around his little finger so easily...

I spent the weekend at the office working on the presentation, making sure it was ready for Sharon's meeting on Tuesday, going over every detail, trying to make sure each slide was perfect and the whole thing flowed. I checked every number three times with the source material. I sent copies to each of the editors involved in providing the data for their input.

It kept me busy all day Saturday and Sunday.

I didn't see Josh during that period, but he made sure to text me.

I continued to give the excuse that I was working late and needed to go right to bed when I was done for the night.

On Saturday afternoon, he called me while he was out shopping.

My cell rang and I checked the call display to see whether it was him, although there were very few people in the entire world who knew my number other than Steph -- Sharon, Josh and Cindy from the office. That was pretty much the extent of it and since both of them were only steps away, I knew it was him.

"Hello, Josh."

"Hello, Ella. I'm down at Mr. Ho's place by the office and am wondering what to get for supper."

"It all depends," I answered, smiling at his blatant attempt to talk me into having dinner with him.

"Depends on what?" he asked, his interest piqued.

"On what you feel like eating, of course," I replied and stared off into the distance, trying to imagine him standing at the fruit and vegetable stalls at the small grocers down the street from the main office in the financial district. I could see him picking up pieces of fruit and smelling them, feeling the cucumbers, checking out the fresh seafood in the display case.

"I want to know what *you're* interested in eating."

"Oh, I already have my dinner taken care of. Sharon brought us some homemade lasagna and garlic loaf for supper. But thanks for thinking of me."

"Rats," Josh said, and I could hear the disappointment in his voice. "You wouldn't prefer some General Tso's chicken and rice? Some nice egg rolls?"

"Sadly, not tonight. We're working through supper to get this finished."

"Okay, but don't say I never tried."

"I could never say that."

I hung up and smiled to myself, enjoying his attention, regretting that I really couldn't take time off even if I wanted to. I didn't want to -- not really. Josh was like a triple chocolate fudge sundae with whipped cream on top. You know you shouldn't eat it, but that doesn't stop you from wanting it.

Josh wouldn't be good for me. He was a super-rich business mogul who would marry some society girl like his ex. I was out of his league and I knew it. The last thing I wanted or needed was to spend the rest of my life feeling looked down on because I wasn't the right kind of person.

EVER HOPEFUL THAT I'd given in out of sheer exhaustion from saying no, Josh texted me on Sunday afternoon.

JOSH: *I bought a couple of really great tenderloin steaks and some sweet corn from the grocer down the street. I could grill them up on the BBQ on my roof-top patio if you'd like to join me. The view is fantastic and I promise you, the company couldn't be finer.*

I EXHALED, wanting to go to him, but at the same time, kicking myself for being so weak-willed.

. . .

227

ELLA: Sorry. Sharon bought us a couple of containers of Kung Pao Chicken and rice for supper. Working late again!

JOSH: Can't blame a man for trying...

ELLA: At some point, I would think a guy might get tired of being turned down...

JOSH: You are obviously unaware of my incredible persistence. Some would call it obstinacy. Or maybe blindness... But I prefer to call it impressive staying power. *Grin*

ELLA: LOL

ELLA: No comment. Not enough data to judge.

JOSH: I can help you with that. I like to ensure a woman has adequate knowledge of my best attributes.

ELLA: You think that's your best attribute? I would think it would be your moral character or intelligence or compassion or wit...

JOSH: Those, too.

ELLA: Have a great evening and enjoy your tenderloin. As for me, I'll be working on Sharon's presentation on the spring schedule for her meeting.

JOSH: You could come by later for a nightcap...

ELLA: I'll be so tired by the time I get home, I'll be good for nothing but sleep.

JOSH: If you change your mind...

ELLA: Good night. Sleep tight.

I PUT my cell away and tried to focus on the presentation, but Josh's persistence had me smiling to myself.

Around four in the afternoon, a woman entered the office with a tray of coffee and a box of donuts in her hand. She was striking, with black hair and patrician features, dressed immaculately in a business suit. She went right into Sharon's office and I thought nothing of it until I got a call from Sharon to join them.

The door to Sharon's office was cracked open and I was just about to open the door and go inside when I heard them mention Josh's name. I stopped and listened, curious what they'd say about him.

"...and he was looking for a wife and he had me vetting candidates. Can you believe it?" the woman said.

"Joshua asked you to find him a wife? Seriously?" Sharon asked, her voice shocked.

"Yes," the black-haired woman answered. "He said he was too busy to find one himself. He needed to get married to receive instalments on an incentivized trust his father left for him. He would only get money on his wedding anniversaries. A cool twenty-five million each year. So, he asked me to find suitable women and arrange the meetings."

"That's so utilitarian. It's disgusting, really, when you think about it. I never would have thought of Joshua like that."

"He's a business man, in the end. He said he was too busy for romance, but he needed that twenty-five million dollars to help his paper get off the ground running. The boys all thought they'd get a one-fifth share of the fortune, which would have been close to two billion each, but no. His father didn't believe in inherited wealth. He wanted them to work for their own fortunes."

"That sucks," Sharon replied.

I stood in the darkness of the hallway and felt like my blood had turned to ice. Josh hired the headhunter to find him a wife so he could get twenty-five million dollars? He was willing to have me as his little fuck buddy while he looked for a real wife?

As much as I didn't plan on getting married any time soon, it hurt me to think that I wasn't good enough for him to consider as a potential wife. In fact, I felt like I was going to cry.

I left the hallway and went to the staff washroom and did just that. While I cried, I realized that I didn't want to just have a dirty fling with handsome and wealthy bachelors like Josh. I wanted something real.

While I sat on the toilet and wiped tears away, I texted Josh.

ELLA: I'm sorry I can't come with you to Bali, but I just can't do casual sex. I need something more. Something deeper. I was with my ex for years and I realize that I'm on the rebound and you can't trust yourself when your heart has been broken. But the last two weeks have shown me that I just can't do meaningless but pleasurable. I'm worth more than that. Good luck with your life but it's better this way.

MY FINGER HOVERED over the send button. Did I really want to do it? Josh told me that he was down on romance because of his bad experiences, but he was willing to hire a headhunter to find him a wife so he could get married for money.

It just didn't seem like the man I had come to know over the past few weeks, but I had to admit that if he really was trying to find a wife so he could get his first instalment and was happy to use me as a fuckbuddy until he met a woman good enough to be his wife, I couldn't be with him.

I tapped *send* and then went back to my office and sent a message to Sharon that I didn't feel like coffee or a donut and to go ahead without me.

Then I cried my eyes out alone in my office.

CHAPTER TWENTY-FOUR

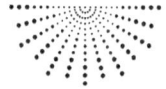

JOSH

I READ over her text several times, rubbing my jaw and trying to figure out what happened to change her mind.

ELLA: I'm sorry I can't come with you to Bali, but I just can't do casual sex. I need something more. Something deeper. I was with my ex for years and I realize that I'm on the rebound and you can't trust yourself when your heart has been broken. But the last two weeks have shown me that I just can't do meaningless but pleasurable. I'm worth more than that. Good luck with your life but it's better this way.

SHE WAS TURNING ME DOWN. I'd thought after our little rendezvous in the photocopier room that she was interested in more, but apparently, she'd changed her mind. Her excuse was that she was on the rebound and couldn't trust herself. In the end, she realized she couldn't do casual sex. She was worth more than that.

She was.

She was definitely worth more than causal sex.

I texted her right back.

JOSH: You're right. You are worth more than that. I only know I want to be with you, any way I can get you. If that's not enough for you, I understand. I want meaningful as well but you can't know in advance how a relationship will develop. I'm more than willing to see where our relationship goes, and won't put any requirements on it. If it develops into more, I'll be happy. If you decide it's not enough, I'll be sad, but that's always your decision. Just don't end it before it really even begins.

GIVE ME – give us – a chance.

THEN I SENT it and waited for her response.

Nothing.

I put my cell away and spent the rest of the afternoon trying to keep my mind off her and the question of what made her change her mind so suddenly. She had spoken of how down she was on marriage and how she needed to pursue her career and give that all her attention. What happened between the time I saw her last and earlier when she sent that text?

I spent the evening in a funk, trying to distract myself from thoughts of Ella but failing spectacularly.

Later that night, while I was lying in bed in the darkness, unable to stop thinking of what happened with Ella, I pulled out my cell and sent her another text.

JOSH: If the world was fair, you and I would be having text sex right now...

There was no response, and I just couldn't let it end that way. So I sent her another text.

JOSH: *Ella, please tell me what happened between the photocopy room and your text giving me the brush off. What did I do – or didn't do – to make you change your mind? I thought we were on the same page when we were alone. What happened?*

ANOTHER LONG PAUSE OCCURRED, but then I saw the little dots jumping and I knew she was finally responding.

ELLA: *Marcella Binetti dropped by for a quick visit today. You never told me about your father's will and that you had hired a headhunter to find you a suitable wife.*

I GRIMACED when I saw the reference to the will and Marcella. She must have told Ella about working for me to find a wife. But obviously, she didn't tell Ella everything.

JOSH: *Did she tell you that it was her idea, not mine? Did she tell you that I couldn't go through with it, primarily because I met you and I knew I couldn't even consider dating anyone else? Did she tell you that I told her to stop looking, and that I would find someone who I actually loved myself? That hiring her was too mercenary? I bet she didn't.*

THERE WAS no response for a few moments. I waited, wondering if that would be enough to convince her.

. . .

JOSH: If you don't believe me, ask her yourself. Go ahead. I give you permission to talk to her and tell her about our relationship. Ask her to give you the whole story. Please, before you decide anything, talk to her and get the whole story. That's all I ask.

I WAITED but she didn't reply, and I realized that I had to leave it up to her now. She would call Marcella or she wouldn't and she would decide to keep seeing me or she wouldn't.

Part of me wanted to call Marcella up and give her hell for talking about our business relationship, but that would do no good. She and Sharon were friends from a long way back and I should have known that somehow, news of my looking for a wife using a headhunter would slip out. It would be just too juicy a piece of gossip not to.

I thought Marcella was more professional than that, but she and Sharon were best friends. I should have been more professional myself and not even considered it.

Sleep was a long time coming and I had to admit defeat finally and take my cock into my own hand, engaging in a bout of solitary masturbation, imagining Ella being with me instead, riding me instead of resorting to my hand. The small burst of endorphins from my orgasm did little or nothing to soothe the ache I felt at the prospect of losing Ella before I really even had her.

THE NEXT MORNING, I went through my usual routine, my mind occupied with how I could convince Ella to give me another chance. I was so focused on the problem that I almost ran into a cement pylon left in the center of the bike lane, but managed to avoid it at the last moment.

"Hey!" A worker dressed in an orange vest and hardhat called out when I nearly struck him. "Watch where the hell you're going, bud!"

"Sorry!" I called out and kept going, slowing down a bit and trying to focus on the ride instead of my situation.

Usually, I'd let a relationship drop without protest if it had just started and wasn't progressing, but there was something about Ella I couldn't resist. I knew she was substantial. Someone I could happily spend time with, doing nothing, and enjoying every minute of it, whether we were fucking or just talking quietly afterwards, cooking a meal, or talking shop. I knew I'd kick myself if I let her slip away, but at the same time, I didn't want to be a stalker who couldn't take no.

When I arrived at the office for the day, after showering and dressing and grabbing a bagel and coffee at the coffee shop across the street, I called David.

"Hey," he said, his voice chipper.

"Hey," I replied, smiling when I imagined him sitting by his pool in sunny LA.

"What's up?" he asked.

I took in a breath. "So, there's this woman."

"Tell me about her," he replied, not missing a beat.

"She's perfect."

"No, she's not. She's a human, Josh."

"She just told me to fuck off, in so many words."

"What did you do to deserve that?"

"She found out that I hired a headhunter to find a wife so I could get the first installment of the trust fund."

"You did *what?*" he said, his voice incredulous. "You actually hired a headhunter to find you a wife? That doesn't sound like you. You're a hopeless romantic."

"I didn't really hire her. She was meeting with me about

staffing for the paper and I complained about the will. It was her suggestion, not my idea. I didn't go through with it, because I met this woman and I knew I couldn't meet anyone else until I knew where the relationship was going."

"So?"

"So, she found out and thinks I'm a heartless mercenary jerk."

"Of all the men I know, you are not a heartless mercenary jerk. If she doesn't know that by now, she's either dim or you haven't shown her who you really are. If you've told her how you feel and she turns you down, let her go."

"I can't let her go." I rubbed my forehead. "I don't know what's wrong with me."

He chuckled. "You're in love."

"I just met her two weeks ago," I said in protest.

"You're in love."

"How can you tell?"

"You wouldn't be calling me otherwise," he said with a laugh. "If she was just a fuck, you wouldn't think twice about her and you wouldn't be calling your little brother for advice."

"Come to think of it, I don't even know why I'm calling you, of all my brothers. You're the one who never plans on getting married or falling in love."

"Oh, I intend to fall in love, but I just plan on doing it over and over again. I don't want to deprive the female race of my attentions." He laughed out loud at that. "But you and I are fundamentally different. You need more than that. I know, I know-Christie hurt you. Don't let your experience with her change you into a cold hard-hearted loner. That's not you."

I didn't respond for a moment, letting it sink in.

"Look, even I can tell you're in love with this woman. Own it. Go and tell her you're in love with her. Give her a chance to tell you she's in love with you or she isn't. Then, if she doesn't love you back, let her go."

236

"How could she love me? We just met two weeks ago."

"Hey, stranger things have happened. If you feel like you can't be without her, *tell* her."

"Okay."

"There. That's settled," he said, sounding pleased. "Call me back and let me know what happens. If she tells you she's not in love with you, come out here for a week and we'll go surfing and try to make you forget her."

"Okay."

"Bye, big brother. Love you."

"Love you back, little brother."

Then I hung up.

ALL MORNING, I paced my room like a caged lion, going over and over in my head what I'd say to Ella. No more texting or email or even phone calls between us. I'd go to her office and I'd do what David said. I'd tell her I'd fallen in love with her and that I wanted to find out where our relationship went.

Of course, I was swamped with meetings and I had business to attend to, so it wasn't until late that afternoon that I had a long enough break to even consider speaking to her. When I finally went to her office, I popped my head in only to find that it was empty.

I checked with the receptionist at the front desk.

"Oh, Ella? She left the office for the day. She and Sharon have been working overtime to get Sharon's presentation ready. I think she went home."

"Thanks," I said and went back to my own office. I sat behind my desk and considered my next move.

I'd have to go to her place if I wanted to talk to her in person. After taking care of some more business I couldn't let slide, I grabbed my jacket and went to the parking garage to get my car and drive to her new place in Chelsea. I had the address from the cashier's check I'd purchased for her. Part of me felt guilty for going there, considering that she didn't invite me, but I'd only do what David suggested – I'd tell her how I felt and then let her decide what happened next.

I'd honor her choice – continue our relationship and see where it went, or end it there and then. I hoped she'd choose to continue and that she felt the same way I did, but I had to be prepared that she saw me as too much trouble or maybe, she just wasn't that into me as I was to her.

I parked my car a block down from her apartment building and walked the rest of the way there. Before I got there, I stopped at a small shop and bought a bouquet of roses and carried them, unwrapped, to her front door. I stood at the entrance and pressed the buzzer to her apartment, waiting, glancing up at the camera in the corner of the entry, smiling and holding up the flowers for her to see.

There was no answer.

I buzzed again, but nothing.

Was she there and just not answering?

I went back down the stairs and stood back near the curb, looking up at the front of the building. According to the address I had, she was on the third floor. She said her window looked out into a courtyard, so I went around the block to the back alley and walked down to the area behind her building. There, three floors up, was what I assumed was her window. There was a small courtyard at the ground level with a walkway and a small alcove with a bench and a planter. It wasn't much but it gave the space a pleasant atmosphere. I glanced up and checked the window out. There was no way I could climb up to it, so I stood back and picked up a pebble off the ground. It was small and round, about the size of a bean or pea. Perfect.

I threw the pebble at the third-floor window and waited,

hoping she'd hear the *plink* of the pebble against her window.

Nothing.

I found another pebble and lobbed it up, and again, there was nothing.

She was either gone or ignoring me.

After the fifth pebble, I gave up and went back around the front of the building. I had to decide what to do – I could stay in the neighborhood and hang out, waiting for her to return, or I could leave the flowers in the entryway, with a note asking her to call me.

I decided to leave the flowers and sent a text so that she'd know they were outside.

JOSH: I'm standing outside your apartment with a bouquet of roses in my hand, hoping you'll let me in so we can talk this over.

If she was home and ignoring me, she'd likely throw them in the garbage and I'd never hear from her again. If she was out, when she arrived home, she'd find them there and maybe think I was nice to leave the flowers for her. Maybe, it would soften her heart and she'd call me.

All I could do was try. The rest was up to her.

I hated walking away with nothing resolved, but one thing I'd learned by going through my breakup was that you couldn't force someone to love you.

They either did or they didn't and there wasn't much you could do about it either way.

CHAPTER TWENTY-FIVE

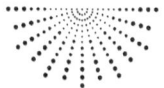

ELLA

I LEFT THE OFFICE EARLY, but before I left, I put a call in to Marcella Binetti. I felt really awkward calling her, considering we'd only just met and I had to talk to her about something really personal, but I wanted to know if Josh was telling me the truth.

"Hello, Marcella," I said and chewed a fingernail. "I wonder if I could come by your office and have a quick chat."

"Of course, Ella. Please come by. I'll be in until six at least."

She gave me the address, which was just down the street a few blocks. I had some time off because of all the hours I'd put in over the past few days, and since Sharon had encouraged me to take some time off, I did.

I said goodbye to Cindy at the front desk, and took the elevator down to the lobby, wondering if I would run into Josh. I hoped that I didn't. I wanted to talk to Marcella before I saw him again. If I did ever see him again, that is... I still hadn't decided whether to go to Bali or not.

241

I arrived at her building and checked in with the front desk security guard, who issued me a pass. Then I took the elevator up to her office on the twenty-third floor. A receptionist ushered me into a big corner office and there, behind a big oak desk, was Marcella.

She stood and came to meet me at the door, shaking my hand.

"Come in and sit down," she said, leading me over to a small seating area with a sofa and chair across from each other over a coffee table. Everything in the office was high end and elegant, like Marcella herself.

She offered me the chair so I sat and adjusted my skirt, and then I waited for her to sit down herself.

She smiled and folded her hands. "So, Ella. I assume you're hoping that I can find you a good paying job. Perhaps in another publishing house? I know the position you currently have is unpaid and temporary..."

I shook my head, then had to take in a deep breath.

"Actually, no. I love my position at Macintyre Publishing. I wanted to ask you about Joshua Macintyre."

"Oh?" she asked, her eyes wide. "Why would you ask me about him?"

"He told me to talk to you. He said I should ask you about," I said and hesitated, not knowing how to word things. "Well, you should know that we've been sort of seeing each other for the past couple of weeks. I overheard you and Sharon talking about him and that he hired you to find him a wife so he could inherit his money. As you can imagine, I felt hurt. I confronted him and broke off our relationship. He told me I should ask you to explain."

"Oh, dear..." She sat back, tilting her head to one side. "You overheard us yesterday," she said and sighed. "I'm so sorry about that. I didn't mean for you to hear our gossip. Yes, I met with Josh just after he found out about his father's will. It was a shock to him, because none of the boys had any idea they wouldn't be splitting the family fortune. Instead, their father created incentivized trust funds for them. In order to get a disbursement, they had to fulfil certain requirements. The first was they had to get married and stay married for at least a year. If so, they'd each get $25 million dollars on their first anniversary and every anniversary that they stayed married. It was their father's way of encouraging them to give up the bachelor's life and settle down."

"Is that even legal?" I asked, for it sounded like blackmail or extortion.

"Yes, it is entirely legal. Josh wasn't happy about it. He recently had a very hard breakup as I'm sure you know. He wasn't at all keen on getting married or looking for a wife. He even joked that I should find him a wife because he was too busy. I said, why not? I could do it because I have files on hundreds of very capable young women, many of whom would be more than happy to meet Josh and get to know him. Maybe become his wife."

"And?"

"And, I tried my best. I provided him with the very best candidates I had on file at the time. Women from very privileged backgrounds, with degrees and who were attractive and successful, and who agreed to meet him. He turned each one of them down, finding excuses. One wasn't nice enough. One was too nice. One had a career that was trifling. One was too serious."

"Did he ever say anything about me?" I asked.

"No," she said, frowning. "He never indicated he was seeing anyone, but now that I meet you, and learn that the two of you have become involved, I suspect he was comparing all the candidates to you, and finding he was just not interested in anyone else."

She raised her eyebrows meaningfully.

That thought made me smile. I covered my mouth with a hand, hoping to hide it because it felt too proud and there was no way of knowing if she was right about him. Still, a little zing of happiness went through me at the thought that Josh had compared me to the women Marcella found for him and turned them all down as a result.

"I was wondering why he was being so reluctant," Marcella said, her eyes narrowing. "Now, I know. He had you as his comparator. You have good breeding, coming from a powerful political family in New Hampshire. You have a degree from an Ivy League College. You have a career and ambition. You're lovely on top of it. I can see why he wasn't interested in anyone else."

Marcella smiled at me, a look of glee in her eyes. "It's a loss for me because I could have made some money off his desire to find a wife, but I've always been fond of Joshua. He's a wonderful person and upstanding young man. It makes me personally happy to know he found you on his own without any help from me."

I shook my head, because she was getting way ahead of herself.

"Wait," I said and held out my hand. "We just started seeing each other. It's not like that."

"Maybe not for you, but I suspect it is for Josh. Besides, your relationship with him was important enough for you to come and speak to me, to hear what I had to say. It was important enough to Joshua to admit what happened and send you to me with his blessing. I'd say there's something between you two that is more than just mutual attraction." She wagged her eyebrows. "Maybe you just don't realize it yet."

I tried not to grin, because the idea made me very happy. It surprised me, but I hadn't realized how much I felt for Josh, in addition to being incredibly physically attracted to him. Thinking about us becoming a couple sent a surge of excitement through me, and a feeling of desire mixed with affection. Of a deep need for him as a man.

I saw his face in my mind's eye – his handsome face, masculine with blue-gray eyes, a well-trimmed beard, his hair long on top, falling into his eyes in this sexy way. His incredible build. His intensity as a lover.

I felt a jolt of desire when I thought about going away to Bali for a weekend with him, alone on a tropical island all-inclusive resort. Nothing but sun, surf and sex...

"Thank you for being so open about this," I said and stood up, deciding I'd heard enough and still feeling quite awkward to be talking to Marcella about it. "I have to go, but I appreciate your willingness to meet with me so quickly."

She stood and escorted me to the door. "Please, feel free to contact me in the future if you are looking for a different opportunity. I'm sure with your credentials, I could land you a plum position with a publishing house."

I smiled and we shook hands before I left. Then I took the elevator down to the main floor and walked out into the late afternoon pedestrian traffic.

I stopped in the middle of the sidewalk and the pedestrians walked around me, flowing like a river of people. I had dreamed of being here, in Manhattan, in Mid-Town Manhattan in particular, the publishing world's center of gravity. Now, here I was – working for a major publisher, living in a cute studio apartment in Chelsea, and I had one of the wealthiest bachelors in America inviting me to spend a dirty weekend with him in a tropical paradise.

"Hey, lady, get the hell off the middle of the sidewalk!" a man called out at me, bumping into me. I came out of my trance of happiness and quickly went to the side of the building, out of the way of the thickest pedestrian traffic.

I didn't go back to my place right away. Instead, I went to

Central Park and walked around the lake, trying to clear my head and figure out what I should do.

I sat on a bench by the pond, and watched some geese swimming around. On the street, a couple of horse-drawn carriages clip-clopped by, the sound of their hooves making me think of when I was a child and used to go on hayrides in the fall.

I was filled with a sense of melancholy, and wished the answer would come to me so I could finally feel settled, but there was no bolt of lightning or clear message from above, telling me what to do.

I had to figure it out myself.

I took out my cell, and checked my messages.

Sure enough, there was one from Josh.

JOSH: I'm standing outside your apartment with a bouquet of roses in my hand, hoping you'll let me in so we can talk this over.

I SMILED at the mention of leaving roses, pleased that he was trying so hard to win me back even if I didn't know if I would let myself go.

I texted him.

ELLA: I met with Marcella.

JOSH: And? I hope she cleared up a few facts.

ELLA: She did.
JOSH: So, what are your thoughts?
ELLA: I'm not sure. I need to think of things for a while.
JOSH: What things? You must know that after I met you, I

didn't want to meet any of Marcella's candidates. None of them compared to you.

I DIDN'T KNOW what to say in response, but it made me smile to myself. It was what Marcella had said, and it warmed my heart to see him repeat it.

JOSH: Ella... I've fallen for you. I think we're good together. I want us to give this – whatever it is between us – a real try. Come to Bali with me.

THAT CONFESSION – that he'd fallen for me – sent a jolt of desire through me. I actually closed my eyes and covered my mouth, because it made my heart tug, but I needed time.

ELLA: I need some time to process it all.

JOSH: Of course. Whatever happens, the tickets are still good for Friday so if you want to give this a real serious try, I'll be waiting at the Emirates Lounge, hoping you show up with only your bathing suit and a change of clothes along with you. Where we're going, it will be clothing optional most of the time and I intend to keep you very busy and very naked...

I SMILED TO MYSELF. That prospect sent a surge of warmth through my body. I glanced up at the sky, grinning like an idiot. It was Tuesday. I had to work Wednesday and Thursday, but then I had Friday off until the following Wednesday. The ticket to Bali was for Friday at noon. We'd fly for hours with a layover in Saudi Arabia, and then we'd fly to Bali for three glorious days in an amazing resort. With our own pool and beachfront.

I didn't text Josh back because, as excited as I felt about Bali, I was still uncertain about whether I should go. I put my cell into my bag, and after it was almost dark, I went back to my apartment and found a bouquet of beautiful red roses at the front entry. I brought them inside and stood at my tiny sink, trying to decide what to put them in. The tallest glass I had was too short and frail to hold twelve roses. I remembered I had a big jar of Catelli Spaghetti Sauce for dinner the other night when I was dreaming of meatballs and made some. It was out in the recycling so I went downstairs to the back of the building and bent over the bin, fishing around in the old tin cans, the plastic bottles and soda cans, until I found it. I brought it back inside, washed it out and then cut each rose stem down so that all twelve fit inside and the jar didn't tip over.

I spent some time cleaning my tiny apartment to distract myself. I needed to talk to Steph, although I already knew what she'd say.

Regardless, I needed to hear it before I made my decision. As soon as I was finished cleaning, I'd call her.

My body said yes, my heart said yes, but my brain kept going over the fact that he felt out of my league and that maybe, I was jumping back into the fire too soon. I thought that a nice fling with a handsome boy-toy like bicycle courier Josh might be a way to get over Jerkface, but billionaire publisher mogul Josh felt like he was more than just a fling.

I could already feel my heart being taken by him, and was afraid he'd break it.

CHAPTER TWENTY-SIX

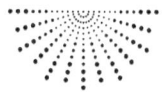

JOSHUA

I SAT ALONE in my apartment and waited for her to reply, and say something about the flowers, but she didn't.

Discouraged, I went out and bought a carton of takeout fried chicken from a small place down the street. I grabbed a six-pack of beer from the corner liquor store and went back up to my apartment in the building by the park.

I could have been out with the boys from work, drinking at a classy bar, ogling the pretty women there, maybe picking one up for a night of easy meaningless sex, but somehow, that felt empty to me now. Sure, maybe it was what I enjoyed five years earlier, before I met and became engaged to Christie, but now?

It felt like a charade. Like an empty waste of time.

A bunch of lonely men pretending to be having fun, laughing it up, getting slightly drunk or stoned, when all we really wanted was something more. A deeper connection to someone who had your back, who looked forward to seeing you each morning and who wanted to spend time with you at the end of each day. Where the sex wasn't meaningless, but was instead deep and intense because you knew exactly what did it for her and she knew what did it for you, and you both delivered.

I thought I had that with Christie, but I was self-deceived. I'd kept myself emotionally locked up ever since we split, and it was only running into Ella, and helping her out when she was in need, that opened me up again to how it felt to be human with another woman.

My cell dinged and I had to wipe my hands off quickly before picking it up off the coffee table to check it out.

ELLA: The flowers are lovely. Thank you. I put them in this spaghetti sauce jar because it was the only thing big enough to hold them without falling over. I actually had to go out back behind the building and get the jar out of the recycling bin. You can imagine me bending over into it, fishing around in the cans and jars, almost falling inside.

I smiled, my grin huge. Well, at least I knew she didn't throw them into the trash.

JOSH: I'm glad you like them. I was worried you'd have thrown them into the trash, but I'm glad you got to reuse that spaghetti sauce jar. Reduce, reuse and recycle is my motto.

She didn't respond back, nor were there any bouncing dots indicating a response was coming and I felt sad. I wanted her to come over right then and there so we could be together instead of me being alone texting her.

JOSH: So, I suppose that means that I missed out on a nice spaghetti dinner... Did you make meatballs?

Then, she did start to answer and I had hope for the first time in a long time.

· · ·

ELLA: Actually, I did make meatballs but alas, my cooking skills are not up to Mrs. Corleone's or whoever it was who made them at that restaurant we went to.

JOSH: I could probably ask for the recipe the next time we go. They like me there. I'm a regular.

THERE WAS a pause and I waited with a smile on my face to see how she'd respond.

ELLA: I saw what you did there...

JOSH: What did I do???

I WAITED but there was no reply. *Damn...* I really had to work hard to get her to stay engaged.

JOSH: So, I have it from sources who are in the know that the resort in Bali has the very best fresh fish and seafood, and it's served daily at an all-day buffet and restaurant. We could order in and stay in the room for the entire time we're there, or we could get dressed up one night when we need a break from all the nakedness and go sit in the lovely outdoor dining room that is described as, and I quote, "open to the magnificent tropical night sky filled with a million stars."

. . .

I WAITED BUT AGAIN, no response.

Then, she texted me an image of the roses in the Catelli spaghetti sauce jar. The label had been partially scraped off, but it was clear enough to know what brand. She'd had to trim the stems so that the roses didn't fall out of the jar, but it was still a nice bouquet.

JOSH: I want to come by and see your apartment.

Of course, I wanted more than just to see her apartment, but I was truly curious about her place. I wanted to see where she lived so I could picture her there.

ELLA: I could send you a video of the place. It's pretty small and would only take about five seconds to cover everything. There's a Murphy bed, and a small desk, a two-seater table against the wall beside the kitchenette, and a television mounted to the other wall. The bathroom is about four by four feet with a tiny shower, toilet and miniature sink. And there's one full wall of brick. It's tiny, but it's mine, all mine.

JOSH: Sounds amazing.

JOSH: So, no invite over for a late-night visit?

ELLA: I'm exhausted after working four straight twelve-hour days, frankly.

JOSH: Three days of sun, surf and ... whatever your heart desires is the remedy for that.

ELLA: I thought Bali was the fulfilment of your fantasies, not mine.

JOSH: Your desire is my pleasure.

There was a long pause and I knew I was pushing a bit too much, but I didn't want to lose her now. I had to keep pressing her to let herself do what I thought she really wanted – I thought – I hoped – that she wanted to be with me, but was afraid. That was my fault for not being truthful to her right from the start about who I was. If I had, she would have trusted me more, and understood that whatever we felt was both mutual and real.

JOSH: Ella, if I could go back in time to the day we met in the elevator, I would tell you the truth about who I was, so you wouldn't be concerned about me being honest. It was just so nice to be liked for me, just Josh. Not THE Joshua Macintyre Jr. That was all. I didn't do it to deceive you. I did it to make you relax and be yourself. It worked and you were real with me. You can't know how much that meant to me, especially after what happened with my ex.

ELLA: I understand. Look, I'm still processing everything, but I really appreciate the thoughtfulness of the flowers. Now, I'm seriously exhausted and have to say goodnight.

JOSH: Goodnight. I hope I see you on Friday...

That was it. She didn't text me back, but I felt a whole lot better about things after texting with her than I felt before. Now, if only I knew for certain she would meet me at the Emirates lounge, I could sleep well and look forward to my final day of work before Bali.

I had decided I wouldn't go if she didn't, because while I really needed the escape, I knew it would hurt too much if she didn't show up.

Unable to sleep because my mind was working too hard, I grabbed my bike and my reflective vest and helmet and went out into the Manhattan evening to ride, work off some of my excess energy.

I rode beside the park along my usual path, driving down side streets to get to the bike pathway along the Hudson. Usually, physical exertion like that cleared my mind, and I rode along, my mind focused on my breathing and the path ahead, the traffic around me and my destination.

I arrived back at the building, a considerable sweat worked up and a lot of stress worked off. I went back up to my apartment and had a shower, all the while thinking of Ella, wondering if she'd show up on Friday. I wanted to text her and try to feel her out, but at the same time, I didn't want to annoy her or be a jerk, so I held off.

Instead, I went to bed and tried hard not to think of her, for I was exhausted and I knew that if I thought too much, my mind would go back to our one real encounter and I would need to take care of business. But try as I might not to think about her, my mind went there and I wondered whether Ella would show up on Friday at the airport lounge.

I didn't know what the future held for us, but I was going to try to give the relationship every chance I could to succeed. Both of us had been hurt by cheaters, and both of us needed to find our way back to trusting again.

All I knew was that when I was with her, I was happy. I enjoyed her – her smile, her wit, and of course, she was beautiful, ambitious and smart. But most of all, she had a good heart.

Whatever happened between us, I felt that was certain and that was what really mattered.

THURSDAY, I spent the day mired in work, going over all the projects I had on my desk, making sure I could take time off over the next five days and that everything would be taken care of in my absence. I truly didn't want to answer any work-related emails or take any business calls the entire time we were there. I would have my assistant field all calls and only put through true emergencies. Nothing less than a five-alarm fire would interrupt me while I was on vacation.

Then, I picked up my suitcase and left for JFK, wondering as the taxi drove there whether she would show up or leave me hanging. I went to the Emirates Lounge, and took a seat in one of the chairs by a window, and began my vigil.

I checked my cell. I had arrived an hour before I needed to check in, and made sure that I could watch the doorway so I could see Ella the moment she arrived. The moments passed, and I kept my cell open, checking email and my social media, hoping that if she decided not to come, that she'd at least text me so I would know before the flight left. I hoped that she would have let me know by now if she wasn't coming so I could either reschedule or cancel, depending.

The fact she hadn't gave me hope.

Exactly thirty-two minutes after I arrived, I saw her walk through the doors into the lounge. The relief I felt was intense. I checked and sure enough, she had a suitcase in hand and hadn't just come to see me off.

I stood and she came right over, her face flushed, her cheeks pink.

She smiled. "I tried to be here an hour before, but my taxi got stuck in traffic."

I took her hand and pulled her into my arms, kissing her, my arms slipping around her to pull her closer. She kissed me back, her enthusiasm a sign she was fully with me. No hesitation.

"You came," I said and stroked her cheek, smiling. "I wasn't sure you would."

"I wasn't sure I would either, but I didn't want to regret not going one day when I'm an old lady living in a retirement home."

She smiled up at me, and I laughed at that image. My mind immediately went to us sitting together in that retirement home, an old grizzled couple, holding hands.

"Better to have loved and lost than never to have loved before."

Then I kissed her again, because I now truly believed that line from Tennyson. No matter what happened between us, I knew then I had to find out.

EPILOGUE

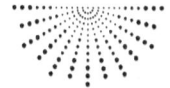

ELLA

"WHAT DO YOU THINK?"

Josh stood behind me at the patio door, his arms around my waist, his chin resting on my shoulder so that his lips were beside my ear.

"It's amazing," I said, squeezing his arms, for the scene was truly fantastic.

Our rooms looked out over the beach and beyond it, to the Pacific, which was now calm, a bright moon illuminating a bank of clouds against a starry sky. I could hear the roar of the surf and it was distant enough to be calming. Outside our room was a personal swimming pool and a set of lounge chairs. A few yards away, surf washed against the beach.

"So," I said and turned around in his arms. "This is your fantasy. Tell me what you want me to do."

He stared into my eyes for a moment then shook his head slowly.

"Just be you. Just be with me. I don't need to play out any fantasy scenario to feel this is worth every moment. What matters is that we're here together for three full days of doing nothing but enjoying the location, the good food, the peace and quiet and of course, each other."

"That's it?" I asked and gave him side eyes. "No kinky sex thing you want me to do? No role playing or games of bondage with silk scarves tied to the bedposts?" I smiled as seductively as I could, hoping to get a grin out of him and an admission.

He pressed his obviously aroused body against me. "I did say that I wanted you all to myself for the entire weekend and that we would spend the entire time fucking our brains out. We can try the scarves later, if you want but right now, just being with you is enough for me."

I stood on my tip-toes and kissed him, pressing my breasts against his chest, grinding my hips against his erection.

"It's more than enough," I said when the kiss broke.

Then he pulled me over to the bed and I soon forgot all about everything except him, and that was the entire point.

He pulled me on top of him as he lay down on the bed. I lay there, my thighs straddling his hips, my knees on either side of his and looked down into his eyes.

"You said you wanted me to ride you." I smiled and leaned down to kiss him, feeling his smile against my lips. He brushed hair from my face, tucking a strand behind my ear. "I don't mind being on top," I said, my voice throaty.

I kissed him, then moved down lower, my mouth pressing against his flesh, down over his well-developed pecs, to his washboard abs and lower. His cock was hard and dripping, and I licked him from the base of his erection to the tip before taking the head into my mouth.

"Oh, *God. Jesus*, Ella, that's so good..."

I smiled, enjoying that I could please him so well.

Finally, he pulled me up from his cock to kiss him once more. I cupped his cheek, and ran my fingers through his hair while I kissed him, my tongue searching for his. The kiss seemed endless, and my body grew more aroused as his hands groped me, squeezing a breast, sliding around to guide his cock against me. I ground myself on his erection, sliding against it, my lust growing as I used his body. He reached over to his open suitcase on the other side of the king-sized bed and pulled out a condom, handing it to me.

I took it and opened the package, then unrolled it over his cock, impressed at how hard and thick he was.

He leaned back on his hands.

"Now, rub yourself against me."

"Your wish is my command," I said, sliding up and down against him, rubbing my clit against his erection like a wanton woman.

"Ride me," he said in a husky voice. I moved up and positioned myself over him. He held his erection in one hand and I lowered down onto him, gasping as he filled me up. I sat still, enjoying the sensation of this hard thickness filling me up so completely.

"Your clit is so hard," he said and rubbed his thumb against it. That, combined with the sensation of his cock inside of me felt so good that I groaned out loud.

He leaned forward and licked the curve of my breasts, before taking one nipple into his mouth and sucking hard. A jolt of pleasure coursed through me, right to my clit, my back arching.

"I won't take long," I gasped. I was so ready, I knew that with a few strokes of his thumb on my clit as I rode him, I'd go over the edge.

"Neither will I."

His thumb stroked me while I rode him and the pleasure was so great, I closed my eyes and bit my lip.

"Open your eyes," he said, his voice demanding. "I want to watch you."

I did, staring into his blue-gray ones, holding his gaze as I moved on him, each move against his thumb driving me even closer to my own orgasm.

"You're so nice and wet. So hot..."

He cupped one breast, squeezing it, mouthing the nipple, then sucking it and I couldn't help but gasp.

"You're so *big*," I gasped as the pleasure built inside of me. "I'm going to," I said, my eyes closing despite my best attempt to keep them open. "That's *so*..."

My body tensed as my orgasm started and I shuddered as waves of pleasure spread up into my belly and down my thighs.

"Oh, *God*..."

"Don't stop," he said, his hands helping me, moving me up and down on him when my orgasm began to wane. I continued to ride him, my hands on his shoulders, and soon, he grimaced in pleasure while his own orgasm began.

"Oh, *God*," he groaned, his body shuddering through his orgasm.

Finally spent, he lay back and I collapsed on top of him, our bodies still joined.

We recovered for a few moments, breathing in deeply, his hands stroking my hair and then moving down my back to my buttocks.

"That was so good," he said, smiling.

"It was," I said and smiled back.

Finally, I slipped off him and lay on my back beside him, staring up at the ceiling fan, which moved in a slow spiral above us.

"I'm glad you came to Bali," he said and rolled over so that he was on his side. "Don't expect to do much else besides fuck me the entire time we're here."

I rolled over and faced him, smiling coyly. "I wouldn't have it any other way."

Then we lay in each other's embrace and enjoyed the afterglow.

As I lay there, Josh's body warm against mine, the sound of the surf a distant roar, I thought to myself that I had fantasized about a life in Manhattan, escaping the disappointment of my previous life, and building a new one. I didn't imagine for an instant that the first man I'd run into – literally – would be the one to capture my heart, but he did.

Neither of us knew where this would go, and that was okay.

Both of us agreed that we wanted to find out together.

END OF PART ONE

Part Two, Tease Me, is available at your favorite eBook retailer!

IF YOU ENJOYED THIS BOOK, please consider leaving a review. Reviews help authors reach more readers so if you have five minutes, please review on your social media or wherever you buy your books.

EXCERPT FROM TEASE ME

CHAPTER ONE

Ella

I passed the spot where Josh and I first met, and a surge of happiness filled me.

Who would have thought that the first man I literally ran into in Manhattan would be the man I would fall for and would spend my days and nights with? I sure didn't expect it, but as I walked along the sidewalk towards the Macintyre building, I smiled to myself remembering our first encounter. This time, I crossed the street at the crosswalk and went to my favorite coffee shop for my morning cup of java, and when I came back, sure enough, Josh was on his bike, riding up the street -- in the bike lane.

I stopped and waited for him on the sidewalk.

"Fancy meeting you here," I said when he arrived at my side. "Even snow won't stop you from riding that thing."

"I laugh at snow," he said and removed his helmet for a kiss. "We're going to have to stop meeting like this."

I leaned in and pressed my lips against his, smiling the whole time while a zing of desire for him flashed through my body.

"You're the boss," I replied.

"Don't say that," he said and shook his head. "I've recused myself from all matters on the book publishing side of the business now that Rob Kennedy has finally taken over. I'm totally focused on *The Chronicle* and keeping MBC afloat. You won't see me around except maybe once a year when I come by for a board meeting."

I pouted. "No more copier room smooches?"

He laughed. "Well, I can't promise that. I might be tempted to come down for more smooches for you in the copier room or hallways when people are busy. And," he said and slipped his arm around my waist, pulling me closer. "If you accept my invitation

264

to stay with me now and then at my apartment, there will be much much more. Like tonight, for example."

"I'll be happy to accept your invitation."

"You have a standing invitation," he said. "Any night you feel like sleeping in my huge bed, you're welcome."

He kissed me, and this time, it was more passionate. For a moment, I lost myself in him, in the sensation of his lips on mine, his tongue touching mine.

We pulled back and stared into each other's eyes.

"Damn, woman," he said under his breath. "We just got finished less than an hour ago and I already want more."

I smiled coyly. "Sorry, Mr. Macintyre, Sir. I have a job to do."

"You do love to tease me," he said as I deliberately flounced off with a flick of my hair and walked towards the building entrance. I arrived at the front doors with him in tow, his bike at his side.

"I do," I said and blew him a very tiny kiss, just in case any of his other staff or business associates were around. I didn't want to embarrass him. We took the elevator up to Macintyre Publishing's offices and he kissed me once more when the doors opened, and we saw we were alone.

The kiss went on and on, and we got away with no one else riding on the elevator with us until my floor.

"Later," he said and pointed to me. "I need my fix."

"Don't worry," I replied and smiled as the elevator doors closed. "You'll get yours."

I popped my head in to see Sharon on my way to my office. We had a meeting in a half hour and I wanted to make sure it was going forward.

"Good morning," I said. "Are we on for eight thirty?"

She glanced up from her desk and gave me a smile. "We are. Bring your best choices and we'll go over them."

"See you at eight thirty."

I went to my office, which was now starting to look like a

person worked there and not a makeshift room with a desk and plastic sheeting. I had a different desk now, with a hutch and ergonomic chair, plus my own filing cabinet and a chair for any visitors. The office was tiny, but it had an actual door and a window, looking out over the building beside ours.

I loved it.

I'd even decorated it with Thanksgiving themed items -- a paper turkey sat on the shelf behind my desk and I had a metallic Happy Thanksgiving sign on one wall. I'd have to take that down to make way for Christmas now that Thanksgiving was officially over.

It would have been hard for me, only a few months ago, to imagine my life the way it was now. I was depressed after my breakup with Jerkface, and I didn't want to stay in Concord, knowing that he was there, working and probably now fucking Bunni on an even more-regular basis. I wanted to escape.

Moving to Manhattan to take an unpaid internship was the best decision I'd made in a very long time.

I spent the next thirty minutes preparing for my meeting with Sharon, but my peace and quiet was shattered by the loud ring of my cell. I had programmed it so that when my father called, an old car horn blared. I knew it was him immediately, and I could prepare mentally for our talks.

"Hi, Dad," I said, wondering why he was calling me at this time in the morning. "To what do I owe this pleasure?"

"Hello, Dear," he replied, his voice sounding distracted. "Your mother and I are making a trip to Manhattan this weekend and will be staying for most of the coming week. Something came up and I have some business to attend to. She wanted to spend some time with you while I'm otherwise occupied."

"That's great," I said, even though I'd seen them the previous week for Thanksgiving. "Where are you guys staying?"

"The Ritz downtown. Your mother wanted to be close to your

apartment so you two could do some sightseeing. I'll be in meetings the entire weekend."

"What's up?"

"Just some party business before the new session. I know you aren't interested in politics, so I'll just say it's party business and leave it at that."

"Upcoming by-election?"

"Something like that. Sudden death of an old friend and colleague."

"Oh, I'm sorry, Dad. Who was it?"

"Just a former member of the State legislature when I was a member. We've got to find the right person for the seat and so will be meeting all weekend to strategize."

I made a huge and very audible yawn and then a very loud snore for his benefit and he laughed out loud.

"See, I told you that you wouldn't be interested."

"Right now, I'm reading thriller manuscripts and I'm focused on things that are a bit more exciting than by-elections. Politics is not my thing."

"I know that only too well. I won't bore you with the details, but I know your mother would love to do some early Christmas shopping and you two go to a spa and have the full treatment, maybe go for a nice lunch or two. Whatever it is you two do when you get together."

"I'll be glad to see you both."

"So, what's new with you? Any good books? Are you writing? Have you met any decent young men?"

I laughed at his peppered questions. "Dad, I just spent the long weekend with you and Mom," I said. "I already told you that I've got new friends at work and I'm super busy reading manuscripts. I'm really happy to be living here."

"I know. I just wanted to give you a chance to come clean in case you were actually lonely and wanted to move back."

"Not on your life," I said with a laugh, knowing he was only half-teasing me. "I love it here."

"I know your mother misses having you in Concord, but she wants you to be happy, so I'm glad you are. I'll call you when we arrive. Maybe you can meet us for supper tomorrow."

"Do you want me to meet you at the airport?"

"That's not necessary," he replied. "We're getting in during the day, so you'll be at work. We'll call you with a time for dinner."

"Sounds good. Love you Dad," I said.

"Love you back, Punkin," he replied, using his pet name for me.

I hung up and leaned back, smiling to myself. I was glad to see them, but at the same time, I hoped they didn't take up all my time on the weekend. Josh and I spent the Thanksgiving weekend apart and we wanted to make up for lost time. We were having so much fun with each other, spending our weekends together, that I didn't want to deprive myself.

Still, it would be nice to see them both again. I could take my mom to some of the places I'd grown to love visiting and of course, seeing my dad when he was through with his political meetings.

I spent the rest of the day focused on my work, and of course, received quite a few texts from Josh.

JOSH: *I already miss the photocopier room...*

ELLA: *You made your bed and now you have to deprive yourself of my company.*

ELLA: *Speaking of which, my parents are coming down to Manhattan for the weekend. My dad has some back-room political meetings he has to attend and so I'll be spending the weekend with them.*

JOSH: *They just had you for four whole days.*

ELLA: *They are the parental units.*

JOSH: Do I finally get to meet the Carlsons?

ELLA: Not on your life. I don't want to mention that you and I are seeing each other so if you want me, you'll have to come by late at night after my daughterly duties are finished.

JOSH: I'm insulted. Why don't you want me to meet your parents?

ELLA: My father is a notorious fourth-degree kind of man.

JOSH: Oh, yeah? You don't trust me to stand up to his scrutiny? I'm crushed...

ELLA: I don't want any drama. Besides, my mother will pester me to no end about you. I don't need the aggravation.

JOSH: I feel somehow slighted. But as long as I get you at night, I guess I'll take what I can get.

ELLA: I'll be yours from, say, nine-thirty at night until breakfast. I'll probably meet them for breakfast before my father's meetings and then will be with my mother the rest of the time until after dinner.

JOSH: I'll find something else to do with myself until nine-thirty. But I am disappointed. I would have liked to meet your parents. Your father is notorious.

ELLA: That's exactly why I'd rather not spring you on them at the moment. He is notorious.

JOSH: Okay. If that's what you want. Just so you know, I clean up pretty decently when I have to meet important people. I know what fork to use and all that...

ELLA: Josh! It's not that I don't think you'd pass muster, but I just don't want this weekend to be all about my new boyfriend.

JOSH: So, I take it that I _am_ your new boyfriend? I'm beyond the fuck-toy stage and I'm now into the regular squeeze category?

ELLA: Regular squeeze sounds about right, although I do like the fuck-toy stage, too.

JOSH: It was a lot of fun, I have to admit.

269

ELLA: It was. Now, I have to go so quit distracting me or my boss will have my hide.

JOSH: That damn boss... Can I stop by later? I'll be on that floor for something.

ELLA: Okay but you should have an excuse. I don't want the whole office to know we're seeing each other.

JOSH: That's twice I've been crushed in this one textual exchange, Ella. I'm feeling a little insulted here...

ELLA: People know about my past. They know about your past. They'll think we're both crazy for seeing each other.

JOSH: Okay...I'm stopping by and will be in and out in two minutes tops. A quick kiss and grope are all I need.

ELLA: That I can give. Any time. Now, I have to go and get work done. I hear the big boss is a real stickler for productivity.

JOSH: I've only heard nice things about him.

ELLA: Later. :)

I put my cell away, smiling at our exchange. He was always in a good mood, and was always a bit playful, which I enjoyed. He made me happy.

For the rest of the day, I waited for him to pop by and by the end of the day when he still hadn't, I felt a bit glum. While I didn't want the entire office staff to know I was seeing the big boss, I didn't mind him popping by for a quick kiss and squeeze. He could always find some reason to pop in to see Sharon or something. They were friendly enough that he could always use that excuse.

At five thirty, which was the official end of my day, I gathered up my things and said goodnight to Amber, who was working the front desk. I took the elevator down to the main floor and made my way out of the building. As I left the front door, I was accosted by Josh, who stepped out from behind one of the columns at the front of the building. He laughed when I squealed and pulled me into his arms.

We kissed, our focus completely on each other, while people walked around us on the sidewalk.

"I didn't think you were going to show up," I said when the kiss ended.

"I wanted to keep you in suspense."

"You wanted to tease me," I said, and gave him side-eyes. "You were making me all excited, wondering when you'd show up and what you'd do."

"I admit it. Anticipation makes it always so much more exciting. Now, how about some dinner? Since I'm going to be deprived of you as a dinner companion all weekend, I'd like to get in as much time as possible for the next couple of days."

"I'm all yours," I replied and stepped onto my tip-toes to kiss him.

"I like that." He kissed me back.

When we were finished, he took my hand and together, we walked along the street to his car, which was parked about a block away from the building.

He opened the passenger door for me and I got inside. After he got in beside me, he took my hand and kissed my knuckles.

"What do you feel like? Something healthy or some junk?"

"Mmm," I said and tried to think of what I wanted to eat. "Something junky. My mother is a health nut and so we'll probably be eating clean all weekend."

"How about some of Uncle Joe's Barbecue?"

"Perfect."

We drove off and went to Uncle Joe's, which was one of Josh's favorite restaurants. It was a tiny hole in the wall that looked like it belonged down by the bayou in Louisiana instead of Manhattan. He'd taken me there twice before and the food was so good, and there was always too much of it. I took home leftovers and ate them on my lunch break the next day, so it was a way for a single girl to stock my fridge for a meal or two.

We arrived at the restaurant and went inside, taking a tiny table beside the window looking out over Lexington. It was busy outside, and we were lucky to get in without a wait, but we'd chosen the best time to go. Most people got off work at six, so we beat the usual rush which really got started around six thirty or seven o'clock.

Josh ordered for us, and we sat and held hands across the table, watching outside and talking about the day while we waited for our food to come.

"I'm curious," Josh said, his tone becoming a little hesitant. "Why you're trying to avoid me meeting your parents. Is it too soon? We've been dating since September. I know your father was heavily invested in Jerkface as his future son in law, but still, I'd think he'd be happy to see you meet someone new. I clean up pretty well, all things considered..."

I sighed, not wanting to get into the whole business about his father's television reporters doing a big expose on one of my father's business partners.

"It's too soon," I said and squeezed his hand. "Let's just enjoy ourselves."

"I'd like to meet the Governor of New Hampshire one of these days," he said. "So, I hope that the next time they come to town, you bring me along. What about Christmas? That would be a good time to meet the parents."

"We'll see." I smiled and nodded, not committing to anything. He seemed assured that we'd still be together at Christmas, which was still three weeks away. That was a long time in a new relationship and after the nightmare that was my previous romance, I wanted to be cautious without too many expectations. Not that I was already thinking of us breaking up, but the chances of us being long-term partners was pretty slim. Even I had to admit that.

I didn't want to tempt the Gods, so I smiled and diverted the conversation to *The Chronicle* and how the search for good staff was going. Luckily, Josh was only too happy to tell me about his work staffing the new paper.

For the rest of the evening, I tried to just enjoy Josh in the moment instead of thinking ahead to what might or might not happen between us. I didn't want to hope too much.

I'd made that mistake before and wasn't going to make it again.

END OF EXCERPT

Buy it now at your favourite e-book retailer!

ABOUT THE AUTHOR

S. E. Lund writes erotic, contemporary, new adult and paranormal romance. She lives with her family of humans and animals in Beautiful British Columbia Canada on the side of a mountain and in sight of an active volcano. She dreams of living in a warm climate where snow is just a word in a dictionary.

For More Information:
www.selund.net
selund2012@gmail.com

If you would like updates on new releases and sales, special promotions and other news, sign up for S. E. Lund's newsletter. She hates spam and so will never share your email with anyone!

https://www.subscribepage.com/x8t1t7

ALSO BY S. E. LUND

Other Books by S. E. Lund:

CONTEMPORARY EROTIC ROMANCE:

BILLIONAIRE ROMANCE:

The Macintyre Brothers Series

Tempt Me: Book 1

Tease Me: Book 2

Tame Me: Book 3

The Mr. Big Series

Mr. Big Shot: Book 1

Mr. Big Love: Book 2

Mr. Big Daddy: Book 3

Mr. Big Deal: Book 4

The Unrestrained Series

The Agreement: Book 1

The Commitment: Book 2

Unrestrained: Book 3

Unbreakable: Book 4

Forever After: Book 5

Everlasting: Book 6

Drake Forever: Book 7

Endless: Book 8

Limitless: Book 9

The Drake Series (The Unrestrained Series from Drake's Point of View)

Drake Restrained

Drake Unwound

Drake Unbound

Military Romance / Romantic Suspense

The Bad Boy Series

Bad Boy Saint: Book 1

Bad Boy Sinner: Book 2

Bad Boy Soldier: Book 3

Bad Boy Savior: Book 4

The Boyfriend Series:

Boy Toy: Book 1

Man Bun: Book 2

PARANORMAL ROMANCE:

The Dominion Series

Dominion: Book 1 in the Dominion Series

Ascension: Book 2 in the Dominion Series

Retribution: Book 3 in the Dominion Series

Resurrection: Book 4 in the Dominion Series

Redemption: Book 5 in the Dominion Series

For more info:

www.selundauthor.com

selund2012@gmail.com